Heroes ar

Jon Elsby

Also by Jon Elsby

MEMOIR
Wrestling With the Angel: A Convert's Tale (print)

BIOGRAPHY
Hilaire Belloc: Reputation and Reappraisal
 (exfoliations.blogspot.com)

THEOLOGY
Coming Home (print)
Light in the Darkness (print)
Reassessing the Chesterbelloc (ebook)

Heroes and Lovers

Jon Elsby

_____cHp_____
CentreHouse Press

British Library Cataloguing in Publication Data
A catalogue record for this book is available from the British Library

ISBN 978-1-902086-22-4

CONTENTS

Part Three
32 Short notes—

Foreword

A ny book subtitled *The Great Tenors* makes, at least by implication, a large claim. Are these the only great tenors? Is the choice made supposed to be definitive? Are tenors who have been excluded deemed to be less than 'great', whatever that may mean?

The answer to all three questions is 'no'. The choice is, in part, subjective. It reflects the extent and limits of my knowledge (the tenors I have heard, and about whom I know enough to say something), and also my tastes (like everyone else, I find some voices more sympathetic than others). There are glaring omissions. Early tenors are very perfunctorily covered – but then they have been thoroughly covered in classic works by P. G. Hurst, Michael Scott, and J. B. Steane, among others. The French school is inadequately represented, and the Eastern Europeans are hardly mentioned at all. There is no reference to such fine tenors as Jan Kiepura, Wiesław Ochman, Paulos Raptis, Benno Blachut, Vilem Přibyl, Ivo Židek, Virgilius Noreika, Vladimir Atlantov, or Vladimir Galouzine, to cite a few examples. The only excuse I can plead is authorial ignorance. I simply don't know enough about them – their lives, careers, or recordings – to say anything to the purpose about them.

Some readers will doubtless resent what they will see as an undue prominence given to British singers. There are three reasons for this – and none of them has anything to do with nationalistic pride. The first is that I have had many opportunities to hear those singers in person and on record. The second is that I happen to like the

1

repertoire in which they excel. And the third is that I think they have been neglected and underestimated by some other writers.

So this is a personal choice of some great tenors. My selection is not exhaustive – no selection could be – but I would advance the more modest claim that all the tenors discussed in the following pages are worthy of inclusion.

So much for the subjective element. But, unless a book is to be what Stravinsky called 'a rave for one sort of mediocrity and a roast for another', the author must offer a rationale for his critical judgments. He must appeal to objective facts and sustainable interpretations of them to justify his opinions. I have tried to do so – with what degree of success is for others to judge.

Of course, I do not expect everyone to agree with my views. But I hope that, if nothing else, this book might provoke someone else – perhaps someone better qualified than I am – into writing his own book on the subject and making his own selection of the great tenors. If it does, I shall be the first to order a copy.

The Great Tenors
Part One

1 Introduction

What makes a great tenor? Why does the tenor nearly always get the girl? Why are they so highly paid? What is a tenor anyway? The short answer to the last question is that a tenor is the highest natural male voice with a range of approximately two octaves up to and including (please God) a top C. But even this definition is highly disputable. Is a counter-tenor not a natural voice? Many would argue that it is, and that the term *falsetto* is a misnomer. Come to that, is the tenor a natural voice? Not everyone would agree that it is. As the American heroic tenor, James McCracken, remarked, 'The human voice wasn't meant to sing a high C. It wasn't meant to sing a high B flat.' The tenor's high notes are far above the pitch of the human speaking voice. Nearly all adult male speaking voices are baritones, the rare exceptions, whose voices never broke, being altos. No one speaks as low as a bass can sing or as high as a tenor can. And not all tenors need, or even have, a top C. Wagnerian tenors tend to be B flat tenors and rarely have to sing higher. Mozartean and Handelian tenors also seldom have to sing notes above B flat. A tenor who is content to restrict himself to operatic roles which make no call on notes above high B flat or B natural, or to the concert repertoire, can get along very well without a top C. Conversely, a tenor who wants to specialize in the early nineteenth-century *bel canto* repertoire, or in such high-lying character roles as the Captain in *Wozzeck*, the Astrologer in *Le Coq d'Or*, Mephistopheles in *Doktor Faust*, or the Police Inspector in *The Nose*, will need a range that extends at least to a top D natural and preferably beyond – to E flat, E natural, even to a top F. Most of us think we could recognize a tenor if we heard one. But could we? Some tenors sound like baritones – listen to Ramón Vinay or Hans Hopf. Conversely, some baritones sound like tenors – listen to Dietrich Fischer-Dieskau or Roderick Williams. The dividing line between tenors and baritones is thinner and more porous than you might think. Some singers possess a range that defies categorization. The American baritone Leonard Warren could sing a full voice high C, and Jussi Björling had an unusually solid lower register for a tenor whose range extended to a ringing top D flat. It is easy to see why even experienced voice teachers sometimes make mistakes when classifying a student's voice.

Taking in turn the other questions I have raised, what makes a great tenor varies according to the type of tenor we are talking about. There are many different types (see the table opposite), and a great tenor might belong to any of them. What people usually mean when they talk about great tenors is those tenors who specialize in the central operatic repertoire for the lyric-dramatic (or *lirico spinto*) voice. But it does not follow that only such tenors can be considered great. The tenor doesn't always get the girl. Indeed, for some kinds of tenor, it is irrelevant to speak of getting the girl at all. A tenor who specializes in the Baroque or concert repertoire, for instance, will be judged on technique, musicianship and interpretative subtlety rather than charisma and sex appeal. And not all tenors are highly paid. The superstars – the Carusos, Giglis, Björlings, Domingos and Pavarottis – tend overwhelmingly to be those who sing the central lyric-dramatic tenor roles already alluded to. Tenors who sing, for instance, the Evangelist in the Bach Passions, or *Lieder* and art song, will certainly not be comparably well paid, and may even struggle to make a living through singing alone.

So the picture is rather confusing. However, for most purposes, the various tenor voices can be categorized as in the table opposite.

Heroes and Lovers

VOCAL CATEGORY	DESCRIPTION	EXAMPLES
haute contre or *tenore contraltino*	A very high tenor suitable for certain roles in the French Baroque and *bel canto* (esp. Rossinian) repertoire. Also for some more modern roles such as the Astrologer in *Le Coq d'Or*, the Police Inspector in *The Nose*, or the tenor solos in Orff's *Carmina Burana*. Range will extend to a top E.	Hugues Cuénod, Jean-Paul Fouchécourt, Barry Banks
tenore leggiero or *tenore di grazia* or light-lyric tenor	**Either** (a) a light, bright voice with an extensive upward range, reaching to top D or even higher (*I Puritani* requires a top F), suitable for the *bel canto* repertoire, **or** (b) a light voice with a lower range (extending to top B or C) who will be suitable for the early, Baroque, classical, and some modern repertoire, and for *Lieder* and art song.	(a) Alfredo Kraus, Juan Diego Flórez (b) Peter Pears, Ian Bostridge
tenore buffo or *Spieltenor* or Trial ténor	A character voice; suitable for roles where acting is as important as singing. Range depends on repertoire: most character roles do not need high notes but some, e.g. the Captain in *Wozzeck*, do. The majority of *comprimario* roles as well as some principal parts fall in this category.	Piero de Palma, Graham Clark, Charles Anthony
lyric tenor	A sweet-toned voice with some power, especially at the top of its range. The range will normally extend to top C, and perhaps higher. Typical lyric roles include Nemorino in *Elisir d'Amore*, Rodolfo in *La Bohème*, Pinkerton in *Madama Butterfly*, Alfredo in *La Traviata*, and the Duke in *Rigoletto*.	Beniamino Gigli, Giuseppe di Stefano, Heddle Nash, Nicolai Gedda
Mozart tenor	A sub-class of the lyric tenor, specializing in the operas of Mozart and, probably, in *Lieder*. The range need not extend beyond a top B flat. Consummate musicianship, taste, and a sound technique are at least as important as beauty of tone. Roles include the title role in *Idomeneo*, Don Ottavio in *Don Giovanni*, Ferrando in *Così fan Tutte*, Belmonte in *Die Entführung aus dem Serail*, and Tamino in *Die Zauberflöte*.	Richard Tauber, Anton Dermota, Léopold Simoneau, Fritz Wunderlich

VOCAL CATEGORY	DESCRIPTION	EXAMPLES
tenore lirico spinto or *spinto tenore* or lyric-dramatic tenor	A voice with much of the sweetness of the lyric tenor and some of the extra power or more penetrative timbre of the dramatic tenor. The range will extend to a top B or C. Typical *spinto* roles include most of the Verdi tenor roles, Enzo in *La Gioconda*, Cavaradossi in *Tosca* and Canio in *Pagliacci*.	Enrico Caruso, Jussi Björling, Carlo Bergonzi, Plácido Domingo
tenore robusto or *tenore di forza* or heroic tenor or dramatic tenor	A voice which may be either baritonal and weighty or bright and steely in timbre and will be, in either case, very powerful and/or penetrative throughout its range. The range will extend at least to a top B and preferably to top C. Typical heroic roles include Radames in *Aida*, Énée in *Les Troyens*, Samson in *Samson et Dalila*, Calaf in *Turandot*, and the title role in *Otello*.	Giovanni Martinelli, Mario del Monaco, Jon Vickers, James McCracken
high heroic tenor	A voice of great power and brilliance, typically with a bright, forward sound (although some may be dark and baritonal, with a cavernous quality to the top notes) and an extensive upward range, reaching C# or even D natural. Typical roles are Raoul in *Les Huguenots*, Arnold in *William Tell*, Gualtiero in *Il Pirata*, and the title role of *Poliuto*.	Giacomo Lauri-Volpi, Helge Roswaenge, Franco Corelli, Franco Bonisolli
Heldentenor	A voice of immense power and stamina, strong in the middle register and with a range that extends at least to B flat; the top C is required only by the young Siegfried. Typical roles will range from the slightly less demanding youthful *Heldentenor* roles such as Erik, Lohengrin and Walther von Stolzing to the almost impossibly demanding heavy *Heldentenor* repertoire such as Tristan and Siegfried.	Lauritz Melchior, Walter Widdop, Ben Heppner, Johan Botha

TABLE: CATEGORIES OF TENOR

These categories are not watertight. Some singers range across two
or three categories and one, Nicolai Gedda, even ranges across all
of them. Of course, he does not sing every role in each category –
no one could – but his operatic roles range from the light lyric
(Nemorino, Count Almaviva) through the *buffo* (Monsieur
Triquet, Danilo), the lyric (Faust, Rodolfo), the entire Mozart *Fach*,
the *lirico spinto* (Max, Don Jose), and the heroic (Hermann,
Arnold) to the *Heldentenor* (Lohengrin, Huon): a very impressive,
and probably unique, achievement. And many tenors change from
one category to another as their voices develop with age. Giovanni
Martinelli began as a *lirico spinto*, developed into a high heroic
tenor, and ended his career as a *tenore di forza*. Caruso and Björling
both developed from pure lyric tenors into *spintos*. So, to a lesser
extent, did Gigli. Such changes are not uncommon. But neither are
they inevitable. Some voices darken, and gain in power and weight
with age. Some do not. Tito Schipa, Heddle Nash, and Alfredo
Kraus, to cite three distinguished examples, ended their careers
exactly where they began: in their cases, there was no appreciable
vocal development.

So what makes a great tenor? It is impossible to say, though
Caruso's prescription – 'a big mouth, a big chest, ninety per cent
memory, ten per cent intelligence, and something in the heart' –
comes as close as any, at least where tenors of his own type are
concerned. There are many ways of being a great tenor. What do
Ian Bostridge and Mario del Monaco have in common? Not much.
Yet both are great tenors, or would widely be considered so. And
the same might be said of other incongruous pairings – of, say,
Francesco Tamagno and Richard Tauber, or Lauritz Melchior and
Peter Pears, or Fernando de Lucia and Julius Patzak, or Jon Vickers
and Hugues Cuénod. Tenorial greatness, it would seem, is more
easily recognized than defined.

A great tenor need not have a great voice. Of those mentioned,

Pears, de Lucia, Patzak and Cuénod have very disputable claims to vocal greatness. Even Vickers was controversial: the power of his voice was universally admitted, but many found the timbre unsympathetic. All these tenors were great by virtue of what they did with the voices they had: their interpretative insight, their imaginative phrasing, dramatic intensity, tonal colouring, dynamic variety, technical skill, virtuosity, clarity of diction, ability to 'sing off the words', and so forth.

The supreme example of a great tenor without a great voice is probably the English tenor **John Coates** (1865–1941). Sir Thomas Beecham described Coates as 'one of the half dozen most interesting artistic personalities in England' and the tenor's recordings, despite the fact that some were made late in his career, when he was in his sixties, amply justify the high praise. Yet Coates did not have a great voice. What he had was intelligence, which, together with good taste, a wide culture, a lively imagination, interpretative insight, a phenomenal capacity for hard work, a scrupulous and conscientious approach to everything he sang, outstanding musicianship, a fundamentally sound technique, and a robust constitution, enabled him to undertake an astonishingly varied repertoire with success. His operatic roles ranged from Faust and Hoffmann via Dick Johnson and Radames to Lohengrin, Tannhäuser, Parsifal, Tristan, and Siegfried. He was acclaimed as a Wagner singer in Germany as well as England. He sang extensively in oratorio and was one of the greatest interpreters of Elgar's Gerontius, much admired by the composer himself who referred to Coates as 'Arch-chanter John'. He was a superb *Lieder* singer and sang the full range of English song, from the lute songs of the Elizabethans, to Purcell, to his own contemporaries. He was described by the exacting Michael Scott, no easy critic to please, as 'one of the finest English singers on record'. And he achieved all this with a voice of only moderate size, range, and quality.

Conversely, there are tenors who are endowed with outstanding natural gifts but do not quite make the grade. Somehow they fail to qualify as 'great'. They lack a certain quality that is easy to recognize but very hard to describe. Examples might be the great *Heldentenor manqué*, Ernst Kozub, remembered on record chiefly as Erik in Klemperer's *Fliegende Holländer* and for being replaced as Siegfried in the deservedly celebrated Solti recording of Wagner's Ring cycle on the Decca label by the more reliable Wolfgang Windgassen; and Ferruccio Tagliavini, in many respects the natural successor to Gigli and possessor of a meltingly beautiful lyric tenor, and yet without quite that elusive quality that makes even the most jaded listener sit up and take notice. Anyone who listens to half a dozen Tagliavini recordings – which is apt to be rather an enervating experience – and then plays one by the young di Stefano, will see what I mean.

The tenor hasn't always been the romantic lead. In the early days of opera, the *castrati*, many of whom were singers of fabulous vocal power and agility like Caffarelli, Senesino, and Farinelli, occupied the position now taken by sopranos and tenors. It was only after the practice of castrating boys before puberty in order to preserve their voices was banned as cruel and unnatural that the tenor came into his own, first in the operas of Mozart, then in the works of his German and Italian successors: Beethoven, Weber, Schubert, Rossini, Pacini, Donizetti and Bellini. Now, several generations later and with a large and well established standard operatic repertoire to draw on, the tenor's position as *primo uomo* seems unassailable. Whether the hero of the evening is a *tenore di grazia* like Lindoro, or a *Heldentenor* like Tristan, or something in between, he is, at any rate, nearly always a tenor of some description.

To some extent, singers *choose* how to sing. Granted any singer has a natural endowment which cannot be altered, he chooses what vocal method to adopt, what repertoire to concentrate on, which aspects of his voice to develop, and which to suppress. Tenors like Martinelli, del Monaco, and Corelli could have sung using less breath, could have cultivated elegance of manner and beauty of tone rather than power and intensity, had they wanted to do so. Conversely, tenors like Gigli and Björling could have neglected the cultivation of the head register in order to generate greater power, had they wanted to do so. Lucie Manen, with whom Peter Pears studied in the latter stages of his long career, observed that Pears had reserves of power that he never used, but could have drawn on. Evidently, he preferred to maintain the flexibility of his voice, which served him better in his chosen repertoire than brute force would have done.

It is often said that tenors are rare compared with other voice types. Actually, while the baritone is the commonest male vocal type, tenors and basses, the two deviations from the norm, are equally rare. What makes tenors seem rarer is that many either choose other careers or, if their voices permit them this option, choose a safer living as a baritone. In high baritones like Leonard Warren, Dietrich Fischer-Dieskau, Hermann Prey, Ettore Bastianini and Piero Cappuccilli, one has often suspected a tenor in disguise. The reason is simple. The tenor's 'money notes' – roughly speaking, the notes from A flat upwards – being far above the normal pitch of a human speaking voice, are risky. A voice taken so far above its customary pitch might crack. The tenor takes that risk every time he sings a high note. Of course in a well-trained voice with a good technique, the risk is minimal, but it is there all the same. No tenor contemplates Otello's *'Esultate'*, or the final high B flat of *'Celeste Aida'*, or a role such as Arnold in *William Tell* or Arturo in *I Puritani* with equanimity. He knows that he is walking a high wire without a safety net, a hair's breadth from disaster. That is why the tenors who specialize in that central Italian and French repertoire are so exciting. That is why they are (or seem to be) so rare. And that is why they are so highly paid.

2 The early tenors of the recorded era

The recorded era began in the last years of the nineteenth century. At first, recordings were made with piano accompaniment because the primitive apparatus could not cope with an orchestra. Later, from about 1906 onwards, singers were recorded with orchestras of a sort (wind instruments, having a more penetrative tone, were often substituted for strings) but throughout the era of acoustic recordings, orchestral accompaniments sound wretched. One simply has to accept them for what they are. Luckily, the tenor voice itself recorded well – its frequencies lay in the middle of the limited range that the acoustic process could record most faithfully. So, while female voices are apt to sound bird-like (sopranos) or fruity (contraltos), and baritones and basses often sound woolly, the tenor voice records pleasingly. We have a much better idea what Caruso sounded like than we have of Melba.

For most opera lovers, the recorded era began with Caruso. But, in fact, quite a few earlier tenors made recordings, and they tell us something about the style of singing favoured in the pre-Caruso years.

For a start, they tell us that the way high notes were sung was different. Caruso carried the fullness of his chest register up to the top of his range, producing an ineffable effect of effulgent power on the top B flat and B natural. Earlier tenors used less breath, producing a lighter, narrower sound at the top of their range, using more head resonance. Their style and technique had more in common with the tenors of the *bel canto* period – Nourrit, Rubini, and

Mario. Caruso, too, had been schooled in that style, but he deliberately adopted a more muscular, virile approach, which subsequently influenced all his successors. Tucker, Bergonzi, Corelli, Pavarotti, Domingo, and Carreras were all followers of Caruso.

Then, we notice that earlier tenors were not pigeonholed in matters of repertoire to the same extent as their modern counterparts. John Coates' versatility has already been mentioned. The repertoire of another fine English tenor, **Walter Hyde** (1875–1951), was equally astonishing. Hyde began his career in musical comedy and sang principal roles in *HMS Pinafore*, *The Mikado*, and *Ivanhoe*. Later, his repertoire included, in addition to leading roles in several operas by British composers, the following—

- Wagner's Froh, Loge, Erik, Lohengrin, Siegmund, Walther, Tannhäuser, and Parsifal;
- Mozart's Don Ottavio, Belmonte, Pedrillo, Ferrando, and Tamino;
- Puccini's Pinkerton and Dick Johnson; Leoncavallo's Canio;
- Gounod's Faust and Roméo; Bizet's Don José and Haroun (*Djamileh*); Offenbach's Hoffmann; Saint-Saëns' Samson; Berlioz's Faust (*Damnation de Faust*); Debussy's Pelléas; Charpentier's Julien (*Louise*); Ambroise Thomas' Laertes (*Hamlet*);
- Mussorgsky's Dimitri (*Boris Godunov*); Rimsky-Korsakov's Mikhail (*Ivan the Terrible* or *The Maid of Pskov*).

In addition to this operatic fare, Hyde's concert repertoire included Bach's cantata *Phoebus and Pan*, Handel's *Ode on St Cecilia's Day*, Berlioz's *Te Deum*, Mendelssohn's *Elijah*, Elgar's *The Apostles*, and Coleridge-Taylor's *Hiawatha*.

How could any tenor encompass such a variety of roles? Gounod's Faust and Roméo and Offenbach's Hoffmann were in the repertoire of Alfredo Kraus, a *tenore di grazia*. The Mozart roles, too, suggest a light-lyric tenor. But then we find some of the heaviest Wagnerian roles co-existing in Hyde's repertoire alongside those much lighter parts. No modern tenor – not even Gedda or Domingo – has undertaken such a diversity of roles.

In those days, the combination of Handel and Wagner was quite often found in the repertoire of British tenors, although it was virtually unheard of elsewhere. Parry Jones, Tudor Davies, and Walter Widdop were other tenors who sang Wagnerian roles as well as the traditional Handel oratorios, which were as much a staple of British singers as the Shakespeare plays were of British actors. Widdop possessed a voice of truly Wagnerian power, but the other tenors named here did not. How were they able to acquit themselves satisfactorily in roles which should have been far beyond their means?

The answer must lie, to some extent, in the playing of the orchestras. Modern orchestras are expected (and encouraged by superstar conductors) to play as loudly in opera as in purely orchestral music, and to show little or no regard for the singers.[1] In the early years of the twentieth century, they must have played with more restraint. And it may be that some of their instruments were incapable of generating the same volume as their modern counterparts. Otherwise, one would have thought, tenors like Coates and Hyde would have been inaudible beyond the prompter's box in roles such as Tristan, Siegfried, and Tannhäuser.

Apart from orchestral playing, other factors must have been at work. One wonders how large were the auditoriums in which Hyde and Coates sang their Wagnerian roles. Did they appear mostly in small houses, where their voices would carry more easily? Were the orchestras smaller or the instruments of different manufacture? Were the interiors of the theatres in their day built out of acoustically friendly materials, such as wood? One would give much to know the answers.

Just as Caruso conditioned our expectations of the traditional Italian tenor, so the Great Dane, **Lauritz Melchior**, conditioned our expectations of the Wagnerian *Heldentenor*. To a unique degree, Melchior was able to combine tonal beauty, stentorian volume, and limitless stamina. What other tenors achieved by a careful husbanding of their resources, Melchior achieved with an almost insolent ease. While other tenors were virtually spent before the end of Act Three of *Tristan*, Melchior sounded as though he could have sung the whole part over again, if he had wanted to. His voice had retained the dark colour of the baritone he had once been, but his range had extended to include bomb-proof high notes. In the upper register, the voice – its power undiminished – was keenly focused to prevent the tone from spreading. Melchior, as Michael Scott has observed, was not so much a *Heldentenor* as a force of nature.

But Melchior's predecessors sang Wagner differently, just as Caruso's predecessors sang the Italian and French repertoire differently. Listen to the recording of Siegfried's Forging Song by the Russian tenor **Ivan Ershov** (1867–1943). He sang the dramatic tenor repertoire, including many Wagner roles, at the Mariinsky Theatre to great acclaim. Yet there is nothing of the baritone in his voice. The high notes are bright and penetrative but without either the breadth and richness of Caruso's or the weightily baritonal colour of Melchior's. Again, the earlier Wagnerians, like their counterparts in the French, Italian, and Slavonic repertoires, used more head resonance and cultivated a brighter, narrower, headier sound in the upper register. Typically, their voices seem to have been more flexible than those of their modern successors, with a wider palette of colours and more dynamic variety.

The lyric tenors before Caruso are best exemplified by **Fernando de Lucia** (1860–1925) and **Alessandro Bonci** (1870–1940). In both, one can hear the fast *vibrato* characteristic of the period (for an example, listen to Bonci's magical 1905 recording of '*A te, o cara*' from *I Puritani*), but also a flexibility in the execution of *fioriture* and a capacity to shade and vary dynamics which all but disappeared from vocal art for the next forty years.[2] In both, one notices the exceptional degree of integration of the head voice with the lower registers, and the way their use of the head voice permits them to float soft high notes or execute *diminuendos* on high notes – skills which few of their successors could command.

The *ne plus ultra* of the Italian heroic tenor before Caruso was **Francesco Tamagno** (1850–1905). A comparable tenor from the French school was **Léon Escalaïs** (1859–1941). Both had bright, powerful voices with brilliant, pealing high notes. Both also were skilled in the graceful execution of ornaments. And both had been trained in the operas of Rossini, Donizetti, Bellini, Meyerbeer, and Verdi, but eschewed the *verismo* repertoire. Tamagno declared that he thought *verismo* roles would be bad for his voice (though he made an exception for the title role of *Andrea Chenier*). The reasons are not hard to find. The *veristi* worked with a wholly different grammar of expressive devices from their *bel canto* predecessors. Where the earlier composers had worked within an exclusively musical language, employing trills, mordents, *gruppetti*, *fioriture*, *appoggiature*, and so on for expressive purposes, the *veristi* favoured a less singerly, more actorly approach. *Their* preferred expressive devices were extra-musical: singers were expected to laugh, sob, shout, yell, howl, and scream – in short, to employ whatever naturalistic means were necessary to communicate feelings to the audience. They were also expected to be capable of producing stentorian volume in the middle and top registers over a relatively dense orchestration. Power replaced flexibility, and the capacity to generate excitement became more important than the ability to produce a consistently beautiful tone, or to colour the voice sensitively in response to the words or their musical setting.

Of course, these observations apply only to opera singers. When we turn to the concert repertoire, the situation is different. Technical shortcomings are relentlessly exposed in performance of *Lieder* and art- song in general. Nor is the choral repertoire more forgiving. The Passion settings and cantatas of Bach, the masses of Haydn and Mozart, and the oratorios of Handel, Berlioz, Mendelssohn and Elgar, make severe technical, stylistic, and interpretative demands of tenors. The mannerisms of the *veristi* would have been entirely out of place in the concert hall.

In both the concert and the operatic repertoire we have to make an effort to hear earlier tenors as their contemporaries did. We have to get past the differences of style, vocal method, diction, and idiom. If we think their diction 'funny', or their use of *portamento* in Mozart exaggerated or unstylish, we shall miss a great deal of inestimable value in their art. Moreover, we shall be committing the anachronistic fallacy of applying the standards of our time to the products of an earlier age. We need to remember that our own standards are not absolute, and the performances of our contemporaries will sound just as strange to our descendants in 2100 as the performances of the 1900s sound to us.

If only we make the effort to listen to these earlier singers attentively and sympathetically, we shall be amazed at the depth of interpretative artistry and the sheer beauty of sound that we discover in their recordings. They evoke the manners and mores of a vanished age as surely as the Sherlock Holmes stories of Arthur Conan Doyle evoke a bygone world of London fogs and hansom cabs. The value of their recordings, in artistic and historical terms, cannot be overstated.

Notes
[1] I remember attending a performance of *Götterdämmerung* in London when the soprano singing Brünnhilde (who shall be nameless) might as well have been miming for all the difference it would have made.

[2]The skills associated with the age of *bel canto* reappeared in some surprising places. They can be heard in the singing of Richard Tauber (listen to the fluency of his runs in Mozart's *Il mio tesoro* or to the accuracy of his ornamentation in Almaviva's music from Rossini's *Barbiere di Siviglia*), and in that of Peter Pears (listen to his rapid and fluent runs on the words 'excellently bright' in his first recording of Britten's Serenade for Tenor, Horn, and Strings).

3 *The popular tenors*

Tenors are not confined to the opera house and the concert hall. They have also been stars of music hall, cabaret, radio, stage (i.e. musical theatre other than opera), and screen. Ever since popular music began to separate itself from the European classical tradition, some tenors have chosen to specialize in the popular repertoire – ballads, *chansons*, songs from operettas and musicals, and romantic songs like '*Tristesse*', 'Because', '*Granada*', and '*O sole mio*' – sometimes combining that repertoire with well-known operatic arias. These tenors were often highly accomplished vocalists with mellifluous light-lyric voices and a technical mastery of the head register which allowed them to float soft high notes and blend *falsettones* with their chest voice. For listeners who found the more strenuous delivery of the true operatic tenor too forceful for their taste, and who may not have cared much for operatic music, the popular tenors offered a form of singing, and a musical repertoire, that they could appreciate and enjoy.

Essentially, until the first crooners appeared, popular singers and classical singers sang in the same way. They had a common vocal method and technique, predicated on the need to be heard in concert halls or on the stage without the assistance of electronic amplification. Even the most light-voiced singers knew how to project their tones so as to be heard in the galleries or from the back rows.

The line between popular and classical singers was not impossible to cross. Popular tenors like Webster Booth and Mario

Lanza had also sung in opera. And classical singers sang popular repertoire. Caruso, Gigli, and Schipa all sang Neapolitan songs; McCormack and Heddle Nash sang drawing-room ballads and Irish songs; Joseph Schmidt, Richard Tauber, and Fritz Wunderlich all sang operetta and Viennese popular songs; Richard Crooks sang the tuneful, sentimental songs of Stephen Foster; and, in our own time, Pavarotti, Domingo, Carreras, and Alagna are just four of the many tenors who have proved adept at the art of crossover. I must also mention a neglected favourite of mine, the American tenor **Eugene Conley** (1908–81), who, in addition to his operatic recordings, recorded some wonderful versions of songs by composers such as Victor Herbert and Guy d'Hardelot (Helen Rhodes), replete with stunning top notes (his range extended to a ringing and unforced top D).

Between them, the popular tenors sang a varied repertoire. **Cavan O'Connor** (1899–1997) and **Josef Locke** (1917–99) – the former immortalized in his son Garry's racy and very entertaining memoir *The Vagabond Lover*, and the latter memorably incarnated by Ned Beatty[1] in the film *Hear My Song* – were two of the most successful popular tenors from the first half of the twentieth century. They sang many of the same songs, but each had a signature song – one with which he was identified in the minds and affections of the public. In Cavan O'Connor's case, the song was 'I'm Only a Strolling Vagabond'; for Locke, it was 'Hear My Song, Violetta'. Both had attractive light tenor voices of a kind well suited to the romantic ballads they specialized in.

Webster Booth (1902–84) became best known for his long musical partnership with his wife Anne Ziegler. Their duets are still cherishable, but Booth also had a distinguished career as a soloist, singing opera and oratorio, as well as songs like Tosti's 'Goodbye' and Stephen Adams' 'Nirvana'. Anyone who imagines that popular tenors are somehow second-rate should listen to Booth's recordings of arias by Handel, Mozart, and Verdi. He will hear an artist of consummate taste and considerable technical skill – qualities that Booth also brought, along with an appealing light-lyric tenor, to the popular repertoire he sang.

Different again was the American **Arthur Tracy** (1899–1997), known as the Street Singer. One of the most popular performers of the 1930s, he disarmingly confessed to putting 'all the schmaltz I had' into his songs. Whatever he did, it was highly effective. His versions of songs like 'Marta', 'Rambling Rose of the Wildwood' and 'When I Grow Too Old to Dream' have a beguiling charm characteristic of popular tenors at their best. His repertoire naturally concentrated on American popular songs of the period rather than the Irish or British songs favoured on this side of the Atlantic, but the musical idiom was similar. At that time, popular music had not been wholly taken over by African-American musical forms and styles which were alien to the classical European tradition.

Not all the popular tenors were from the anglophone world. The francophone Corsican **Tino Rossi** (1907–83) sang, with ineffable Gallic charm, a mixture of French *chansons* (e.g. '*Un Violon dans la Nuit*' and '*J'attendrai*'), classical arias ('*Je crois entendre encore*' from Bizet's *The Pearl Fishers*, which he sings in a defiantly non-operatic style, with much *portamento* and deliberate lifting to certain notes – practices common in popular song but reprehended in classical singing), and songs adapted from classical pieces (e.g. the Chopin-based '*Tristesse*'). High notes are invariably taken in a delicate head voice. His performances often have a slightly melancholy, elegiac quality which was part of his appeal to audiences: there were evidently certain moods which he captured better than anyone else. His sweet-voiced, elegant delivery puts one in mind of Bruno Landi (1900–68), a sadly all-but-forgotten Italian operatic tenor who specialized in the light-lyric repertoire.

The epitome of the popular tenor, and the most commercially successful of them all, was the Italian-American **Mario Lanza** (1921–59). The more sensational facts about Lanza's private life are well known – the battles with alcohol and binge-eating, his wildly fluctuating weight, his philandering, and his tempestuous marriage – and his early death from a heart attack was both foreseeable and avoidable. Critics are inclined to be supercilious about his operatic recordings, sometimes with good reason – his rhythmic sense was defective, his interpretative skills were limited, and he lacked the self-discipline to make the most of his great natural gifts. But there can be no doubt about those gifts. The voice itself is a splendid instrument, even if it is not always used with much taste or self-restraint. It is also much weightier than those of the popular tenors we have discussed so far – a *lirico spinto* tenor in fact. Time and again, the sheer quality of the tone, and a certain irresistible charisma about the performances (though some might call it crude vigour), sweep aside any critical reservations. Pavarotti, Domingo, and Carreras have all testified to the electrifying effect that Lanza's performance in the film *The Great Caruso* (a typical Hollywood 'biopic', wildly inaccurate) produced in them. A tenor capable of leaving such an abiding impression is not to be despised.

The Welsh comedian, actor, writer, and singer **Harry Secombe** (1921–2001) was another tenor whose renditions of songs from the shows (one of which – 'If I Ruled the World' from *Pickwick* – became his signature tune), hymns, and popular songs and arias made him a highly marketable commodity. The voice is a penetrative high tenor, with a range beyond high C. The top notes are solid and reliable. The timbre itself is not especially ingratiating, but the warmth of Secombe's personality comes through in his singing, and it is probably this, along with the spectacular top notes, that accounts for his success as a vocalist. He retained his voice and top notes into later life, proving the fundamental soundness of his technique. A curious episode in Secombe's career is that Geraint Evans tried to persuade him to sing the comic character role of Bardolph in Verdi's *Falstaff*, but he declined, perhaps feeling that he would be out of place on stage in the company of professional opera singers.

The English-born Welsh tenor **David Hughes** (1925–72) began as a pop singer but, after suffering a heart attack at the age of thirty-six, decided to fulfil a lifetime's ambition by retraining as an opera singer. He made the transition successfully, singing principal roles with the Sadler's Wells and Welsh National Opera companies, but he continued to sing light music alongside his operatic activities. His attractive, Italianate tenor was equally well suited to romantic ballads and the lyric repertoire in opera. Sadly, this gifted artist died, aged only forty-seven, after suffering a second heart attack onstage at the London Coliseum during a performance of *Madame Butterfly* – a performance which he courageously completed in spite of his condition.

The Scottish tenor **Kenneth McKellar** (1927–2010) specialized in Scottish traditional songs, often settings of the poetry of Robert Burns. Classically trained, he was an accomplished singer, gifted with a beautiful lyric tenor voice and equipped with a secure technique, which enabled him to give impressive renditions of the music of Handel, among other composers. Although he sang with the Carl Rosa Opera Company early in his career, he quickly decided that the operatic stage was not his métier and pursued a varied career as a concert artist, also appearing on stage in pantomime. In his case, classical music's loss was popular music's gain.

To judge from the careers of Andrea Bocelli, Paul Potts, and Russell Watson, the popular tenor is still with us, and able to flourish, despite an ambient culture which one would have thought unpropitious for that kind of singing. In popular music since the

War, there has been a perceptible movement away from classically trained voices to more 'natural' singing styles – in other words, to that approximation to the ordinary spoken voice that is characteristic of pop singers today. West End and Broadway musicals no longer require classically trained singers: they rely instead on actors who can sing (after a fashion), and electronic amplification. Microphone singing is essentially different from classical singing, which eschews any form of artificial assistance or enhancement. Paradoxically, the supposedly more natural style of the modern popular singer turns out to be less natural than the cultivated art of the classical singer.

Notes

[1]Josef Locke's singing voice was supplied in the film by Vernon Midgley, son of the fine English tenor Walter Midgley and an accomplished artist in his own right.

4 The British tenors

I have said a little already about British tenors, but they are so often unfairly maligned as a species that more needs to be said.

Britain is not generally thought of as a land of tenors. Many western European countries, notably Italy, Spain, France, and Germany, have produced a succession of great tenors, and there have been several from the Americas. Eastern Europe and Scandinavia have also produced an abundance of world-class tenors. But Britain? Who are the great British tenors?

The problem is that, when people talk about the great tenors, what they have in mind is the sort of tenor who specializes in the central roles of the Franco-Italian lyric-dramatic repertoire – a territory which extends roughly from Rodolfo to Radames and from Faust to Samson. On the whole, and with a few exceptions, this repertoire is not congenial to British tenors. Certainly, despite the domestic success of several fine tenors with the English, Scottish and Welsh National Opera Companies, there has been no tenor native to the British Isles to rival the best from other nations. Leaving the Italians and the Spanish aside as *hors concours* for the sheer number of great tenors they have produced, there has been no real British equivalent of Ansseau, Thill, Björling, Tucker, Cura, Villazón, Kaufmann, or Calleja.[1] The strengths of the typical British tenor lie elsewhere.

Where, exactly? Well, generally speaking, the most typical British tenors may be located somewhere on a spectrum which has Heddle Nash at one end and Peter Pears at the other. That is to say, they are lyric tenors, and their voices may be either sweet, like Nash's, or slender, like Pears'. The influence of Pears and the repertoire he crafted on the subsequent generation of British tenors was seminal. If we think of the outstanding British tenors among Pears' contemporaries and of the post-Pears generations, we think of the following: **Richard Lewis, Alexander Young, Ian Partridge, Robert Tear, Philip Langridge, Anthony Rolfe Johnson, Arthur Davies, Mark Padmore, John Mark Ainsley, Ian Bostridge, Toby Spence, James Gilchrist,** and **Andrew Kennedy.**[2] They were the most prolific recording artists; and what we find, when we look at the repertoire they sang or listen to their recordings, is a certain family resemblance. There is a kinship in timbre, style, vocal weight, colour, and technique, range, repertoire, and something more elusive: something covered, if hardly explained, by the phrase *a commonality of culture.*

The typical British tenor sound is formed by the combined influence of seven factors, viz.—

1 the British choral tradition, especially that of the cathedral and college choirs and of the numerous choral societies;
2 the British song tradition from Byrd to Britten, including madrigals and part-songs, which is much richer, more diverse, and more vital than the native operatic tradition;
3 the scarcity of opera houses and opera companies in Britain compared with Italy and Germany, which means that British tenors must either cultivate a wide concert repertoire, or, if they want to specialize in opera, go abroad;
4 the number of small groups of singers, such as the BBC Singers, the Deller Consort, the Hilliard Ensemble, the Sixteen, and Red Byrd, in which many British tenors gain early experience;

5 the voice, style and vocal method of Peter Pears, and the operatic and concert repertoire created largely by Benjamin Britten and specifically tailored to the requirements and possibilities of Pears' voice and art;

6 the revival, in the late twentieth century, of interest in the Baroque and early music, which provided a new repertoire to which British voices and vocal training were peculiarly suited; and

7 last but not least, the English language with its consonantal clusters and peculiar diphthongs instead of the liquid consonants and open, rounded vowels of the Romance languages.[3]

This combination of influences produced a school of tenors of high accomplishment and certain shared vocal characteristics: voices that are light, slender, agile, adept in coloratura, well schooled in method and technique, and pure in sound, but inclined to whiteness; a wide culture, extending beyond music to art, literature, history, Christian liturgy and philosophy, while also embracing a catholic musical taste and knowledge; and a vocal repertoire which extends backward in time to early, Baroque, and classical music (properly so called) and forward to Britten, Tippett and beyond, but includes relatively little of the nineteenth century, apart from oratorio and art song, especially *Lieder*.

In this field, British tenors have established a preëminence rivalled only by the best of the Germans. It is true that no British tenor could tackle the Italian and French roles as nobly as Caruso or Domingo, but it is also true that Caruso and Domingo could not sing the Evangelist in the Bach Passions, or the Monteverdi Vespers, or Elgar's *Gerontius*, or Britten's *Peter Grimes*, or Schubert's *Winterreise*, or the songs of Vaughan Williams, Finzi, and Warlock, as eloquently as our typical British tenor. When it comes to breadth of repertoire, or the musical quality of the works undertaken, the British tenor has nothing to fear in comparison to his Latin counterparts.

Anyone who wants to explore the recorded legacy of British tenors has rich resources to draw upon. Recent years have seen an enormous growth in the number of recordings of the British song repertoire – in my own collection, I can find four versions of Britten's *Serenade for Tenor, Horn and Strings* (by Peter Pears, Robert Tear, Philip Langridge, and Ian Bostridge), seven of Warlock's *The Curlew* (by René Soames, Ian Partridge, James Griffett, Adrian Thompson, Andrew Kennedy, Mark Padmore and James Gilchrist) and no fewer than eight of Vaughan Williams' *On Wenlock Edge* (by Tear, Partridge, Gilchrist, Bostridge, Anthony Rolfe Johnson, two by Mark Padmore, and one by the American tenor George Maran – a welcome sign that interest in British composers is not confined to British artists).

Apart from British song, modern British tenors have been extensively recorded in other repertoire – madrigals, German *Lieder*, French *mélodies*, art song from Eastern Europe and America, oratorios and liturgical settings from the Baroque to the modern age (and everything in between), Baroque cantatas, early and modern opera, certain unclassifiable works like Bantock's *Omar Khayyam*, Coleridge-Taylor's *Hiawatha*, George Dyson's *The Canterbury Pilgrims*, and George Lloyd's *The Vigil of Venus*. All of this deserves exploration.

Also worthy of exploration – but much harder to find – are the recordings of earlier British tenors from John Coates, Edward Lloyd, Walter Hyde, and Gervase Elwes to Joseph Hislop, Heddle Nash, Walter Widdop, and Tudor Davies. YouTube is a valuable resource here. The pre-Pears British tenors are more varied than one might expect, both tonally and in terms of the repertoire they tackled. Their recordings deserve, and repay, close attention.

THE SAD CASE OF CHARLES CRAIG

Among the minority of English tenors who buck the trend, **Charles Craig** (1919–97) stands out. He is often said to be the finest Italianate tenor Britain has ever produced. The competition is surprisingly stiff. His predecessors included Frank Mullings, Alfred Piccaver, Joseph Hislop, John McCormack, Tom Burke, Walter Widdop, Tudor Davies, Heddle Nash, Arthur Carron, James Johnston and Henry Wendon, and his successors included David Rendall, Edmund Barham, Arthur Davies, John Hudson, Julian Gavin (Australian-born but British-naturalized), Rhys Meirion, and Peter Auty. Not all of them were suited to the *lirico spinto* repertoire, but quite a few were. Yet the general *on dit* is that, from the point of view of the repertoire for the *lirico spinto* tenor,[4] Craig was probably the best of them.

His credentials are impressive. From 1957 to 1985 he performed leading tenor roles at London's Royal Opera House and at the English National Opera. He was especially renowned in the title role of Verdi's *Otello*, which he sang in Chicago, Berlin, Vienna, Naples, Munich, Venice, Salzburg, Turin, Lisbon and Düsseldorf. In London, his roles included Otello (with the ENO), Cavaradossi, Pollione (which he sang opposite the Norma of Maria Callas at Covent Garden), Radames, Manrico, Pinkerton, Turiddu and Canio. Other roles in his large and varied repertoire included Nadir, Arturo (in *I Puritani*, in which he sang opposite Joan Sutherland), Don Ottavio, the Duke of Mantua, Don Carlo, Benvenuto Cellini, Faust, des Grieux (in Puccini's *Manon Lescaut*), Calaf, Samson, the Prince (in Dvořák's *Rusalka*), Babinsky (in Weinberger's *Schwanda the Bagpiper*), Andrea Chenier, Luigi (in *Il Tabarro*), Sou-Chong (in *The Land of Smiles*), Prince Vassily Golitsyn (in *Khovantschina*), Sergei (in *Katerina Ismailova*), Bacchus (in *Ariadne auf Naxos*), Aegisthus (in *Elektra*), Florestan, Lohengrin, Siegmund, Siegfried (in *Götterdämmerung*), and

Rodolfo (in *La Bohème*). He was finally able to sing his signature role, Otello, in his home city in 1980, when he gave a series of critically acclaimed performances at the Coliseum for the ENO. In 1983, he sang the role in two performances at Covent Garden, substituting for an ailing Plácido Domingo. Two years later, aged sixty-six, he gave his final stage performances, as Cavaradossi at the ENO. His voice was still in excellent shape and the top notes rang out with the clarion strength of old – a testament to his superb technique and iron constitution, as well as his ability to sing within his limits, without forcing or striving for more power than the voice naturally possessed, even in the most demanding roles.

Clearly, then, Craig had a major career. So why should he be considered a sad case? First, because he was a late starter. There were few opportunities in England for a gifted working-class boy like Craig to study music and singing, or to get started in the profession. Initially, he was employed at Covent Garden but only as a member of the chorus. Had he not been spotted by Sir Thomas Beecham who, with characteristic generosity, paid for Craig to have voice lessons and supported his family until he could establish himself as a singer, he would not have enjoyed a solo career at all. Second, because his recorded legacy was so pitifully small. He recorded a few (very few) recital discs when he was in his prime, and also highlights (in English) from *Madam Butterfly* and *Il Trovatore*. He also recorded Delius's *A Mass of Life* under his mentor, Beecham – but it is one of the composer's least attractive pieces and hardly the most suitable work for a display of an Italianate, *lirico spinto* tenor's talents. For the rest, there are only highlights from *The Land of Smiles*, *Un Ballo in Maschera*, and *The Student Prince* (all recorded in English), and a live recording of *Otello* from the stage of the London Coliseum. Fine though it is, and while there is much to be grateful for, there is also much to regret: all the usual shortcomings of live performances (stage and audience noises, occasional mistakes, and uneven balance); the fact that the performance is in English rather than Italian, which makes comparison with other recorded versions problematic; and that EMI waited until Craig was in his sixties before recording him in his greatest role. Why did the record companies not offer Craig more work when he was in his prime? Why did they not record him in the studio, and in his best roles? The third reason for thinking him a sad case is that he was not given enough opportunities by the major London companies during his best years. Why did Covent Garden prefer imports such as James McCracken, Richard Cassilly, Jon Vickers and Carlo Cossutta as Otello when they had one of the world's finest exponents of the role on their doorstep? Why did they not support Craig in the same way, and to the same extent, as the Metropolitan Opera in New York supported *their* home-grown tenor, Richard Tucker?

Let's consider what might have been. Craig was only six years younger than Richard Tucker. They were more or less contemporaries. Yet we have ten operatic recital discs from Tucker, and many more discs of song. And we have thirteen complete operas in studio recordings: two versions each of *Aida, La Forza del Destino,* and *Madama Butterfly,* and single versions of *Lucia di Lammermoor, La Traviata, Il Trovatore, Rigoletto, La Bohème, Cavalleria Rusticana,* and *Pagliacci.* In each of these, Tucker was surrounded by a major international cast. His soprano partners included Lily Pons, Maria Callas, Anna Moffo, Lucine Amara, Gianna d'Angelo, and Leontyne Price. He sang with noted baritones, like Frank Guarrera, Robert Merrill, Leonard Warren, Giuseppe Valdengo, and Tito Gobbi. Now, Craig appeared in the world's opera houses in comparably stellar company. And his voice was in many respects similar to Tucker's. Both had dark, powerful tenors, with ringing, virile top notes (though Craig had the greater upward extension). Both started as lyric tenors but moved into *spinto* and then dramatic roles as their voices darkened and their careers progressed. Both had long careers, and preserved their voices, thanks to their excellent vocal technique and a prudent choice of repertoire. Both admired, and, to some extent, modelled themselves on, Beniamino Gigli, especially early in their careers. Craig probably possessed the more robust voice: certainly, he had the wider and more demanding repertoire, singing roles such as Otello and Siegmund, which Tucker never attempted.[5] Just suppose that we had a dozen recital discs by Craig, and that we also had thirteen studio recordings of complete operas in which he sang opposite some of the most highly regarded singers of his day – the people he regularly partnered in the world's opera houses. Then ask yourself this: in those circumstances, would Charles Craig seem at all inferior to Richard Tucker?

Perhaps I may be allowed a personal reminiscence. I was fortunate enough to hear Charles Craig sing what was probably his greatest role – the title part in Verdi's *Otello* – at the ENO in 1980. I was amazed that a tenor in his sixties, after a long career singing some of the most demanding and strenuous roles in the entire operatic repertoire, could still sound so fresh and secure. The voice was dark and rich in timbre. The high notes rang out with power and brilliance. The registers were fully equalized, the tone virile, pure and unforced throughout its range. Dramatically, it was an assumption of compelling honesty and dignity: this Otello was not just a tenor with a suitably heroic voice – he actually seemed the commander he was supposed to be.

I have no doubt that Craig deserves a place among the world's great tenors. This is not an idiosyncratic view. He is mentioned admiringly in Kurt Pahlen's *Great Singers from the 17th Century to the Present Day*, and is one of the very few British tenors to have sung principal roles in Italian operas in the major Italian houses. That, in spite of all this, he has been denied the recognition he deserved in his native country by both record companies and opera houses is shameful. I remember hearing the great English lyric baritone, Sir Thomas Allen, say many years ago in a radio programme, 'It hurts me when I think how Charles was treated.' At the time, I didn't understand what he meant. But I do now. Charles Craig was *our* Richard Tucker. If only he had been given the same chances. Perhaps then he might have had the international recognition, public honours, and financial rewards to which he was entitled.

Notes

[1] It is only fair to add that there have been many fine British tenors who regularly sang the Italian and French repertoire, either in the original language or in English. Some of the modern ones can be heard on Chandos's Opera in English series.

[2] The fine Scottish tenors Neil Mackie and Mark Wilde deserve mention, as do Martyn Hill, Adrian Thompson, and two young tenors – Ben Johnson and Robin Tritschler – who show that the British tenor tradition is alive and well. The Welsh tenor Stuart Burrows, the supreme Mozartean of his generation, is dealt with in the next essay. He is untypical of the tenors examined here.

[3] In fact, most, if not all, other European languages are probably easier to sing in than English because of their purer, more rounded vowels.

[4] It is worth remembering too that Craig sang not only Italian roles but also roles from the French, Czech, Russian and German repertoires, and that his repertoire embraced roles ranging from the pure lyric (Rodolfo, Pinkerton, the Duke of Mantua) to the heroic (Otello, Lohengrin, Siegmund, Siegfried).

[5] One respect in which Craig was totally dissimilar to Tucker was temperament. Tucker possessed an abundance of chutzpah, whereas Craig, unusually for a tenor, was a notably modest man.

[6] Actually, it is noteworthy that Craig's repertoire was much wider than Tucker's. Tucker, who was shy of top Cs, would never have tackled the

high-lying role of Arturo in *I Puritani*, nor would he have ever sung any of the heroic roles which Craig fearlessly tackled, such as Otello or Siegmund.

5 The Mozart tenors

The art of Mozart singing is such a specialized activity that it merits a section of its own. Of all the great composers, Mozart is one of the most beneficial for the voice, especially for young singers – but he is also one of the most relentlessly demanding. He requires a first-class technique, exemplary musicianship, and interpretative ability of the highest order. Singing Mozart fosters the development of good vocal habits, enables the singer to consolidate his or her technique, and does not require young voices to force, as the orchestra is modest in size.

The true Mozart tenor does not require an extensive upward range. If we except the early (and rarely performed) *Mitridate Re di Ponto*, Mozart tenor roles do not go above the tenor's top B flat, and even that note is rare. They do, however, demand the ability to survive a generally high tessitura with ease (for example, Tamino's '*Bildnisarie*', Belmonte's *Wenn der Freude Tränen fliessen*, or Ferrando's *Ah lo veggio quell'anima bella*), and to negotiate sometimes fearsome flights of coloratura (for example, Don Ottavio's *Il mio tesoro*, Belmonte's *Ich baue ganz auf deine Stärke*, or Idomeneo's *Fuor del mar*). They also demand the ability to delineate a character through strictly musical means without ever resorting to the expressive devices appropriate to the nineteenth-century Italian repertoire – *portamento*, for instance, is as foreign to Mozart as it is to French opera and song. And as for the vocal manners and mannerisms of *verismo* – don't go there, is the best advice to an aspiring Mozart singer.

In recent years, we have grown accustomed to hearing only very light tenors in Mozart roles. But this practice is unhistorical. As we have seen, the English tenor Walter Hyde sang everything from Mozart to Wagner. Leo Slezak, a renowned Otello and Tannhäuser, also sang Belmonte in *Die Entführung aus dem Serail*. The Welshman Tudor Davies, a genuine *spinto* tenor, sang Tamino. Even without such exceptional examples, we can think of Mozart tenors (Richard Tauber and George Shirley, for instance) whose voices may not have been especially large, but who possessed a characteristically dark, virile tone such as we seldom hear in Mozart today.

If the modern approach to Mozart is somewhat homogenized, that cannot be said of earlier generations. There is plenty of material on record for anyone in quest of a truly individual approach to Mozart to explore. The Mozart recordings of **Richard Tauber** (1891–1948) are a good place to start. Not only do we hear a notably virile voice, but we also hear a vivid personality, great dynamic variety including a meltingly beautiful *mezza voce*, and a phenomenal technique. Who else has sung long runs with such fluency as Tauber in his recording of *Il mio tesoro*? Probably only **Hermann Jadlowker** (1877–1953). Jadlowker was trained as a cantor and he had both the tendency to a somewhat throaty delivery and the extreme fluency in the execution of runs characteristic of tenors who have undergone cantorial training. Both can be heard in his classic recording (in German) of Idomeneo's *Fuor del mar* (*Noch tont mir ein Meer in Busen*). The coloratura singing is of breath-taking virtuosity. It is extraordinary to hear a voice of Wagnerian size and colour singing runs in full voice with such accuracy and brilliance.

Mention of Wagnerian size recalls that Beecham's Tamino in his 1938 recording of *Die Zauberflöte* was the Danish tenor **Helge Roswaenge** (1897–1972), possessor of not only a stentorian heroic voice, but also of one of the most brilliant top Ds ever recorded. He is not the sort of tenor one would expect to find in a Mozart opera – and certainly today he wouldn't be allowed anywhere near one. He makes surprisingly heavy weather of Tamino's music, rarely sounding fully at home in the Mozartean idiom. He is heard to better effect in Belmonte's *Hier soll ich dich denn sehen*, where his singing is manly and characterful, if lacking in elegance.

In the 1950s, probably the two leading Mozarteans were the Slovene tenor **Anton Dermota** (1910–89) and the French-Canadian **Léopold Simoneau** (1916–2006). Their voices make an interesting comparison, neatly pointed up by Elisabeth Schwarzkopf, who referred to Dermota's Mediterranean timbre ('a southern voice, dark, creamy, always covered, never open'), contrasting it with Simoneau's brighter, more Björling-like sound.[1] Both contributed notably to recordings of complete Mozart operas in the early days of LPs. Their vocal characteristics were reflected in their interpretative art. Simoneau's Björling-like timbre went with a rather cool manner (his Mozart is more memorable for the exceptional elegance of his vocal delivery than for dramatic involvement), while Dermota's Mediterranean voice was accompanied by a southern temperament, making him a rather more ardent Ferrando, for example, than one is used to hearing. His contribution to Karajan's soporific account of Mozart's Requiem is one of the few arresting features of a disappointing recording.

The next generation produced two outstanding Mozarteans: the Swede **Nicolai Gedda** (1925–2017) and the German **Fritz Wunderlich** (1930–66). Their voices are not dissimilar in weight and colour, and their repertoires overlapped in more than Mozart. Both were deservedly renowned exponents of Viennese operetta, for example, and of the lyric tenor repertoire in general. Nearly all of Wunderlich's recordings are in his native German, but he sings the language so beautifully and expressively that it would be churlish to complain. A rare excursion into Italian is a delightfully uproarious version of '*Funiculi, funiculà*', which rivals Gigli's in sheer exuberance. In Mozart, he is surely the perfect Tamino, and the concluding phrases of the '*Bildnisarie*' have seldom sounded less effortful than they do in his rendition. He also makes an unwontedly characterful and heroic Don Ottavio. Gedda, by contrast, is a musical chameleon, sounding completely at home in whatever language he happens to be singing in – French, Italian, German, Russian, Czech, English, or Latin. His Mozart, unfailingly musical, yet never bland or lacking in character, is nearly always gratefully heard, although it must be admitted that a 1974 *Così fan Tutte* finds him singing energetically, but in rather rough voice. However, his early recordings of Mozart and other repertoire show why, after hearing the twenty-three-year-old Gedda for the first time, the impresario, Walter Legge, cabled his wife, Elisabeth Schwarzkopf, to say that a great and heaven-sent singer had fallen into his lap.

The African-American tenor **George Shirley** (b. 1934) possesses an unusually dark voice for a lyric tenor. He sang much apart from Mozart, accumulating an enormous repertoire of more than eighty roles. On record he makes a more forceful Ferrando than one is accustomed to hearing (and none the worse for that), and a superb Idomeneo, acquitting himself well in the longer and more taxing version of '*Fuor del mar*'. A contemporary of Shirley was the Welsh tenor **Stuart Burrows** (b. 1933), an outstanding Mozartean who happily was recorded in several of his best roles. Like many other notable exponents of Mozart, Burrows ranged more widely, singing French and Italian *bel canto* roles, and even the part of Jack in Tippett's *A Midsummer Marriage* on disc. His voice is a lyric tenor of unusual beauty of timbre and equipped with a flawless technique – his breath control and fluency in the execution of ornaments are exceptional. The voice also seems larger than the majority of Mozart tenors. Although he certainly enjoyed a distinguished career, he deserves, in my view, to be more celebrated than he is. One of the truly great tenors of our time.

Several other tenors from the British Isles deserve an honourable mention in any survey of Mozarteans, among them **John McCormack** (1884–1945); **Heddle Nash** (1894–1961) and **Richard Lewis** (1914–90), both of whom sang many Mozart roles at Glyndebourne; **Anthony Rolfe Johnson** (1940–2010), and **Ian Bostridge** (b. 1964).

There are also, and not surprisingly, a good number of Austrians and Germans, including **Julius Patzak** (1898–1974), **Walther Ludwig** (1902–81), **Werner Hollweg** (1936–2007), **Peter Schreier** (b. 1935), and **Werner Krenn** (b. 1943). Of these, Patzak and Schreier deserve special mention more for the individuality of their voices and their exceptional interpretative intelligence than for sheer beauty of tone. Both bring the *Lieder* singer's art of word-pointing to their operatic work. The Swedish tenor **Gösta Winbergh** (1943–2002) remains one of the few to have made a successful transition from light-lyric roles to the most dramatic parts in the repertoire, singing several Wagner roles as well as Florestan in *Fidelio* and Calaf in *Turandot*, and bringing to those roles a glowing lyricism they did not often get. But it is probably for his mellifluous and elegant Mozart performances in the early part of his long and successful career that he will be best remembered.

All these fine singers had an individual way with Mozart, a way of shaping and colouring a phrase that could etch it in the memory of a listener. They also had individual and recognizable voices – they were not just undifferentiated light-lyric tenors. The modern age has produced a number of light-lyric tenors of great technical accomplishment, but without highly individual voices or interpretative qualities that distinguish them from each other. There is a certain sameness about their performances, an anonymity, a lack of real individuality that sometimes leaves one with the impression that they are interchangeable. That could not have been said of earlier Mozarteans; and, for all the moderns' pleasant, well-schooled voices, their vocal and interpretative homogeneity marks a sad decline in the art of the Mozart tenor.

Notes

[1]See *Elisabeth Schwarzkopf: A Career on Record*, Alan Sanders and J. B. Steane, Duckworth, 1995.

6 The Heldentenors

Brief mention has already been made of the *Heldentenors*, especially of that king of the breed, Lauritz Melchior. The Great Dane set the gold standard – one which, in the opinion of many respected judges, has never been equalled. But there have been several admirable *Heldentenors* since, and some of them are covered here.

But first, what is a *Heldentenor*? How do we tell an authentic *Heldentenor* from a close relative, such as the Italian *tenore robusto*? The facetious answer is that the *Heldentenor* properly so called is the size of a double wardrobe and has a voice to match. He will be, in all probability, tall, broad, and burly. It is not unusual for *Heldentenors* to be well over six feet tall and to weigh more than 250 lbs (c. eighteen stone). For some reason, a massive physique is (nearly always) necessary to generate the massive vocal power required by the Wagner tenor roles.[1] Those roles also call for exceptional stamina. Tristan, for instance, is not only very strenuous; it is also very long. A Tristan who gets to the end of Act Three without feeling – and sounding – utterly spent, is a rare thing indeed.[2]

It is hard to combine the Wagner roles with French and Italian repertoire because the approach to the high notes is different. Some tenors have managed to bring this off, generally for a short period and by strictly limiting their appearances in Wagner. It will also usually be found that, after a time, they ration their appearances in French and Italian operas to the ones with lower-lying tenor roles.

Few Wagner roles go higher than top A, but many lie predominantly in the upper middle part of the range, so that a top A feels like a high C. A tenor who specializes in such roles might also sing Samson or Radames: but he won't be likely to sing Arnold in *William Tell*, an excruciatingly high-lying part, or even Manrico in *Il Trovatore*, which, though generally low-lying, contains, in '*Di quella pira*', a couple of unwritten but customarily inserted top Cs. These will usually be quite enough to deter a *Heldentenor*, with his quasi-baritonal range, from attempting the part.

We have already met some of the first generation of *Heldentenors* on record in the chapter on the early tenors. But there were others, notably **Jacques Urlus** (1867–1935), **Franz Völker** (1899–1965), and **Max Lorenz** (1901–75). All these tenors possessed powerful voices, but also finesse. They sang with sensitivity as well as power. They showed that Wagnerian singing was not simply a matter of brute force. It was necessary to combine a certain muscularity of delivery with the sensitivity to words of an accomplished *Lieder* singer.

British Wagnerians have included **John Coates**, **Walter Hyde**, **Frank Mullings** (1881–1953) **Parry Jones** (1891–1963),**Walter Widdop** (1892–1949), and **Alberto Remedios** (1935–2016). Of Coates and Hyde, we have already spoken. Mullings, admired by many good judges in his day for the power of his acting as much as anything else, emerges on record as an honest singer of some intensity, but with an imperfect vocal method, which may have mattered less in the flesh than it does on repeated hearings on disc. Parry Jones did not have the most sensuously beautiful of voices, but it was strong and steady, and controlled by a keen intelligence. Widdop was one of the best Wagnerian tenors of his day, and all his recordings are a joy to hear. Alberto Remedios, a much later singer, was the English National Opera's resident Siegmund and Siegfried in their Ring cycles in the 1970s, and also a lyrical Walther in *Die*

Meistersinger for the same company. He had a voice of more than adequate power, but he stands out as one of the most lyrical *Heldentenors* on record.

In the generation after Melchior, five notable Wagnerian tenors emerged: **Set Svanholm** (1904–64), **Ludwig Suthaus** (1906–71), **Günther Treptow** (1907–81), **Wolfgang Windgassen** (1914–74), and **Hans Hopf** (1916–93). None of them took Melchior's place (no one could), but they were all highly regarded, at least by some critics and some of their fellow musicians. Svanholm, a rare example of a *Heldentenor* who was neither tall nor physically enormous, possessed a serviceable voice inclined to dryness. He is often praised for his musicianship, but I have to confess that I have found little to like or admire in the recordings that have come my way. The voice is unlovely, pinched and effortful at the top, and there is no real concept of *legato*. He is probably heard at his best in a 1948 *Das Lied von der Erde* with Kathleen Ferrier as the contralto soloist, and Bruno Walter conducting. Suthaus, a splendid Tristan on Fürtwängler's legendary 1952 recording, tended to be overshadowed by his contemporaries – a circumstance for which his less-than-heroic stage presence (it has been unkindly said that he looked like Jeeves) may have been responsible. Treptow and Hopf, both weightily baritonal in sound, are not as well represented on disc as could be wished. Treptow makes a rather mature-sounding and decidedly unromantic Walther on Hans Knappertsbusch's *Meistersinger*, and Hopf is an ungainly Tannhäuser on Franz Konwitschny's recording, although both were capable, as they proved elsewhere, of delivering powerful and exciting performances.

By some distance, the best of Melchior's immediate successors was **Wolfgang Windgassen**. He had the most beautiful voice among them, and he was a conscientious and musical artist. Luckily, his art is well captured on disc, and nowhere better than in Georg Solti's Ring cycle for Decca. Though it catches him late in his career (and he was not the first choice), this recording is a fine monument to Windgassen's accomplishments in Wagner. Less generously endowed vocally than Melchior, 'live' recordings show that he was obliged to husband his resources carefully, and that, even so, he often sounds tired by the end of a performance. It is a testimony to his intelligence and integrity as an artist that, in spite of this, he is one of the finest Wagnerians of the recorded era.

The Chilean tenor **Ramón Vinay** (1911–96) is probably best remembered today as the mighty Otello in Toscanini's deservedly famous recording (as well as in several 'off the air' versions) but he also sang Wagner roles, including Tristan, at Bayreuth with great success. The voice was stupendous in size and noble in tone, but he never really managed the technical transition from baritone to tenor. Instead of trying to produce a narrower, brighter sound in the upper range, he carried the baritone fullness up to the top B – a risky step. Not surprisingly, after he had sung the heroic tenor repertoire for some twenty years, the strain became too great, the high notes disappeared, and he was obliged to revert to baritone roles.

The next generation yielded four good, if not outstanding, *Heldentenors*. Vocally, the best of them may have been **Ernst Kozub** (1924–71), but poor health and an early death prevented him from fulfilling his potential. Two Americans, **Jess Thomas** (1927–93) and **James King** (1925–2005), had notable careers, the former rather light of voice by *Heldentenor* standards but an intelligent and sympathetic interpreter; the latter, solid and reliable but not the most exciting of singers. Better than either was the Canadian **Jon Vickers** (1926–2015), whose incandescent performances as Tristan burned themselves indelibly into the memories of all who were lucky enough to hear them. Vickers recorded Tristan for Karajan and Siegmund twice (for Leinsdorf and Karajan). There is also a live performance of *Parsifal* on disc, but that was the full extent of his Wagnerian repertoire. He never sang either of the Siegfrieds or Lohengrin or Tannhäuser or Walther. Superb though he was in the roles he *did* sing, the fact that he sang so few Wagner roles (and none at all by Richard Strauss) calls into question his title to be called a *Heldentenor*. It is probably best to regard him as *sui generis*.

The next decade saw the emergence of a trio of German Wagnerians who were to dominate the scene for most of the following twenty years: **René Kollo** (b. 1937), **Siegfried Jerusalem** (b. 1940), and **Peter Hofmann** (1944–2010). In one respect, Kollo is the most remarkable *Heldentenor* on record: he is the only one to have recorded all the main Wagner tenor roles (except Siegmund), including the early *Rienzi*. The results, however, have been variable. John Steane comments that, at its best, Kollo's voice 'resounds with a pure, well-projected tone that is like silver of great price', but also notes a plethora of intrusive aspirates and 'at declamatory climactic points [...] resort to a throaty, guttural kind of production for emphasis'.[3] More generally, one notes an unevenness in his performances on record. He recorded Mahler's *Das Lied von der Erde* twice (for Solti and Bernstein) and both versions find him in poor voice; in each recording, the strenuous opening song is as much a trial for the listener as it seems to have been for the tenor. His Erik in Solti's *Der Fliegende Holländer* is not a thing of beauty either: a kind of Wagnerian *bel canto* role, it finds him in rough voice and wanting in elegance. His Lohengrin for Karajan, on the other hand, is a fine one, sung with a pure, gleaming tone and ample power. The safest rule is, *caveat emptor* – his recordings should be sampled before buying.

Siegfried Jerusalem sounds, at first, too light for a *Heldentenor*, but his Wagnerian repertoire and vocal longevity tell a different story. In fact he shows that it is not necessary, even with modern orchestras, to have a voice that knocks down walls in order to sing Wagner. Jerusalem, with what is essentially a lyric tenor with some power, a penetrative timbre, and a lower than average *tessitura*, has sung all the major Wagner tenor roles, including the fearsomely demanding Tristan and the low-lying Siegmund. He has also successfully essayed roles as lyrical as Lionel in *Martha* and Tamino.

Peter Hofmann's career as a *Heldentenor* was comparatively short. There were various reasons for this. His technique was unfinished. He chose, unwisely, to combine his operatic career with a parallel career singing rock music. And his health failed (he developed Parkinson's disease). His recordings are few and even more variable in quality than Kollo's. A version of Gluck's *Orfeo* in which he sings the title role in the baritone key is, frankly, awful. When we turn to Wagner, the news is (sometimes) better. His Parsifal is well sung, dramatically involved, and deeply moving. Hofmann's career probably owed as much to his exceptional good looks as to his vocal and interpretative qualities.

Peter Seiffert (b. 1954) is another German tenor whose brilliant, bright-toned Wagner performances have attracted favourable notices in recent years. On disc, he also makes a more-than-usually heroic Max in *Der Freischütz*, a part often given to a much lighter tenor. The American **Gary Lakes** (b. 1950) is another lyrical-sounding Wagnerian. On disc, he makes a decent impression as Berlioz's Énée in *Les Troyens*, although the high notes are disappointing.

A Commonwealth quartet comprising the Canadian **Ben Heppner** (b. 1956), the South African **Johan Botha** (1965–2016), the New Zealander **Simon O'Neill** (b. 1971), and the Australian **Stuart Skelton** (b. 1968) have also been outstanding in recent years, on stage and in the recording studio, and in more than the Wagnerian *Fach*. Heppner, for example, is a superb Prince in Charles Mackerras's recording of Dvořák's *Rusalka* and is equally fine in a 'live' recording of *Les Troyens* under Colin Davis. Skelton has sung masterfully in a wide repertoire on disc, including Elgar's *Dream of Gerontius*, John Foulds' *A World Requiem*, and Schönberg's *Gurre-Lieder*. And the late, much-lamented Johan Botha, on disc a magnificent Lohengrin, also, in a BBC recording of *Das Lied von der Erde*, delivered what, for me, is the ideal performance of the tenor's songs – one that delivers both declamatory power and genuine lyricism. O'Neill is the possessor of a strong but not especially ingratiating voice, but he compensates for the lack of sensuous beauty of tone with excellent musicianship and interpretative intelligence.

This brief and by no means exhaustive survey of *Heldentenors*, if it achieves nothing else, will have given the lie to persistent rumours that the breed is dying out, or that true *Heldentenors* are naturally as scarce as hens' teeth. In fact, over the recorded era, there have been more good *Heldentenors* than good Mozart tenors. But to say that is to beg the question, what is a *Heldentenor*? Lauritz Melchior had no doubt: a real *Heldentenor* must have begun his career as a high baritone, and he must have succeeded in grafting on to a voice still baritonal in range and colour, bomb-proof high notes up to a top C. His voice must be preëminently suited to Wagner and to very little (if anything) else. In short, he must be, as nearly as possible, a carbon copy of Lauritz Melchior.

But as we have seen, there is more than one way to sing Wagner, and there is more than one kind of voice that is suited to the *Heldentenor Fach*. Some *Heldentenors* are weighty and baritonal – Melchior, Hopf, and Vinay, for instance. Others have bright, tenorial voices with a trumpet-like top register – Seiffert, Heppner, and Botha, for example. Some favour a powerfully declamatory approach. Others sing in a more lyrical, Italianate style. Some focus almost exclusively on Wagner. Others sing a wider repertoire of heroic roles. The non-Wagnerian operas most commonly found in the repertoire of *Heldentenors* include *Fidelio*, *Der Freischütz*,

Jon Elsby

Oberon, Euryanthe, Elektra, Salome, Daphne, Die Frau ohne Schatten, Ariadne auf Naxos, Aufstieg und Fall der Stadt Mahagonny, Aida, Otello, La Forza del Destino, Don Carlo, Andrea Chenier, Cavalleria Rusticana, Pagliacci, Tosca, La Fanciulla del West, Turandot, Rusalka, Dalibor, The Queen of Spades, Boris Godunov, Les Troyens, Carmen, Le Prophète, Samson et Dalila, Káťa Kabanová, Oedipus Rex, Peter Grimes, Billy Budd, Tiefland, Die tote Stadt, and _Wozzeck._ Being a _Heldentenor_ does not necessarily preclude having a broad repertoire. The only requirements for other roles are that they should be capable of being sung well by a voice of heroic proportions, and that their _tessitura_ should not be too high.

Notes

[1] I hope it is not ungallant to point out that most of the Wagnerian sopranos are built on similarly generous lines.

[2] I had the pleasure of hearing Stuart Skelton sing Tristan for the ENO in 2016. Uniquely in my experience, he sounded at the end of Act Three as if he could have sung the entire role over again.

[3] See J. B. Steane's essay on _Tannhäuser_ in _Opera on Record_ (Hutchinson, 1979).

The Great Tenors
Part Two

7 Caruso: the master of them all

There is a well-known story about Giovanni Martinelli, Caruso's successor in dramatic roles at the New York Met, according to which a woman approached him at a party and asked whether Caruso was really as good as people said he was. Martinelli replied, 'Madam, if you put Gigli, Lauri-Volpi, and me together and made us into one tenor, we would not be fit to kiss Caruso's shoes.' It is known that Jussi Björling both idolized Caruso and feared comparison with him. Robert Merrill recalled that, before he and Björling recorded the Oath Duet from *Otello*, he had to walk the tenor round the block several times to calm him down, so intimidated did he feel by the prospect of competing with the celebrated recording by Caruso and Titta Ruffo. And Richard Tauber begged his friends never to play a record of his after one of Caruso's.

These stories aptly illustrate the way Enrico Caruso (1873–1921) is regarded by his fellow tenors, who, as a breed, are not noted for their modesty. Yet the unanimity with which they acknowledge Caruso as their master is very striking. Equally striking is the fact that that unanimity of opinion extends also to other singers, music critics, conductors – indeed, to virtually all musically informed persons. There is scarcely a dissenting voice to be found. Even sopranos, few of whom have a good word for tenors (or a polite one, at any rate), revere him.

Such unanimity of educated opinion deserves respect. But is it justified? Or does it depend on a pious legend which originally arose from Caruso's untimely death and which, with the passage of time, has hardened into an indisputable 'fact'? The question is a natural one, and it deserves a considered answer.

Well, let it be admitted that not all Caruso's records are perfect. A few are not even very good. He recorded a fair amount of rubbish – very inferior stuff, unworthy of his talents. But the same might be said of other singers – of Clara Butt, for instance, or Tauber, or McCormack. In some of his recordings, he was not in his best voice. But that, too, might be said of other singers. The fact remains that, when Caruso was at his best (which was most of the time), and when he was singing material worthy of him, he set a standard unmatched before or since. Anyone who doubts this should try an experiment. Play a selection of Caruso's recordings. Many could be made, but I would suggest the following as a sample: the 1904 '*Sogno*' from *Manon*, the 1906 '*Spirto gentil*' from *La Favorita* and '*M'appari*' from *Martha*, the 1908 '*Deserto in terra*' from *Don Sebastiano*, the 1912 trio '*Qual voluttà trascorrere*' from *I Lombardi* and the Goodnight Quartet from *Martha*, the 1914 '*Brindisi*' from *Traviata* and the Oath Duet from *Otello*, the 1916 '*Ô Souverain, ô Juge, ô Père*' from *Le Cid*, and the 1920 '*Rachel, quand du Seigneur*' from *La Juive*. That selection offers a fair conspectus of Caruso's voice and art at all stages of his career. It covers the full range of his repertoire, from the most lyrical roles to the most dramatic. It includes French and Italian items, duets and ensembles as well as solo arias. It shows how considerate Caruso was of smaller-voiced partners (Alda, Gluck) and how well he could compete with the biggest voices of all (Ruffo).

When you have listened to all those recordings, play – either physically or in your mind's ear – a few of your favourite rival versions. Then, making due allowance for the differences in the quality of recorded sound, consider whether any other tenor measures up to Caruso. Does anyone else equal the beauty of his voice, or the size, or the sweetness of his *mezza voce*, or the perfection of his *legato*, or the purity of his line, or the *squillo* of his top B flats and B naturals, or the baritonal sonority of his middle register, or the excellence of his technique (listen to how cleanly the *gruppetti* in the '*Brindisi*' from *Traviata* are executed)? Could any other tenor produce high notes that ring out as powerfully as Mario del Monaco's and a *mezza voce* that caresses like Gigli's? Could any other tenor equal the sheer agility of Jadlowker, the declamatory vigour of Martinelli, the pure line of Schipa, and the patrician elegance of Bergonzi? Has any other tenor sung with the overwhelming passion of Caruso (listen to, say, '*Testa adorata*' from Leoncavallo's *La Bohème*, Lensky's aria from Tchaikovsky's *Eugene Onegin*, or '*Ah fuyez douce image*' from Massenet's *Manon* to see what I mean)?

Therein lies Caruso's excellence. It was not that he did this thing, or that, better than anyone else. It was that he presented a balanced combination of attributes, each of which was excellent in itself, but which, taken together, constituted a previously unexampled phenomenon. He is the *ne plus ultra* of the Italian tenor.

It is sometimes claimed or suggested that Caruso was simply an immense natural talent – someone who sang as naturally as a bird and never had to think about what he was doing. That view cannot survive even the most cursory inspection of the evidence. In the first place, Caruso was clearly a singer who thought hard about what he was doing. He recorded quite a few items more than once, notably the aria, '*Celeste Aida*', and the *Rigoletto* quartet, '*Bella figlia dell'amore*', both of which he recorded multiple times. In these recordings, we can trace the development of his interpretations over time, and the way in which he made adjustments to accommodate the darker, more heroic quality of his voice as he grew older. In the second place, we know from his letters and from the testimony of those who knew him how hard he worked, and how much it cost him, to maintain his standard and fight off the competition. His contemporaries included Bonci, Slezak and Zenatello, and the younger generation included Hislop, McCormack, Martinelli, Pertile, Lázaro, Schipa, and Gigli. To get to the top was one thing; but to stay there was quite another. John Steane is not alone in surmising that stress contributed to Caruso's final illness and death. And thirdly, Caruso was not a natural tenor. Like Plácido Domingo, but unlike Gigli, Björling, or Pavarotti, he had to learn how to produce the top notes securely before he learned how to sustain them. Art and technique had as much to do with Caruso's excellence as nature.

Finally, let us take down a few Caruso recordings from the shelf, this time not in order to prove a point but for the sheer pleasure of hearing them. We might start with the Garden Scene from *Faust*, of which Caruso made a nearly complete recording which shows that he was one of the few Italian tenors who are truly at home in the French repertoire. Then, perhaps we might turn to *Il Trovatore* for the '*Miserere*' with Alda and the '*Ai nostri monti*' with Schumann-Heink. By way of contrast, we could next have the ravishing '*Magiche note*' from Goldmark's *Königin von Saba* (magic notes, indeed!) or '*Mia piccirella*' from Gomes' *Salvator Rosa*, with its *cadenza* despatched with the sort of accuracy and fluency we associate with much lighter voices. Then a version of '*Come un bel dì di Maggio*' from *Andrea Chenier* which, in its perfect combination of lyrical *legato* singing and fiery yet continent declamation, beats all the others hands down. Since the others include Martinelli, Pertile, Gigli, Tucker, del Monaco, Corelli, Domingo, and Pavarotti, that is no small claim. And, finally, we might want something special to end the evening, so how about Tosti's song '*L'alba separa dalla luce l'ombra*', a setting of a poem by d'Annunzio, which is given a magnificently ardent performance by Caruso, eclipsing even the fine versions by Björling and Tucker?

By then, surely even the most skeptical listener will be convinced that Caruso is the master of them all.

For those seeking further information, there are many biographies of Caruso, not all of them reliable. The most comprehensive, as well as the most accurate, is probably *Enrico Caruso: My Father and my Family* by Enrico Caruso Jr. and Andrew Farkas. Also essential are *Caruso: A Life in Pictures* by Francis Robinson, *Enrico Caruso: His Recorded Legacy* by J. Freestone and H. J. Drummond, and *The Great Caruso* by Michael Scott, which combines biography and criticism in equal proportions.

8 Gershon Sirota:
the cantor of Warsaw

Blanche Marchesi, a distinguished soprano and voice teacher wrote in her book, *A Singer's Pilgrimage*, that, 'although Caruso had a remarkable voice, it was not more remarkable than that of Tamagno (the creator of Verdi's Otello) or the cantor from Warsaw, Sirota'.

Gershon Sirota (1874–1943), who probably came nearer than anyone else to matching Caruso in terms of sheer vocal splendour, is nothing like as well known, despite leaving a sizeable legacy of about 175 recordings, made over a thirty-year period. The reason is not hard to find. Unlike Caruso – indeed, unlike most other tenors mentioned in these pages – Sirota was not an opera singer. He was a cantor, who led services in the Warsaw synagogue for many years. His recordings are exclusively of *chazzanut* – the cantorial music which forms such a central part of Jewish worship. This music is vocally taxing to the last degree. It requires a rock-solid technique, declamatory fervour, at least a two-octave compass, extreme vocal flexibility and agility, exemplary breath control, a good *legato*, expressive enunciation of the text – in short, all the attributes (with the possible exception of sheer stamina) that are required of an operatic singer.

So could Sirota have sung in opera? Undoubtedly, he could. In fact, in his concert tours of America, he included quite a few operatic items in his recitals, with great success. But orthodox Judaism in Sirota's day prohibited men and women from appearing together on stage. Sirota was nothing if not faithful to his creed. His beliefs precluded the glorious operatic career that might otherwise have been his. Instead he became known as perhaps the greatest cantor of the golden age – the period between the wars which was uniquely rich in masters of *chazzanut*.

Photographs of Sirota show a man of the typical tenor build: not particularly tall, but wide-shouldered, thickset and powerful, with a broad head and a neck like a bull. Physically, he resembles many other tenors – perhaps especially Richard Tucker, another great Jewish tenor with East European antecedents and a cantorial background.

What of the voice? It was a rich, dark, full-bodied *tenore robusto* of Caruso-like power throughout its range and with a similar quality of *chiaroscuro* – a wide palette of vocal colours. Like Caruso's, Sirota's voice darkened perceptibly with age. Unlike Caruso's, his range extended to a good top C (for Caruso, the high C was problematic and involved a perceptible gear change). It seems he could execute a perfect trill on almost any note in his compass. His vocal flexibility, in the light of the size of his voice, is astonishing: again and again, he shows the ability to execute runs and ornaments which would defeat many much lighter tenors.

Any listener to Sirota's recordings will be struck by both the vocal power and the expressive quality of his singing.[1] Fervour in petitionary prayer forms an important part of cantorial training, and that goes some way to explaining why so many cantors – Hermann Jadlowker, Jan Peerce, and Richard Tucker are examples – went on to have distinguished careers as operatic tenors. Had Sirota sung in opera, there can be no doubt that the dramatic roles of the French and Italian repertoire would have found in him their ideal interpreter. Roles like Jean de Leyde, Samson, Éléazar, Don José, Radames, Don Alvaro, Canio, and perhaps even Otello, would have lain within his compass. Anyone who has heard his records longs to know what he would have made of them. He is unquestionably the greatest operatic tenor who never was.

Notes

[1]It is interesting that cantors manage to achieve great emotional intensity without descending to the vulgarity and cheap tricks of which operatic tenors are often accused, sometimes with justification.

9 John McCormack:
the tenor as minstrel

The Irish tenor John McCormack (1884–1945) was the only tenor of his period to rival Caruso in popularity. In America, huge audiences turned out to hear him in vast open-air concerts long before Pavarotti popularized 'concerts in the park'. But McCormack was not just a popular singer. He was also a finished and conscientious artist with a taste so fastidious that he would lavish upon the simplest Irish ditty the same care that he brought to an air by Handel. It was said that, whereas McCormack sang everything, even a drawing-room ballad, as if it were an aria by Mozart, Gigli sang everything, even an aria by Mozart, as if it were a Neapolitan song.

There is some truth in the witticism. But it does not tell the whole story. McCormack was certainly not an elitist, and Gigli was certainly not *just* a populist. The truth about any great tenor is complex, and one does not do justice to a complex truth by reaching for glib phrases or slick aphorisms. The John McCormack who sang songs like 'Kathleen Mavourneen', '*Macushla*', or 'I Hear You Calling Me' also made recordings of '*Il mio tesoro*' from *Don Giovanni*, '*Per viver vicino a Maria*' from *La Figlia del Reggimento*, and 'Come, my beloved' from Handel's *Atalanta* (to cite just three of many possible examples) which have set the standard for all tenors ever since.

That McCormack was a great tenor is not in dispute. But in what did his greatness consist? He did not possess a voice of overwhelming magnificence like Caruso. He lacked the ringing top notes of Jussi Björling or the mellifluous quality of Gigli. But there are few tenors on whom the critical verdict is more unanimous. At his farewell concert in London, McCormack included the German folksong, '*All mein Gedanken die ich hab*'. The great music critic, Ernest Newman, a notoriously crabby individual who possessed probably the keenest ears and the highest musical standards of any critic of his day, later wrote: 'Rather than McCormack singing it to us, *we* should have risen *en masse* and sung it to him.'

McCormack's genius is only partly revealed by his operatic recordings. Even so, there are remarkable things here. I have already alluded to two of them, but there are many others – his Handel recordings, for instance, or his exquisite versions of Faust's two arias from Boïto's *Mefistofele*, '*Dai campi dai prati*' and '*Giunto sul passo estremo*'. The two latter arias are sung with a purity of tone and an aristocratic style unmatched by any other tenor on record. But there is a certain lack of detailed expression in these recordings which probably bears out something McCormack himself confessed to Gerald Moore many years later. When Moore asked him whether he had enjoyed appearing in opera, McCormack replied, with a frankness that was typical of him, 'Not at all. I was a rotten actor.' Of course, many tenors have been indifferent actors on stage, but good actors with the voice – Carlo Bergonzi comes to mind. But McCormack's vocal acting was also rather limited. In his famous recording of Mozart's '*Il mio tesoro*', for example – which has been rightly admired for its exceptional musicality and remarkable breath control (he was the first singer on record to sing the long central run in a single breath) – he makes relatively little of the difference between the opening section of the aria and the more martial middle section ('*Ditele che i suoi torti*'), where several other tenors point the contrast more effectively.

It is in song, and especially when singing in his native language, that McCormack really comes into his own. His pellucid diction with its distinctive Irish brogue was an asset in his delivery of the Irish songs he made so popular, but his natural enunciation of the text, where he privileged the natural rhythms of speech over note values, was equally important, and lent to his singing a vividly communicative quality that has been the envy of other tenors. He may have been a poor actor, but he was an incomparable storyteller. He can make a thing of magic out of a song as banal and sentimental as 'The vacant chair'. In his rendering of the Irish rebel song 'The wearing of the green', he sings with the sort of passion and intensity that we normally associate with a more heroic voice – say, with Giovanni Martinelli, a tenor McCormack is known to have admired for 'the fire and ease of his vocalism'. In the Rachmaninov songs he recorded with Fritz Kreisler's violin *obbligato*, both artists make magical effects out of the rather melancholy material.

McCormack's concert tours of America were hugely successful, attracting vast audiences and rapturous applause. Long before the Three Tenors, he popularized mass concerts at open air venues. It testifies to his integrity as an artist that events like these did not corrupt his taste or his art. At all times throughout his career, he was capable of both entertaining crowds and delighting connoisseurs. Nothing he did was ever cheap or intended only to please the gallery. He showed that, whatever self-appointed *cognoscenti* might say, a refined taste, consummate musicianship, and a broad popular appeal, were compatible and could co-exist in one person.

There are surprises in McCormack's enormous discography. He recorded some duets with the Italian baritone Mario Sammarco, including the vocally strenuous '*O grido di quest' anima*' from the first Act of *La Gioconda*. Sammarco possessed a voice of notable size, and one might have expected the much lighter-voiced McCormack to be overwhelmed. He is not. He shows that the classical virtues of purity of tone and clarity of projection count for more than sheer volume. And as for musicality, he simply sings rings round Sammarco, whose vocalism is made to seem crude by comparison. Again, in duet with the formidable dramatic soprano Emmy Destinn, McCormack holds his own without forcing or shouting. But probably his finest duet recording finds him partnering the delectable Italian soprano Lucrezia Bori in '*Parigi, o cara*' from the last Act of *La Traviata*. McCormack's elegant, exquisitely poised singing is matched by Bori in a version equalled only by the famous account by Tito Schipa and Amelita Galli-Curci.

McCormack's career in the opera house was comparatively brief, and various explanations have been put forward for this. He disliked acting and stagecraft was not his forte. But there was also the problem that the top notes went early. This may have been a blessing in disguise. By forcing him to make a virtue of necessity, it freed McCormack to do what he did best: perform as a concert artist. In song, whether art song or popular numbers, he was supreme, making even Gerald Moore, who accompanied every great tenor from John Coates to Nicolai Gedda, wonder 'how many tenors there are in the world who can measure up to this man'. The question remains as pertinent today as it was when Moore first raised it.

10 The strange case of Aureliano Pertile

Aureliano Pertile (1885–1952), who enjoyed an immensely successful career in Rome and Milan during the 1920s and '30s, where he became known as 'Toscanini's tenor' because of the maestro's declared partiality for him, is a puzzle for critics. He attracts equally vehement praise and criticism. Here, for example, is the English critic, Kaikhosru Shapurji Sorabji—

> Of the Canio of Mr Pertile it is difficult to speak with patience, such an exhibition of vulgar hysteria, mad ranting, and utter lack of anything remotely resembling style or beauty of singing will be (one hopes) difficult to surpass.

Yet this same tenor probably attracted more admiration from his tenor colleagues than any other with the exception of Caruso. Lauri-Volpi, del Monaco, di Stefano, Corelli, Bergonzi, Pavarotti, Domingo – all expressed their admiration for Pertile in the most glowing terms. In a characteristically thoughtful and perceptive essay in Volume 1 of his *Singers of the Century*, the late John Steane writes—

> Choice praises (freely translated) include: 'Pertile was to be my model, my ideal, throughout all my long career' (Bergonzi); 'Pertile was a singer who influenced all tenors, in my case in a way that was constant and decisive' (Corelli); 'To him goes the gratitude of all tenors who would draw upon the fountain of the

purest Italian lyricism' (del Monaco); 'Caruso, Pertile, Schipa, Gigli...and then...who?' (di Stefano); 'a serious, conscientious and most musical artist...a technique all his own, inimitable' (Lauri-Volpi).

Steane goes on to quote, at somewhat greater length, the verdict of Luciano Pavarotti on Pertile's art: a verdict which he describes as 'probably the most accurate and thoughtful'—

Ideal interpreter of *verismo* and of the late romantic school (it is sufficient to recall his Otello, confronted to the limits of vocal resource), Pertile is almost certainly the most representative tenor of his time, which was permeated by the culture of *verismo*; and of the Italian musical *verismo* school, he still represents the most pure and valuable aspects, the most humanly and passionately involved.

'Ideal interpreter of *verismo*'...carries, perhaps, the implication that Pertile was something less than an ideal interpreter of everything else – of *bel canto*, for example, or Verdi, or Wagner, all of which figured prominently in his repertoire. Yet even this would be less than the truth. Pertile's recordings of the *bel canto* repertoire – of '*A te o cara*' from *I Puritani*, '*Spirto gentil*' or '*Una vergine*' from *La Favorita*, '*Sulla tomba*' from *Lucia di Lammermoor* – though not in the authentic *bel canto* tradition of de Lucia, say, or Bonci, are not without merit. Their phrasing is distinguished and expressive. The articulation of the words is clear. The juddering tone which so often affects his delivery of declamatory passages is largely (though not entirely) absent, as is the explosive emotionalism which characterizes his singing of the *spinto* and dramatic repertoire. In these lyrical arias, as in the Verdi and *verismo* roles with which he was more closely associated, he shows himself a sensitive, vivid, and musical interpreter, with an instinctive sense of the shape of a musical phrase. He is less elegant than Bonci or Schipa or Lauri-Volpi, perhaps, and less stylish than de Lucia, but he is not coarse, inelegant, or grossly unstylish, as so many later tenors were in such music. He has a way of compelling the listener's attention in everything he does. And in many arias, including some unexpected ones, he makes an unforgettable impression. His Lohengrin, to judge from his recording of '*Merce, merce cigno gentil*', must have been one of the most lyrical and poetic ever heard. His singing of '*Quando le sere al placido*' from Verdi's *Luisa Miller* was rightly described by John Steane as 'quite breathtakingly "inner" and alive'. Pavarotti's verdict – that Pertile represented the purest and most valuable aspects of *verismo*, 'the most humanly and passionately involved' – seems amply justified by these recordings, where Pertile brings to an earlier repertoire the expressive qualities he had learned from his absorption of the characteristic products of *verismo*.

It is not only poetic phrasing that makes Pertile's recordings worth listening to. The voice itself, though not as beautiful as Gigli's or Caruso's, is by no means wholly unsympathetic. It is not hard or forced. It is more freely produced than Martinelli's or del Monaco's, and able to encompass both the lyrical and the declamatory styles, moving easily from one to the other. With the Irish soprano, Margaret Sheridan, he serves up a memorable final scene from *Andrea Chenier*. The opening section, '*Vicino a te*', is tenderly sung and grandly phrased on broad arcs of sound. In the more declamatory section that follows – '*La nostra morte è il trionfo dell' amor*' – both artists give one of the most thrilling accounts that has ever been committed to disc. Pertile manages to be convincingly romantic and heroic in the title role on disc, where his decidedly unromantic appearance is not a drawback.

The admiration of Pertile's tenor colleagues, then, is justified. But what of Sorabji's strictures? Are they merely the eccentric animadversions of an embittered and inexplicably hostile critic? Not exactly. I have mentioned juddering tone and explosive emotionalism. Both feature very noticeably in some of Pertile's recordings, early and late, especially of *verismo* parts – but they can also be found in his versions of some Verdi roles and arias, particularly his complete recording of Manrico in *Il Trovatore*. These faults are present to an embarrassing extent in his recording of '*Vesti la giubba*'. Not only does he indulge in unusually tempestuous weeping in the aria's final phrases, but after the orchestral postlude, he returns unexpectedly for a final bellow, just for good measure! The effect, to English ears at any rate, is irresistibly comic – not at all what was intended.

What was the reason for these apparent lapses of taste on the part of a serious and conscientious artist? I would suggest that they have to do partly with the Italian temperament, which is naturally more expressive and extravert than the English, and partly with the artistic demands of the *verismo* repertoire. The *proprium* of *verismo* was that it required singers to adopt a different expressive style, a different grammar of expressive devices, from that of their predecessors. No longer was it the singers' first duty to make beautiful sounds, or to master the art of devising and executing tasteful ornamentation. Rather their duty was to convey, through the music, the meaning of the text. And if that meant, as it sometimes did, that they had to shout, scream, howl, laugh, cry, yelp, roar, and speak, as well as sing, then so be it. Sometimes it might be necessary to cultivate a deliberately ugly tone – for instance, in (non-*verismo*) parts such as Beckmesser, Mime or Herod (although a respectable ancestry might be claimed for such roles in earlier parts, like Monostatos in *The Magic Flute*, who must sound harsh and menacing, or Basilio in *Le Nozze di Figaro*, who has to affect a wheedling tone). Sometimes it might be necessary to sing sharp of the written note for dramatic emphasis, or to employ an exaggerated *vibrato* (hence the juddering which some critics so disliked). This was a radically different approach to singing from that of the *bel canto* specialists or the early Verdian tenors.

Verismo affected the way singers approached the earlier repertoire. It affected also their vocal method and technique. And its effects were not beneficial, at least as far as their singing of the older repertoire was concerned, as can be heard from listening to recordings of *bel canto* roles and arias from the 1940s and 1950s. Tenors such as Luigi Infantino, Ferruccio Tagliavini and Gianni Poggi had only the most rudimentary idea of how to sing that repertoire, and their technique was not equal to the demands of the music. Their execution of *fioriture* was clumsy and graceless; of runs, sketchy and approximate. But was their extraverted, hell-for-leather style the only, or even the best, way to approach the *verismo* repertoire? Alternatives are suggested by the recordings of *verismo* roles by singers such as Björling, Bergonzi, Domingo and Pavarotti – not to mention Pertile's contemporaries and compatriots, Schipa and Martinelli. Here we find singers who could interpret the *verismo* repertoire without disrupting the vocal line with sobs and aspirates, and without resorting to shouting in declamatory passages. There are undoubtedly musical gains in this approach. But there are losses too. Few comparing, say, the Canios of Björling and del Monaco would maintain that Björling's was the more dramatic interpretation – even if they preferred it for purely musical reasons. The approach of *veristi* like Pertile and del Monaco may have been less singerly, but it was more actorly. Or, to make the same point in another way, it may have been less musical, but it was more dramatic. For those for whom opera is not simply a musical genre, like the symphony, but a unique combination of music and drama, in which neither element is more important than the other, this approach will always have an appeal – even if a slightly guilty one.

Whether a rational justification for the Pertile approach can be offered turns, then, on one's view of the old dictum, *Prima la musica, poi le parole*. Does the music really come first? Can it claim primacy, in importance if not in chronology, over the words? The truth is that they are equally indispensable. Certainly no one would pay to see a performance of an operatic libretto as a play, without music. But would anyone pay to see a performance of an opera from which words were absent, where the vocal parts were played on instruments, or vocalized by singers on meaningless vowel sounds? If the answer to these questions is 'no', then there must be a place in opera for the actorly, or dramatic, approach to the singer's art; and the principal question becomes how to achieve a balance between the requirements of the music and those of the drama or text. Pertile's solution was one possibility. It was not just a matter of playing to the gallery: on the contrary, it was a solution which occurred to an intelligent, sincere, and committed artist. In the *verismo* and late Romantic repertoire, it was supremely successful. The results cannot be dismissed as cavalierly as Sorabji's diatribe suggests. They deserve serious consideration as one possible solution to the perennial interpretative problem of finding the correct balance between the competing claims of music and words, or of beauty and truth.

11 Giovanni Martinelli: the tenor as hero

Giovanni Martinelli (1885–1969), born in the same town as Pertile and (allegedly) in the same year,[1] also has a somewhat controversial reputation. In some ways, he is the obverse of Pertile. Pertile was admired in Italy, but less successful elsewhere. Martinelli was extravagantly admired in New York and London, but met with a much cooler reception on his infrequent visits to his homeland.

The reasons for this divergence of opinion are suggested in the views of two knowledgeable critics, one an ardent admirer of Martinelli, the other a detractor who views his recordings with distinctly modified rapture. The first is John Steane; the second, Michael Scott. Here is Steane, writing in *The Grand Tradition*—

Martinelli's records affect listeners in different ways... [...] There are few who fail to recognize a distinction, but many more who find little to delight their hearing. To some, the recorded voice is rather wearing, sometimes downright unpleasant, lacking in richness and beauty, while to others it is the most exciting sound on earth. He is, then, among the most interesting singers this book has to discuss. [...]

[B]eauty of sound is certainly there on the records, its characteristic form being a kind of shining precision. He drew sound with the thin definition of a pencil line, but glowing brightly as if the pencil were pointed with fire. The sharpness and thrust of this could also be moderated and softened. [...] But it is the brilliance of his full voice that is most exciting. [...]

Sometimes the sound on the high F or F sharp is too open for comfort, and the high notes themselves always seem very very high, so that one feels a tension even if the singer is not experiencing strain himself.

Steane has much more to say about Martinelli, both in *The Grand Tradition* and in two other books: *Voices: Singers & Critics*, and Volume 3 of his *Singers of the Century*, each of which contains an insightful essay on the tenor. He was one of Steane's favourite singers, and probably the one whose records he had studied more closely than any other over a long lifetime of listening carefully to vocal recordings.

Michael Scott's opinion, in the second volume of *The Record of Singing*, is slightly different. He writes of Martinelli—

His was an outstanding lirico-spinto tenor voice, the emission smooth and the registers correctly blended up to a fine high C. A remarkable breath span gave his phrasing a nobility and grandeur that was characteristic and time never robbed him of it. Unfortunately, as his contemporaries noted and as is apparent to some degree in almost all his recordings, he forced; not in the way of a crude vocalist who can do nothing else nor [...] from an excess of uncontrolled temperament, but he used too much breath pressure. The result of this was to make the voice tight and over the years intractable; though it survived all the strain, it lost the quality and the tone became thin and fixed-sounding. [...]

It adversely affected every aspect of his singing. He had a fine conception of legato but the execution was imperfect; instead of letting the voice flow poised on the breath, he squeezed it out like toothpaste; for a musical tension he substituted a muscular one. Especially in later years [...] the unrelenting intensity becomes monotonous and wearisome.

The distinguished American bass, Jerome Hines, writing in his *The Four Voices of Man*, attributes Martinelli's characteristically bright, narrow sound to his adoption of the low larynx or Melocchi method,[2] but adds that it served Martinelli well, since he was still capable of serving up a fiery account of the taxing role of Canio in *Pagliacci* at the age of sixty-eight.

Putting together these accounts, I think we can see that there is little difference between admirers and detractors over the objective facts, but a considerable difference in the subjective way they respond to the facts. It is admitted, by both advocates and detractors, that Martinelli possessed an intrinsically fine voice, but that his vocal method was strenuous, and that the result was a tense, narrow sound which, to some listeners, could be unvaried and wearyingly bright. But, whereas for Scott the 'thin and fixed-sounding' quality of Martinelli in his prime was 'intractable', for Steane it lent to Martinelli's singing, and especially his interpretation of Otello, an unforgettable and unrivalled intensity. Scott refers to the breadth, nobility and grandeur of Martinelli's phrasing, and these were characteristics that other critics also noted. Even at a slowish tempo, he sings Manrico's '*Riposa o madre, Iddio conceda men tristi imagini al tuo sopor*' in a single, huge span of breath – an impressive feat, not replicated by many other tenors. The taxing high phrases at the end of the *Siciliana* from *Cavalleria Rusticana* ('*E s'iddu muoru e vaju 'n Paradisu*') also find Martinelli phrasing more broadly than any other tenor on record.

As to the vocal method, that may have been, to some extent, a matter of necessity. After Caruso's death in 1921, the great tenor's lyric roles at the Metropolitan passed to Gigli, while his heroic roles were given to Martinelli, perhaps a few years before he felt entirely ready to undertake them. Yet even this may have been a blessing in disguise. Martinelli's recordings of the lyric repertoire, though generally well sung, rarely suggest that he felt much affinity for those roles. His Duke of Mantua is deficient in gaiety, and his Rodolfo sounds a rather staid and serious Bohemian. One cannot quite see him joining in the high jinks of his companions with much enthusiasm. From the first, Martinelli, though lively and convivial in private life, seems to have been notably lacking in the lighter-hearted qualities as a singer. He was best suited to the most tragic and dramatic roles of the repertoire – roles which called for a combination of nobility, restraint, declamatory intensity, and conviction in the delineation of the most profound and passionate emotions. As Arnold, Ernani, Manrico, Alvaro, Don Carlo, Radames, Canio, Chenier, Calaf, Samson, Eléazar, and finally Otello, Martinelli was considered, at least in the USA and the UK, unequalled among Caruso's successors.

In Italy, the picture was different. The competition in Martinelli's favoured repertoire from Zenatello, Pertile, Lauri-Volpi, and de Muro was stiff. And Martinelli's squeezed method of tone production, and the *voce fissa* in which it resulted, were disliked by Italian audiences. But, whatever its drawbacks, that method permitted Martinelli to preserve evenness of emission and avoid any tendency for the tone to spread in the upper register, as invariably happens to tenors who force. It is this even more than the recorded evidence that makes one look askance at Scott's allegation that Martinelli forced his tone. Young tenors who force do not usually become old tenors. And Martinelli emphatically *did* become an old tenor. His career as a principal tenor was one of the longest in the history of the Metropolitan, in spite of the fact that most of it had been devoted to singing the most strenuous roles in the dramatic tenor repertoire.[3]

What does the recorded evidence tell us? Certainly the early recordings confirm the outstanding *lirico spinto* tenor voice that Scott noted, and the sheer beauty of sound Steane refers to. The later electrical recordings show signs of vocal decline in terms of beauty of sound, but a gain in interpretative power and intensity. At all times, the exceptional breath control and the noble, spacious phrasing are much in evidence. They can be heard, for example, in '*Come rugiada al cespite*' from *Ernani*, or in the trio '*Troncar suoi dì quel empio ardiva*' from *William Tell*, where he is joined by Giuseppe de Luca and José Mardones. What is perhaps more surprising is the impression one gets of an effortless voice in so many of the early records. The *Siciliana* already referred to is remarkable for the ease of its delivery – has any other tenor made those difficult high-lying phrases at the end ring out so freely, or sung them so smoothly?

By common consent, Martinelli's greatest achievement was his assumption of the title role of Otello. He waited until 1937 before singing it for the first time. Several 'off-the-air' recordings exist, all in dreadful sound. Even if they had been made in ideal studio conditions in the years 1938–40, they would have fallen far short of modern technical standards. As it is, they all demand a considerable effort of the listener. They are well worth it. Of all the great Otellos, Martinelli probably possessed the voice least suited to the demands of the part. He had neither the darkly baritonal splendour of Ramón Vinay nor the pealing, heroic quality (and thunderous volume) of Tamagno or del Monaco. Such considerations, and perhaps also an understandable unwillingness to court comparison with Zenatello or Slezak, the two leading Otellos of his day, were probably behind Martinelli's reluctance to tackle the role. Yet, for many who have listened attentively to one or more of his recordings, he remains the definitive Otello, phrase after phrase being stamped with the authority of his portrayal. The voice may be dry, and it may never have been an Otello voice in the first place, even in its prime. But when one hears the terrifying recrimination against Desdemona (*quella vil cortigiana che è la sposa d'Otello*), or the anguish in the monologue '*Dio mi potevi scagliar tutti mali*', or the threefold cry of *morta* in the Death Scene, one does not easily forget them. Nor do the most heroic moments find him wanting – the Oath Duet, for example, is a thrilling account in which Martinelli's concentrated tone enables him to achieve parity with the resonant dramatic baritone of Lawrence Tibbett.

Perhaps the most telling fact about Martinelli is that, for many knowledgeable opera lovers, his is the first voice that comes to mind when the heroic roles of the French and Italian repertoire are mentioned. Like Callas, he possesses both a distinctive sound that one can 'hear' in one's mind, and an individual way of shaping a phrase so that it lingers in the mind long after the performance is over. That is why, for many people, despite the rival claims of Tamagno, Zenatello, Pertile, Lauri-Volpi, del Monaco, Corelli, and Vickers, he remains the greatest of all heroic tenors for the dramatic French and Italian repertoire.

Notes

[1] Modern research has called into question the claim that Martinelli was born in 1885. His actual date of birth may have been a few years earlier.

[2] This method was most closely associated with Mario del Monaco but, according to Hines, it was also used by Lauritz Melchior, Richard Tucker, Luciano Pavarotti, and (intermittently) Franco Corelli. Less complimentarily, it has also been described as the 'close-all-passages-and-push' method. One drawback of this method is that, at lower volumes, there may be a tendency to flatten in pitch. Both Martinelli and del Monaco were sometimes affected by this.

[3] Jerome Hines testifies, in his *The Four Voices of Man*, that he heard Martinelli, then aged sixty-eight, deliver a successful performance of the demanding role of Canio in *I Pagliacci*.

12 Tito Schipa: the tenor with a great line

Tito Schipa (1889–1965) possessed a small voice, short at both ends of its range, somewhat limited in its technique (he was certainly not what he is often called, a master of the art of the *bel canto*), and monochrome. Yet this was the tenor of whom Gigli said 'There were many fine tenors in the '20s and '30s, but when Schipa sang, we all had to bow to his greatness.' The tribute is the more touching as, artistically speaking, they seemed on the surface to be opposites: Schipa was as patrician as Gigli was plebeian.

But what does that mean? And what made Schipa great, given that his voice was unremarkable in range, volume, and colour? His contemporaries included Martinelli, Pertile, Gigli, and Lauri-Volpi: how was a tenor with such obvious limitations able to stand out against competition of that quality? Why was he able to command their unanimous respect?

The answer is easier to demonstrate ostensively than to articulate. Let's start with three duets: '*Son geloso del zeffiro*' from *La Sonnambula*, '*Parigi, o cara*' from *La Traviata*, and the Cherry Duet from *L'Amico Fritz*. In the first two, Schipa's partner is Amelita Galli-Curci; in the third, Mafalda Favero. In all three, we notice how skilfully Schipa blends his voice with his partner's. Then, we notice the purity of the line. It is never disturbed by aspirates or unevenness in the emission of tone. There is a restraint about the singing that is rare in Italian tenors of this period – the age of *verismo*. Next, we notice how expressive the singing is. In particular, the emotion of *tenderness* has probably never received a more eloquent expression than in these recordings. Finally, we notice that, while the voice is small, it has a melancholy beauty that is all its own.

One expects, from a small voice, agility – fluency and accuracy in the execution of ornaments and runs. But in these respects, Schipa disappoints. Long runs, such as that in Don Ottavio's '*Il mio tesoro*', are seldom attempted, and when they are, the results are ungainly. *Fioriture* are not sung as cleanly as they are by de Lucia, for instance, or, for that matter, by larger-voiced tenors like Caruso, Jadlowker, Tucker, and Domingo. Schipa's strengths lay elsewhere. What chiefly made him remarkable was his ability to fuse 'plebeian gusto and patrician grace', in the words of John Steane. It is a potent mixture. In popular Neapolitan songs, he catches both the gaiety and the sadness in a very personal way, quite different from the uninhibited emotionalism of Gigli but similarly affecting.

Schipa was not a classic *tenore di grazia*. In the first place, the high notes were not his by divine right and he did not have them for long. Later in his career, he often transposed music downwards to make it easier to sing. At no time did he have the upward extension to notes above high C possessed by tenors like Alfredo Kraus or Juan Diego Flórez. His low notes were practically non-existent, as can clearly be heard (or not!) in an otherwise charming rendition of the Neapolitan song, '*La campana di San Giusto*'. But his repertoire contains quite a few surprises. That a small-voiced, light-lyric tenor should sing the roles of Fenton or Rossini's Almaviva is to be expected – but what of the roles of Cavaradossi, Werther, Maurizio (in *Adriana Lecouvreur*), Turiddu, Faust (in *Mefistofele*), Roméo, and Loris (in *Fedora*)? Five of these featured in the repertoire of Mario del Monaco, and five (not the same ones although there was an overlap) in that of Franco Corelli – both heroic tenors with huge voices. Yet Schipa sang all of them. They didn't shorten his career either. Like Martinelli and Gigli, he was still singing well at an age when most tenors are long retired.

Schipa's success in parts that appear, at first sight, too heavy for his voice must be attributed to three things: his ability to infuse an unusual degree of tension into his tone without forcing, his wide dynamic range, and his ability to project his voice clearly in even the largest auditorium. Anyone who regularly goes to the opera knows that there are big voices which are not well projected and therefore do not carry well, and that there are smaller voices which, thanks to their clarity of projection, carry, as if without effort, up to the 'gods' in the largest houses. Schipa fell into the second category. It enabled him to undertake roles which few would have thought within his vocal means. His pupil Cesare Valletti had some of the same qualities, but without quite the unique individuality of Schipa, whose voice is as immediately recognizable as any tenor's on record.

And that returns us to what made Schipa great. It was partly a matter of his vocal timbre, and partly that purity of line we have already alluded to. He had, as we have said, neither the agility nor the upward extension that we expect of a classic *tenore di grazia*. His Mozart is not as technically accomplished as McCormack's or Tauber's. Most of the *bel canto* repertoire would have been beyond him for want of the necessary high notes, the ability to sustain a generally high *tessitura*, or the skill in *fioriture*. But within his chosen repertoire of *arie antiche*, popular Italian songs, and lyric tenor operatic roles, he was supreme. Nor has he been surpassed since. Gigli's assessment remains as true today as when it was first written.

13 The populist art
of Beniamino Gigli

In (I think) 1949, my mother heard Beniamino Gigli (1890–1957) sing at the Royal Albert Hall in what was billed as a farewell concert. In fact, he continued to sing until 1955, when declining health (he was by then suffering from diabetes and cardiac problems) forced his retirement.

By 1949, Gigli was fifty-nine years old and had been singing for some thirty-five years. My mother, who was not especially musical, recalled sitting in the hall as the lights dimmed – and then seeing a short, fat, elderly gentleman with thinning grey hair waddle on to the stage, and thinking, 'Good heavens! Is *that* what we've paid so much money to see?'[1] Gigli bowed to acknowledge the applause, and then began to sing. 'And that,' my mother said, 'was the last time I gave a thought to his looks!' She remembered that, at the end of the advertised programme, Gigli returned to the platform again and again, and waited, cupping his hand to his ear, as the audience called out the names of the Neapolitan songs they wanted as encores. After he had sung eight of these (including the inevitable '*O sole mio*' and '*Santa Lucia*') in addition to his advertised programme, the manager of the Albert Hall appeared and told the still wildly cheering, clapping, stamping audience that Signor Gigli had been more than generous, but he was now very tired and begged that they would allow him to go.

For the rest of my mother's life, Gigli remained her favourite tenor.

Gigli's art was unashamedly populist. He sang from the heart, and his singing touched the hearts of his listeners. Of course, there were carpers. The more fastidious critics deplored his 'cheap tricks', his 'playing to the gallery', his lapses of taste. But Gigli ignored their strictures, and so did the public. He never sang to please purists. He liked to be known as 'the people's singer of Italy'; and he became, arguably, the people's singer of the whole world. Certainly, he more than any other tenor – and he came from a prodigiously talented generation[2] – was the heir to Caruso. Like Caruso, for millions of people who never entered an opera house, he was *the* tenor – the singer who, more than any other, defined for them what the tenor voice was.[3]

Gigli was also the first tenor to make a respectable number of studio recordings of complete operas. In the twelve years between 1934 and 1946, he recorded *Pagliacci, La Bohème, Madama Butterfly, Tosca, Andrea Chenier, Cavalleria Rusticana, Un Ballo in Maschera, Aida*, and the Verdi Requiem. Many critics consider that Gigli's best years were those between 1914 and 1934, which would mean that only the *Pagliacci* recording was made when his voice was in its prime, but even later in his career few other tenors could match Gigli for sheer effortless beauty of tone or for his ability to project personality in everything he sang.

Taste and musicianship were another matter. Gigli was regularly taken to task for his use – or abuse –of sobs, intrusive aspirates, exaggerated *portamenti*, for ignoring the composer's dynamic markings, and even for his allegedly excessive use of his honeyed *mezza voce*. Yet, in all of his recordings, we encounter a singer with a 'face'. Whether the personality is altogether in keeping with the requirements of the role he is playing may be a moot point, but that there *is* a personality is never in doubt. His Riccardo in *Ballo* may be a little undignified for a Governor of Boston, but he is vividly human and a well realized character. In congenial roles – say Rodolfo in *Bohème* or Pinkerton in *Butterfly* – he is superb, catching the playfulness and high spirits of the Bohemian poet and the insouciant gaiety of the young naval officer perfectly. His favourite role was the title role in Giordano's *Andrea Chenier*, and his recording of it shows why. It is a splendid creation, capturing the combination of revolutionary and romantic fervour that drives Chenier. And it is good to hear a lyric tenor in a role often given to heroic tenors, who are apt to make too much of the declamatory passages and not enough of the lyrical ones. It is unfortunate that his last complete opera recording was as Radames in *Aida*: on his own admission, he never had the right voice for the part, although he sang it fairly often in the latter part of his career. But even in that recording, where his essentially lyric voice sometimes takes on an uncharacteristic dryness ('*Celeste Aida*' is not one of the happier moments), there are moments when the old Gigli magic shines through. The Tomb Scene in Act Four is meltingly beautiful, with some exquisite soft top B flats from the fifty-six-year-old tenor. Even in the Nile Scene, to which he is vocally less well suited, his commitment to the role, and the immediacy and authenticity of his responses go a long way to make up for the lack of a genuinely heroic tone.

Whatever language an opera is sung in, the preferability of casting native speakers holds good as a rule. And, for that reason, the recordings of complete works built around Gigli, who was supported by some of the finest Italian singers of his day – the sopranos Lina Bruna Rasa, Maria Caniglia, Iva Pacetti, Toti dal Monte, and Licia Albanese; the mezzos Ebe Stignani, Fedora Barbieri, and Giulietta Simionato; the baritones Armando Borgioli, Mario Basiola, and Gino Bechi; and the basses Ezio Pinza, Tancredi Pasero and Italo Tajo – are well worth seeking out and stand up surprisingly well to the pick of the modern competition. But, important as these recordings are for historical as well as musical reasons, the best of Gigli is to be found elsewhere – in the acoustic recordings, and in the early electricals. In these, we hear what is probably the most glorious pure lyric tenor on record. His acoustic and electrical recordings of Faust's '*Salut demeure*' (there are three versions, all sung in Italian as '*Salve dimora*': two acoustic recordings made in 1918 and 1921 respectively, and a very fine electrical recording made in 1931) show his voice and art at their best. They also show a secure and easy top C. And, interestingly, they are quite different from each other. Clearly, Gigli was not the kind of artist who decides on an interpretation of a piece, and then sticks to it without variation for the rest of his career.[4]

The general view of the Anglo-Saxon critics was that, stylistically and technically, Gigli represented a decadence from the art of Caruso. But in his *Tradition and Gigli*, the eminent voice teacher, E. Herbert-Caesari, put forward a different view. He claimed that Gigli was the last representative of the classical Italian School, and that there was a continuity between the earliest representatives of that school in the sixteenth century and Gigli in the twentieth. Whether that is true or not – and Herbert-Caesari makes a persuasive case for it – it is certainly *not* true that Gigli decisively broke with the Italian tradition. His mastery of the *mezza voce*, the purity of his *legato*, the clarity of his diction, the equalization of his vocal registers, the smoothness of his *passaggio*, and the plasticity of his phrasing, all testify to what he learned from his predecessors.[5] That said, his populist vocal manners owed more to the *veristi* than to the *bel canto* or Verdian schools.

Gigli was not as influential as Caruso. Few of the tenors who followed him tried to imitate him. Gianni Poggi and Ferruccio Tagliavini were prominent among those who did, but young tenors soon had other models for emulation, notably Mario del Monaco and Giuseppe di Stefano. Perhaps they recognized the futility of trying to emulate Gigli: a voice as naturally mellow and responsive as his comes along once in a century – with luck. Such voices are

God-given: they cannot be manufactured. Rightly or wrongly – probably wrongly – the examples of del Monaco and di Stefano seemed, to the younger generation of tenors, easier to follow.

How should Gigli's legacy finally be assessed? For sheer beauty of sound, perhaps his only tenor rival[6] is Jussi Björling. Their voices were totally different in timbre – Gigli's was golden, honeyed, rounded, and mellow, while Björling's was silvery, gleaming, brilliant, and ringing – but they had in common an effortless delivery and an ability to silence criticism just by the quality of their voices. Interpretatively, they were poles apart – Gigli extravert, demonstrative and wholehearted, Björling introverted, reserved and self-restrained – but, despite the differences in timbre noted above, their voices had commonalities other than beauty of tone. They were similar in weight, colour, and size, Gigli's being somewhat more powerful, but Björling's the more penetrative instrument.

In comparison with Björling, Gigli scores points for personality, dramatic involvement, and the purity of his Italian diction. Björling scores points for musicianship, *spinto* capability (his ringing tone is more adaptable to the demands of the *spinto* repertoire than Gigli's pure lyric tenor), and style in French opera (which Gigli sings as if it were Italian). Honours are finally about even.

No tenor since has approached either of them in terms of vocal beauty. For various reasons, however, performance styles have changed considerably since Gigli's day, and his very Italian, heart-on-sleeve emotionalism would not now be tolerated by conductors, record producers, or (probably, though this is less certain) the opera-going public. It was a quality he shared with several contemporaries. Aureliano Pertile, for example, supposedly Toscanini's favourite tenor, was also given to emotional displays in his vocalization – although, in Pertile's case, the emotionalism generally took the form of an exaggerated *vibrato*, a tendency to sharpen pitch under pressure, and a style of singing that aimed not at achieving a cultivated beauty of sound, but at generating a sense of visceral excitement in the listener. And Gigli's great rival, Giacomo Lauri-Volpi, was also accused of playing to the gallery – although the form Lauri-Volpi's exhibitionism took involved not demotic mannerisms (as with Gigli), or the misuse of *vibrato* (as with Pertile), but outrageously prolonged and flaunted high notes, as well as (sometimes) a brazen disregard for the conductor.

Allowing for changes in taste and performance styles, Gigli remains one of the greatest Italian operatic tenors in history. The qualifications 'Italian' and 'operatic' are important. He was quintessentially Italian. He rarely sang in other languages, and, when he did, the results were not happy. Like most Italians, he was a poor linguist. But in his own language, and in the contemporary musical idiom of Italy, he was, in a certain sense, peerless. His repertoire included a few art songs – *arie antiche* and *Lieder* – all of which he sang in a very personal (and endearingly inappropriate) style. For the rest, he sang only one large-scale, non-operatic work, so far as I am aware: Verdi's Requiem, which is as close to Italian opera as you can get without going all the way.

It is clear, from what has already been said, that the critical verdict on Gigli is mixed. This is what Desmond Shawe-Taylor said about him in his *Covent Garden* (1948)—

A paradox among tenors was Beniamino Gigli; a 'strange harmony of contrast', to quote Puccini's translator. On the one hand, a divine voice, certainly the greatest since Caruso (though of a lighter calibre), an admirable (not quite ideally flexible) technique, and an immense gusto, vivacity and charm; on the other hand, sobs, gulps, exaggerated *portamenti*, streetcorner vulgarities which could reduce the sensitive listener in a moment from ecstasy to despair. Gigli represented at once the virtues and the vices of the star system....

Well, to use Shawe-Taylor's own idiom, we have here, on the one hand, balance – an acknowledgement of what may be said in Gigli's favour as well as of valid criticism – and, on the other, an implied claim to superior taste ('street-corner vulgarities which could reduce the sensitive listener in a moment from ecstasy to despair'), which will strike many modern readers, accustomed to more demotic standards of aesthetic taste and judgment, as intolerably precious. Moreover, Shawe-Taylor does not consider the possibility that the 'street-corner vulgarities' might be the price you had to pay for the 'gusto, vivacity and charm' – that they formed what would nowadays be called 'a complete package', and you couldn't have the one without the other.

In successive editions of *The Record Guide*, which he co-authored with Edward Sackville-West, Shawe-Taylor continued to display ambivalence towards Gigli. And we get a similar impression from a cursory reference, dating from 1936, in Peter Pears' *Travel Diaries*—

> Surely the sharper one's taste, the more pure one's artistic performance? […] Personality is a different thing from Artistry. Gigli is Personality. Schumann[7] Artistry?

The question mark suggests that Pears was not entirely satisfied with this verdict. He was right not to be. The implied division between 'personality' and 'artistry' is too sharp. Artistry without personality is a contradiction in terms; and surely the expression of personality in music necessarily involves a degree of artistry.

John Steane offers a more thoughtful assessment. In a fine essay in the third volume of his *Singers of the Century*, he gives due weight to both the outstanding voice (quoting the *Daily Express*'s view that 'Gigli's voice is marvellously steady, rich in tone and flowing in its impassioned delivery') and the alleged lapses in taste noted by English critics, which Steane perceptively links to a temperamental aversion on the part of Anglo-Saxons from displays of overt emotion. This aversion was not, of course, shared by Italian audiences, who were more likely to take exception to Björling's Nordic reserve than to Gigli's Latin emotionalism.

Both Michael Scott in his two-volume *The Record of Singing*, and Nigel Douglas in his *More Legendary Voices*, offer generally favourable appraisals of Gigli. Douglas refers to the 'captivating beauty' of the voice, adding

It is the archetypal glorious Italian sound; there is a sweetness to it, a glowing, soft-grained caressing quality which simply seduces the ear, and which never hardens or coarsens when the voice comes under dramatic pressure. The technical control with which the head and chest registers are blended is flawless [...] and it allows Gigli to ride [...] sweeping phrases as if the singing of opera were the most natural function in the world. [...]

The impact of Gigli's singing, however, is not only due to the beauty of the voice and the soundness of the technique; the additional factor lies in the passion with which he goes about it, whether he is singing grand opera or the humblest little song. [...] This wholeheartedness in his singing was something which he never lost throughout his long career.

Douglas acknowledges the case against Gigli, but only to dismiss it—

[O]ne can again and again find fault on stylistic points if one feels inclined to do so.... [...] You can either condemn these things and condemn Gigli with them, or you can shrug your shoulders and let [him] bathe your day in golden Mediterranean sunshine.

Scott, an exacting critic and by no means easy to please, observes that

The voice is a perfect example of a lyric tenor, the production preëminently smooth and steady, with no faulty or affected vibrato. The range extends to the high C and even in *forte* passages he gives the impression of singing well within his means. The registers are fully developed and his mastery of *mezza voce* is complete; this is one of the most exacting accomplishments requiring perfect breath control and usually more support than in *forte* singing. With Gigli, however, the voice is naturally so responsive that he seems just to let it float on the breath, giving an irresistibly lazy grace to his singing….

Scott does acknowledge the stylistic flaws (the intrusive aspirates and the sobbing *marcato*), describing them as 'tiresome', but it is clear that he also regards them as a price worth paying for the vocal glories and the vivid immediacy of the interpretations.

Even if we have to admit certain reservations in our assessment of Gigli's art, the positives considerably outweigh the negatives. For better or worse, he inherited from Caruso the mantle of '*the* tenor', even in a generation full of talent. It is a testimony to Gigli's manifold excellences as a singer that this was a position that he held without question, yet one which was also without subsequent heir.

Between 1934 and 1946, Gigli made complete recordings of the following: Requiem *(Verdi), Un Ballo in Maschera, Aida, Cavalleria Rusticana, Pagliacci, Andrea Chenier, La Bohème, Tosca,* and *Madama Butterfly.*

Notes

[1]The seats had cost my father 7/6 (seven shillings and sixpence, or 37½p) each – a considerable sum in those days. At the eleventh hour,

he was prevented from going. My mother went with a friend from her office, a girl called Ethel Sargent, who was much more musical than she was. She never forgot Ethel's face, pink with pleasure, as they left the hall after the concert.

[2]Gigli's contemporaries included Giovanni Martinelli, Aureliano Pertile, Giacomo Lauri-Volpi, and Tito Schipa from Italy, and Georges Thill, Heddle Nash, Walter Widdop, Tudor Davies, Joseph Hislop, John McCormack, Richard Tauber, Helge Roswaenge, and Lauritz Melchior from elsewhere.

[3]Although Gigli had many eminent successors – tenors like Jan Peerce, Jussi Björling, Richard Tucker, Ferruccio Tagliavini, Mario del Monaco, Giuseppe di Stefano, Franco Corelli, and Carlo Bergonzi – none of them commanded popular adulation to the same extent as he. Not until Pavarotti, Domingo, and Carreras arrived on the scene did we have other operatic tenors who were capable of transcending the opera house and reaching mass audiences in the way that Caruso, Gigli, McCormack, and Tauber did – without the aid of modern marketing.

[4]It may surprise readers to learn that there are such artists, including some very fine ones. The great Bulgarian bass, Boris Christoff, is an example. He recorded three roles twice – Gounod's Mephistofeles, King Philip II in *Don Carlo*, and Mussorgsky's Boris Godunov. In each case, it would be hard to tell, purely from his interpretation, whether one was listening to the first or the second recording.

[5]If a single Gigli recording were to be chosen to illustrate all these characteristics, it would be hard to improve upon his 1938 recording of Tosti's '*La Serenata*' – a slight song, perhaps, but utterly beguiling in a performance like this.

[6]Here, as always when discussing and comparing tenors, we must prescind from the special case of Caruso, who remains the unquestioned and unchallenged king of the species.

[7]Elisabeth Schumann (1888–1952), a German (later naturalized American) lyric soprano. Incidentally, no one who has heard her recordings would agree with the (surely unintentional) implication here that Schumann lacked personality.

14 Lauritz Melchior: Tristanissimo

'You are not Tristan,' the great conductor Arturo Toscanini reportedly told Lauritz Melchior, 'you are Tristanissimo!'

He certainly was. Standing at six feet three and a half inches and weighing around nineteen and a half stones, Melchior was an impressive figure on stage, screen, or concert platform. He made up in stage presence for what he lacked in acting ability. But it was not just his physical presence that made him the ideal incarnation of the Wagnerian heroes. His heroic voice, iron constitution, apparently limitless stamina, and total lack of nerves, all rendered him perfectly adapted to the fearsome demands of Wagner's mighty music dramas. So, probably, did his exuberant, jovial, larger-than-life personality, without which the strain of performing such a narrow and strenuous repertoire might have been insupportable.

Melchior (1890–1973) was born on the same day as Gigli. But, though both were tenors, they had little else in common. Melchior began his career as a baritone, and his voice retained a baritonal colour even after he retrained as a tenor. It was quite clear from an unusually early stage that his future lay with the Wagnerian repertoire.

That said, like many *Heldentenors*, he was a late developer. After his baritonal beginning, he retrained as a tenor before making a second debut. Success was not immediate, although discerning critics recognized the exceptional potential. The fact is that big voices, like powerful cars, are hard to manage and control. The difficulty is compounded if the voice has a hybrid quality – neither unambiguously tenor nor baritone, but something in between, partaking of the characteristics of each. This is true of many *Heldentenors*, Melchior among them.

For years after his first appearance as a tenor, Melchior worked hard on consolidating his technique and building a repertoire. He did occasionally sing non-Wagnerian roles – Samson and Otello featured in his repertoire – but essentially his career was made in the Wagnerian *Fach*, and especially in the *schwerer Held* roles. He sang all of them – Tannhäuser, Siegmund, Siegfried, Tristan and Parsifal. He sang Tristan – probably the most insanely exigent of all the Wagner roles – over 200 times. Listening to his recordings, one can see why he was in such demand. The voice has a dark sheen possessed by very few, and it never loses that quality, even at extremes of volume. Even at the end of his long career, there is little sign of vocal decline, nor was there ever any sign of forcing. Rather, as Michael Scott observes, Melchior appears to surmount what for other tenors are insuperable obstacles 'with casual, almost insolent ease'.

Melchior was sometimes criticized for an allegedly defective rhythmic sense and a tendency to lose the conductor. His recordings, whether in the studio or 'live', do not support the criticism. On the contrary, they suggest a most musical and scrupulous artist – one who really *sings* Wagner instead of declaiming an approximation to what is written in the score, as so many have done. He does appear to have been one of those artists who, once he has decided on an interpretation of a particular role, locks it into his memory and thereafter reproduces it with little variation. This trait, and a consequent unwillingness to rehearse (what was the point of rehearsing, he reasoned, when he knew his part and what he was going to do with it anyway?), led to Melchior's falling out with Rudolf Bing, the notoriously autocratic (and vindictive) general manager of the Metropolitan Opera House. Bing fired Melchior just before his jubilee season. It was a spiteful gesture and showed an extraordinary ingratitude to a singer who had been the mainstay of the Met's Wagner repertoire for a quarter of a century.

Melchior forged a subsequent career as a television personality and appeared in a few Hollywood movies. At the age of seventy, his physical energy and voice undimmed, he sang the first act of *Die Walküre* in a broadcast performance: a remarkable feat. Seven years later, as Nigel Douglas relates in *Legendary Voices*, Melchior, on safari in Africa, enthralled his fellow hunters by bursting into song one night after dinner, in the middle of the African bush. Virtually to the end of his long life, Melchior retained his exceptional *joie de vivre*, and the heroic energy and powers of endurance that made him unique. He truly was, as Toscanini said, 'Tristanissimo'.

15 Heddle Nash: the epitome of lyricism

The English tenor, Heddle Nash (1894–1961), is as different as could be from his great contemporary and compatriot, the Heldentenor Walter Widdop, yet they shared some repertoire. Both sang the song and oratorio repertoire expected of an English singer and they also recorded some of the same operatic arias, such as 'All hail thou dwelling' ('*Salut, demeure*' from Gounod's *Faust*) and 'Yes! let me like a soldier fall' from Wallace's *Maritana* (which Nash rounds off with a superb top D flat in a head voice).

This is certainly a case where comparisons would be invidious rather than illuminating. Nash is a lyric tenor,[1] at the opposite extreme from Widdop, a *tenore di forza*. His voice is of exceptional sweetness and tonal beauty, one of the loveliest voices of its kind ever to have been recorded. Indeed, for sheer beauty of tone, he has few equals among tenors of any type, nationality or period. He is also one of the most graceful singers on disc, elegant and cultured in everything he attempts. His Duke of Mantua is, for once, truly aristocratic; his Faust, though sung in English, a model of French style; his Tamino, suitably princely. In the Serenade from Bizet's *Jolie Fille de Perth*, he sings ardently and stylishly, and produces an effortless top C in the head voice, an effect he also achieves in both his early recordings of 'All hail thou dwelling'.

Nash belonged to an unusually gifted generation of British tenors – in addition to Widdop, his contemporaries included Frank Titterton, Tudor Davies, Parry Jones, James Johnston, Henry Wendon, Webster Booth, and David Lloyd, not to mention the slightly older John McCormack, Alfred Piccaver, and Joseph Hislop. To stand out in such company is not easy. It is a testimony to Nash's authentic all-round excellence that he was able to do so.

Nash's operatic repertoire of twenty-four roles does not compare with the sixty-four in the repertoire of Richard Tauber, but it is similar to the twenty-eight in the repertoire of Alfredo Kraus. Moreover, he would undoubtedly have sung more operatic roles had opportunities been available. But, first, his career was interrupted by the War; second, he pursued his career almost exclusively in Britain, where opera houses were very few and professional singers had to accept engagements singing in operettas, musicals, and concerts in order to make a living; and third, in Nash's day, the repertoire to which he would have been best suited – the high-lying lyric tenor roles of Rossini, Donizetti, Bellini, and the French repertoire – simply did not exist: instead he was obliged to sing Handel oratorios, which forced him to lower his natural *tessitura*.

Nash is a superb ensemble singer, as recordings of (to name just a few titles) Hedgcock's carol, 'Sleep, My Saviour Sleep' and 'Silent Night' (with Isobel Baillie, Muriel Brunskill and Norman Allin), the Quartet from *Rigoletto*, and the trio 'Turn On, Old Time' from Wallace's *Maritana* (which he recorded quite magically with the Australian contralto Clara Serena and a regular colleague, the baritone Dennis Noble), amply testify. He is also a sympathetic interpreter of English song, with fine versions of songs by Delius and Quilter and of Vaughan Williams' 'Silent Noon' and 'Linden Lea' (among many others) to his credit. His 1945 recording of Elgar's *The Dream of Gerontius* is a classic version which many critics rate as the best on disc. Certainly, his enunciation of the English language is a model of expressiveness, clarity and beauty: no other singer known to me excels him in this respect.

That perfect enunciation of English texts enables him to make things of pure magic out of such trifles as Victorian drawing room ballads (e.g. 'Alice, where art thou?', 'The bloom is on the rye', 'Eileen Alannah'). And here one is struck by something else – namely, that Nash, alone among English singers, has a genuinely romantic quality to his voice and manner, the quality the Italians call *morbidezza*, a word perhaps best translated as 'tenderness'. His only legitimate successor in this repertoire has been the fine Welsh tenor, Stuart Burrows.

Yet there are limitations. In his early recordings, the low notes are weak. His recordings of Don Ottavio's arias – '*Il mio tesoro*' and '*Dalla sua pace*' – are sung in rather English-sounding Italian and, although he manages the long central run in the former fluently and in one breath, he does so by means of a slight *accelerando* and even so sounds as though his supply of breath is exhausted by the end. Nor are the notes in that run articulated as precisely as they are by McCormack, Jadlowker, or Tauber, for example. His French also sounds somewhat English, despite which his recording of Liszt's song, '*Oh quand je dors*' is utterly beguiling, a superb performance. By 1944, when he made his third recording of 'All hail thou dwelling', the voice was no longer as secure as it had been. The high C, though still musical and unforced, sounds uncomfortably close to *falsetto* and is less than perfectly controlled: certainly, he seems to leave it precipitately.

The extreme beauty of Nash's tenor is best appreciated in his early recordings sung in English. He sang in complete recordings of *Cavalleria Rusticana*, *Faust*, *Maritana*, *Così fan tutte*, and (in smaller roles) *Le Nozze di Figaro* and *Pagliacci*. He also sang in complete recordings of *Messiah* and, as already mentioned, *The Dream of Gerontius*, as well as extended excerpts from Puccini's *La Bohème* (a complete Act Four with Miriam Licette and Dennis Noble) and Massenet's *Manon* (of which he recorded highlights with Maggie Teyte). In all of these, his performances are both vocally beautiful, and exquisitely and stylishly sung.

Notes

¹He is sometimes described as a *tenore di grazia*, a light-lyric tenor. However, although his repertoire included some roles generally associated with that voice type – Almaviva, for example – for the most part, he sang roles suitable for a lyric tenor. For example, Rodolfo, Pinkerton, and Turiddu would generally be considered too heavy for a *tenore di grazia* and arguably so would Faust or Roméo, although Alfredo Kraus later sang both of the latter. Gerontius too requires a voice with some power. In my view, all things considered, it is more accurate to describe Nash as a lyric tenor than as a light-lyric.

16 Richard Tauber: the tenor as magician

Richard Tauber (1891–1948) is, in some ways, the most surprising of the great tenors. Although he was associated primarily with the operas of Mozart and the operettas of Lehár, he sang a repertoire of sixty-four operatic roles, including Calaf in *Turandot* – not at all the sort of role one might expect to find in the repertoire of a lyric tenor with a short voice of moderate volume. But Tauber is full of surprises.

Let's start with a recording of a piece one would not expect to find in his repertoire: a duet from Korngold's opera *Die Tote Stadt*. The role is normally sung by heroic tenors of Wagnerian weight. But if we compare Tauber's version with one recorded by one of these behemoths – the weightily baritonal Hans Hopf – the comparison favours Tauber. Hopf's voice – dark, powerful, with a *Heldentenor* ring to the tone – is, perhaps, more exciting as sheer sound; but Tauber's singing has charm, grace, eloquent and exquisitely shaped phrasing, a perfect *legato*, an artistic use of *rubato*, delicately floated high notes, and a sensitive response to the text as well as the music. It is no contest.

Those words often come to mind in comparisons where Tauber is concerned. Take his '*Bildnisarie*' from *Die Zauberflöte* for example. Unlike the Korngold, this is not a rarity. It has been recorded by most of the greatest Mozart tenors of the last hundred years. But none of them can match the airy lyricism of Tauber's 1922 performance, with its perfectly poised head notes and its sense of wonder. This really sounds like a love song – and the taxing final phrases do not sound effortful here, as they do in so many recordings and live performances. Nowadays, when we are accustomed to hearing the Mozart tenor roles sung by light lyric (some might say 'anaemic') voices with a strong hint of King's College about them, the sheer virility of Tauber's tenor comes as a surprise, but a very welcome one. Only George Shirley of more recent Mozarteans matches him in this respect.

The Tauber magic is not confined to German opera. Though he almost invariably sang opera in German whatever the original language may have been, he conveys the elegance of the French, the *morbidezza* of the Italians, the melancholy of the Russians, as successfully as any rivals on disc. His Hoffmann is as graceful as Gedda's, and, thanks to his perfect technique, the high *tessitura* poses no problems. In Puccini, he is a match for any Italian in ardour, and more than a match in musicianship. Anyone looking for the true *bel canto* approach to the execution of ornaments will find it in Tauber's exemplary fluency and accuracy of articulation rather than in Schipa's sketchy and approximate attempts at similar passages.

As a *Lieder* singer, Tauber belongs to a generation before the detailed word-pointing championed by singers like Pears, Schwarzkopf, and Fischer-Dieskau established a new norm. That is not to say that earlier singers like Tauber, Hüsch, and Gerhardt were inattentive to words; but their interpretation of song lacked the verbal specificity of the moderns: their sense of the words was more generalized. On the plus side, their interpretations will strike many listeners as more natural, less mannered, than those of our contemporaries. Tauber's recordings of *Lieder* and art song always fall pleasantly on the ear. The approach is *singerly*, and the tone is full-bodied in a way that that of some later song specialists – say, Pears, Schreier, or Bostridge, for instance – is not, or not always. Their singing is apt to sound a little anaemic after listening to a few recordings of Tauber: next to him, their tone lacks body and warmth. As ever with Tauber, many of the song recordings are utterly magical – some superb Strauss *Lieder* including a lovely version of '*Morgen*' (a wonderfully evocative piece of scene-painting), a beautifully poised '*Mondnacht*' (Schumann), and some splendid Schubert and Grieg, for example.

For many listeners, it is in operetta that Tauber truly comes into his own. He was closely associated with the works of Franz Lehár, who composed several roles specially for him, always including a show-stopping aria – a number which became known as a *Tauberlied* ('Every *Tauberlied* a *Zauberlied*', as Irving Kolodin felicitously put it). The most famous of these was '*Dein ist mein ganzes Herz*' from *Das Land des Lächelns*. Tauber recorded it in German, and again in his inimitable and endearingly accented English. Both recordings show his extraordinary dynamic control. Both also exemplify the inimitable charm of his singing (he is the most romantic of singers). And both are essential for lovers of Viennese operetta.

17 Giacomo Lauri-Volpi: playing to the gallery

Giacomo Lauri-Volpi (1892–1979) was a mass of paradoxes. He was a *tenore di grazia* who gradually metamorphosed first into a *lirico spinto* tenor, and then into a *tenore di forza* capable of singing Otello; a cultured intellectual who flaunted his (often outrageously prolonged) high notes to please the gallery; a deeply religious man with a colossal ego; a tenor with a highly competitive nature who wrote some of the most thoughtful and intelligent criticism of other tenors; and an assiduous student of the history of singing whose own performances were often criticized as anachronistic.

It has been said that, whereas Pertile, with his violently declamatory style, was the forerunner of Mario del Monaco, Lauri-Volpi, with his distinctive fast *vibrato* and sensational top notes, was the forerunner of Franco Corelli. But the analogy is inexact. Lauri-Volpi was a noted interpreter of Arnold in *William Tell*, a role which Corelli never sang. A few private recordings of him rehearsing the role suggest that it would have lain too high for him. Lauri-Volpi's range allegedly extended to an E in alt, although on disc anything above high C is elusive (both his recordings of '*A te o cara*' from *I Puritani* are transposed down by a semitone so that the climactic high note is a top C rather than a D flat). That said, the high notes are impressive – powerful, focused, and with a bright, ringing quality which suggests that, in the opera house, they must have been sensational. Anecdotal evidence confirms as much.

But there is more to Lauri-Volpi than brilliant high notes. The acoustic recordings show a voice of rare quality with an exciting timbre and the characteristic fast *vibrato* already referred to. They also show an artist of some imagination and refinement – his Italian version of Werther's '*Pourquoi me réveiller*' ('*Ah non mi ridestar*') is a fine one, capturing Werther's intense melancholy more surely than most, and *bel canto* arias of Bellini ('*A te o cara*') and Donizetti ('*Una vergine, un angel di Dio*' and '*Spirto gentil*') are sung not only stylishly but with real feeling. On the other hand, there is a fairly persistent tendency to sing sharp, which manifests itself most acutely in Federico's Lament from Cilea's *L'Arlesiana*. This, and a somewhat casual attitude towards the conductor's beat, are regularly cited as Lauri-Volpi's worst faults.

As befits so assiduous a student of the history of singing, Lauri-Volpi was keenly aware of changes in style and taste. He understood perfectly the differences between the *bel canto* style of Bonci and de Lucia and the veristic style of the *tenori Carusiani* – the post-Caruso tenors who emulated the great man's mannerisms without having undergone his technical schooling. Lauri-Volpi himself mastered both styles, and, in his prime, could switch back and forth from one to the other without effort. In the *bel canto* repertoire, he had much of the grace and the interpretative nuances of Bonci (compare their respective recordings of '*A te o cara*'), but he also had the sheer vocal power and the ability to pack a big dramatic punch required by the tenor roles of Verdi and the *veristi*.

Late in his career, he made a few complete opera recordings for the Italian company Cetra. From a technical perspective, the recordings are dreadful. Musically, the performances also leave much to be desired. In *Luisa Miller*, for instance, Lucy Kelston adopts a *can belto* approach to the title role, the supporting roles are not at all well sung, and Lauri-Volpi – by then fifty-nine years old – has little to offer except the still-splendid high notes. His soft singing sounds like unsupported crooning, and there is no feeling for the shape of a Verdian phrase, which makes it hard to believe that this is the same tenor who made so many fine Verdi recordings earlier in his career. Probably the Cetra recordings were made a decade too late.

There remain the earlier recordings – the acoustics and the electricals made up to 1941 (the *Otello* excerpts recorded in that year are superb, but the excerpts from *Luisa Miller* and *La Forza del Destino* recorded just two years later show a hardening of the tone and the registers beginning to separate). In those early recordings, we hear one of the most thrilling tenor voices on disc. It combines the *squillo* of the dramatic tenor with the grace of the lyric tenor in a way achieved by very few others. And there is something else: those recordings prove that, behind all the flamboyance and exhibitionism, Lauri-Volpi was a serious and conscientious artist. There were many fine tenors who sang Lauri-Volpi's repertoire in his day: Gigli, Pertile, and Martinelli, for instance. That he was able to forge a great career in the face of such fierce competition confirms his position among the greatest tenors of the century.

18 Georges Thill: Wagnerian power and Parisian elegance

At one time, France had a flourishing tradition of opera singers capable of rivalling the Italians and the Spanish. Her tenors included Agustarello Affre, Léon Escalaïs, Edmond Clément, Charles Dalmorès, Lucien Muratore, David Devriès, César Vezzani, Gaston Micheletti and Charles Friant. But, by the time of Georges Thill (1897–1984), if we prescind from a few isolated cases in subsequent generations, the line was coming to an end.

Well, it went out in a blaze of glory. Yet, somehow, Thill has never been given his due by critics on this side of the Channel. He sang outside France with success, notably in Buenos Aires, but his appearances in London and New York were few, and were not fondly recalled by the *cognoscenti* – a circumstance which probably prevented him from being justly appraised by anglophone critics. His records, according to John Steane, have been dismissed as 'very good and very dull'. But, as Steane notes, that is unfair. Thill was a pupil of Fernando de Lucia, and from his master he had acquired an impeccable technique which served him equally well in lyric and dramatic roles. An elegant Faust, Roméo, and Werther, he was also a powerful Énée, Samson, and Lohengrin. The perfection of his French diction – unaffected, exquisitely pronounced, pellucid but never obtrusive – is unmatched by any other tenor on record: so clear is his enunciation that one can easily dispense with printed texts. The tone is pure and unforced, rounded, and notably smooth and even in emission. In the 'Song of the Indian Guest' from Rimsky-Korsakov's *Sadko*, he gives one of the finest readings on disc, effortlessly sustaining the long phrases at a slow tempo and producing a flow of gorgeous tone and a ravishing *mezza voce*. Not even notable versions by Schipa, Björling, and Gedda can compete with this, and Gigli's recording, though tonally luscious as always, is ruled out by its intrusive aspirates ('Gigli so-ho-ing his wild notes' as Ernest Newman said).

The quality that strikes the listener hearing Thill for the first time is the sheer beauty of the sound. This is so uncommon among dramatic tenors that it deserves special mention. It is not often that the word 'suave' comes to mind to describe the singing of a dramatic tenor. But, in Thill's case, it seems the *mot juste*. The beauty of tone and elegant manner do not preclude emotional expression. The Tomb Scene from *Roméo et Juliette* and Samson's '*Air de la meule*' ('*Vois ma misère, hélas*') rarely sound as moving as they do in Thill's recordings. As is often the case in French opera, less is more; and the more overtly emotional renditions of these arias – say, Franco Corelli's of the Tomb Scene and Mario del Monaco's of the '*Air de la meule*' – are not nearly so effective, despite their magnificent voices and the obvious sincerity of their respective performances.

For some listeners, Thill's recordings, in French, of the Italian repertoire seem a little cool. They lack the passionate involvement of the more southern races – the Spanish and the Italians themselves. But, in compensation, they offer standards of musicianship and artistry that few rivals can attain. When all is said and done, it is a matter of personal taste whether one prefers the full-throated impassioned delivery of the south Europeans or the greater refinement of more northern singers – of, say, Thill, or Björling, or Gedda.

Thill's supreme achievements on disc were probably his complete recording of Massenet's *Werther* and an abridged recording of Charpentier's *Louise*. Both were made with the leading French soprano of the day, Ninon Vallin. Unfortunately, she hated Thill, describing him as a 'big baby' and a 'bad colleague', and this ill feeling may explain why they didn't make more records together.[1] The loss is ours. One can hardly think of another partnership in French opera (de los Angeles and Gedda perhaps?) that has been comparably successful.

Steane observes somewhere that what we need – and have, briefly, enjoyed in a very few individuals – is a heroic tenor who has not forgotten the grace and elegance of the lyric tenor. Georges Thill is surely one of the few individuals he had in mind.

Notes

[1]Thill's opinion of Vallin, so far as I know, is not recorded, so we do not really know what happened between them or why they fell out.

19 Peter Pears: the first modern tenor

It is impossible to write about British tenors without mentioning the absolutely seminal influence of Peter Pears (1910–86), whose highly individual voice, keen intelligence and consummate artistry, together with the repertoire created specially for him by Benjamin Britten, made him a towering figure in British musical life for four decades. Pears' influence has been so profound and pervasive that there is scarcely a British tenor since his heyday who has escaped it. Such fine singers as Robert Tear, Philip Langridge, Anthony Rolfe Johnson, Ian Partridge, Martyn Hill, Neil Mackie, Adrian Thompson, Ian Bostridge, Mark Padmore, John Mark Ainsley, James Gilchrist, and Mark Wilde, have all shown clear signs of Pears' influence in their vocal method, technique, choice of repertoire, style of singing, and interpretative approach to the music and texts they sing. It was Pears too who first established as an unchallengeable axiom the view that typically British tenors were unsuited to the standard roles of the nineteenth-century French and Italian operatic repertoire. Pears, in his early days as a member of the Sadler's Wells Opera, had, in fact, sung quite a few such roles, including Almaviva in *The Barber of Seville*, the Duke of Mantua in *Rigoletto*, Alfredo in *La Traviata*, Rodolfo in *La Bohème*, and the title role in *Tales of Hoffmann*. He had also sung the Mozartean roles of Ferrando in *Così fan Tutte* and Tamino in *The Magic Flute*. But he later described these roles, especially the nineteenth-century works, as 'most unsuitable' and summarily dropped them from his repertoire. No tenors of the Pearsian type since have attempted them. This is a pity. The example of tenors like Jussi Björling and Nicolai Gedda proves that it is not necessary to have a Mediterranean timbre to succeed in the French / Italian repertoire. Other tenors who lacked that quality, yet proved highly successful in precisely that repertoire, include McCormack, Nash, Tauber, Patzak, Roswaenge, Schock, and Wunderlich. John Steane recalled hearing the young Pears in *La Bohème* at Sadler's Wells and being favourably impressed. Not everyone, it seems, agreed that British tenors ought to eschew the French and Italian roles. It would, I think, be interesting to hear modern British tenors bring their characteristic mix of tonal purity, proficient musicianship, wide culture, high intelligence, sensitivity to words, and interpretative insight, to the standard operatic *Fach*. The results might just surprise the skeptics and scoffers – and perhaps even the tenors themselves.

It was Pears who definitively established the contents and parameters of the repertoire of the typical British lyric tenor for the next two generations: the vocal works of Benjamin Britten; Baroque music (Purcell, Handel and Bach); English song generally, from the Elizabethan lute songs to the works of modern composers; the operas of Mozart; *Lieder*, especially the songs and song-cycles of Schubert and Schumann; oratorios and liturgical works ranging from the Monteverdi Vespers to the Bach Passions and cantatas, from the Masses and oratorios of Haydn and Mozart to Berlioz' *L'Enfance du Christ*, and from Mendelssohn's *Elijah* to Elgar's *Gerontius* and Britten's *War Requiem*. This repertoire, plus or minus a few items, was what nearly all British lyric tenors from Robert Tear to Ian Bostridge sang.[1] It was admittedly short of roles from the central nineteenth-century operatic *Fach*, but, in compensation, it had considerable variety and ranged over approximately 400 years. This compares very favourably with the repertoire of the traditional Italian tenor, which is entirely confined to operas by Italian (and, possibly, a few French) composers active between 1820 and 1925. Such a tenor may indeed sing more – perhaps many more – operatic roles than the twenty-six or so that Pears sang, but outside the opera house his repertoire is virtually non-existent. By almost any objective criteria, Pears is a more versatile artist.

In some ways, Pears is unclassifiable as a tenor. At first hearing, he sounds like a *tenore di grazia* – light-voiced, elegant, vocally agile, but with a lower range than one usually expects from such a voice. But then the '*tenore di grazia*' proves to have reserves of power equal to the demands of roles such as Peter Grimes, Captain Vere, and Oedipus Rex, not to mention Elgar's Gerontius. And some of the songs Pears sang, notably Britten's *Holy Sonnets of John Donne* and Mahler's *Das Lied von der Erde*, make severe demands of a light voice, but find Pears equal to them. This is not altogether surprising. Pears was physically a big man, tall, broad-shouldered, powerful and athletic in build,[2] and big men usually have big voices. His style of singing was a matter of choice, rather than making a virtue of necessity. He could, had he wanted, have sung in a much more robust manner – but that would have meant sacrificing much of the refinement and subtlety he valued, and which is inseparable from his art.[3] Pears resolutely refuses to be pigeon-holed. Even the low range is deceptive, for by the skilful use of *falsettones* he is able to sing the high-lying parts of the Evangelists in the Bach Passions and to manage the very high *tessitura* of Britten's *Holy Sonnets of John Donne* and the *Seven Sonnets of Michelangelo*. He is a basically light-voiced singer who has reserves of vocal power and depths of tonal colour which he can call on, if necessary. Even this unclassifiability is an aspect of his influence, for many of his successors have shared it.

For much of his career, Pears, like Britten, had to contend with prejudice against homosexuals. Ian Bostridge unearthed the following in the second volume of Isaiah Berlin's letters—

Benjamin Britten + Peter Pears, an obvious ménage, appeared & he sang with a degree of sentimentality, deeply & sincerely in love with his own unbeautiful voice, which was embarrassing.

In some ways, it is amusing – even gratifying – to find the distinguished philosopher writing with as much prejudice and philistinism as any pub bore, but it also gives an idea of what Pears and Britten were up against. Now, when it sometimes seems that gay people have been placed beyond criticism, it is difficult to recall how hard life was for them not so very long ago. Certainly, Pears had to contend with his share of prejudice and hostility, especially early in his career. It is sometimes said that Britten would have been a great composer even without Pears, but Pears would never have become a great singer without Britten. This manages to sound witty and clever without being in the least susceptible of proof or disproof. What can be asserted confidently is that Pears *was* a great singer – one of the most gifted Britain has produced – and his influence has been as beneficial as it has been extensive.

The allegation that Pears' voice lacked tonal beauty is so often made that it bears closer examination. By conventional criteria, it is undeniable that Pears did not have a beautiful voice. It does not have the richness or sheen of the best Mediterranean voices, or the seductive ring of a Björling, a Wunderlich, or a young Gedda. There was also a persistent unsteadiness, which could be obtrusive on record in a way it never was in the flesh.[4] John Steane brings out all the facets of the debate about Pears with typical clarity in *Singers of the Century*, where he writes—

Readers, I am sure, can 'play' Pears recorded voice in their heads […] that highly characteristic sound, not quite a wobble and yet not quite steady; not (maybe) describable as pallid or effete yet hardly robust, resonant or forthright; not deficient in volume but not full-bodied in tone; not throaty yet making you think of the throat; not exactly 'mannered' (to use the modern jargon) yet suggesting neither the voice, nor yet the manner, of nature.

Now the records are unmistakable Pears: there never was a recorded voice more immediately identifiable. But 'in the flesh' the balance of forces, the total impression was different. Most crucial, perhaps, was the difference in perceived quality of sound. Pears' voice was remarkably pure, and even to the end it betrayed no sign of coarsening, no accretion of surface-scratch, no scrape or rattle of metallic alloy. Heard in the concert hall, it was a voice which you could settle to listen to as sound: not that his singing ever encouraged that (because sound without sense was not his line of business at all), but the quality of the voice was a pleasure in itself. It was also a much more virile sound. I heard him first in *La Bohème* and as the stuttering Vašek in *The Bartered Bride*, and the year would have been 1945 or '46. His voice then was slender, like his figure, clear-cut, not rich but fresh. At Covent Garden in the early years he needed more power but later the volume increased quite remarkably, so much so that in his final and probably greatest role, as Aschenbach in *Death in Venice*, his voice impressed in all parts of the house as being ample and even full-bodied.

This is a balanced, judicious assessment of Pears' voice, in marked contrast to Berlin's obviously biased view. And when we add to that the assessment of Dietrich Fischer-Dieskau, who in his memoirs refers to Pears as 'the gifted English tenor' and elsewhere described him as 'the most aristocratic of tenors', we have, it seems to me, to acknowledge that Pears' preëminence among English tenors, and the extent of his influence over his successors, are amply justified.

Quite how pervasive Pears' influence was can be seen if we look at an HMV LP, released in the 1970s, entitled *Famous British Tenors*.[5] The tenors in question were active between (roughly) 1900 and 1945, the latter being the year when Pears first came to general notice after the premiere of *Peter Grimes*, in which he sang the title role. The LP includes several lyric tenors of the pre-Pears period (viz. Webster Booth, Ben Davies, Hubert Eisdell, Joseph Hislop, David Lloyd, John McCormack, Walter Midgley, Heddle Nash, Derek Oldham, and Henry Wendon),[6] none of whom sounds even remotely like Pears. Yet, in contrast, nearly all the most eminent British lyric tenors of the post-Pears era resemble him in some degree, tonally and stylistically. Partly, this is the result of the personal influence of Pears himself as an artist and as a teacher. Partly, it results from the growth of a distinctive repertoire associated with Pears, which, as we have seen, comprised the Britten operatic roles, songs and song cycles, which were written specially for him; works written for him by other composers; and certain earlier works with which he was closely associated as a performer, such as the songs of Purcell, Schubert and Schumann, the Bach Passions, and in the latter part of his career, Elgar's Gerontius. Facilitated by his extensive discography and his work as a teacher, a Pearsian performance tradition has grown up around this repertoire which has affected nearly all subsequent British lyric tenors.

It may now be time to recover the older tradition in all its richness and diversity. There are some signs – for example, the emergence of a younger generation of highly talented but comparatively non-Pearsian British lyric tenors, many of whom can be heard in the mainstream Italian and French repertoire at the English, Scottish, and Welsh National Operas – that this process may now be underway. Even the song and operatic repertoire composed specifically for Pears, which he sang so admirably, can be sung in more than one way. At last, we may be able to look forward to interpretations of Britten's works which will owe little or nothing to Pears' example.

To say this is not to denigrate Pears as an artist or as a singer. But it is to say that great artists cast long shadows; and their mantle may lie heavily on the shoulders of those who follow them. Caruso, for instance, adversely affected, through his magnificent but also dangerous precedent, the careers of many later Italianate tenors. So, in a quite different but equally dangerous way, did Mario del Monaco. And what they did for the Italians, Pears did for the British. Not that imitating Pears ever carried a risk of sustaining vocal damage, as imitating Caruso or del Monaco certainly did. But the inhibiting effect of his influence might have prevented several tenors of the younger generation from realizing their full potential. Without inconsistency, we may rejoice in his achievements, but also think that his successors need to emerge from his shadow and find their own distinctive voices, repertoires, and interpretative styles.

Pears made complete recordings of *Dido and Aeneas, The Fairy Queen, Acis and Galatea, Scenes from Goethe's Faust, L'Enfance du Christ, The Dream of Gerontius, Peter Grimes, Billy Budd, The Rape of Lucretia, The Turn of the Screw, Owen Wingrave, A Midsummer Night's Dream, Death in Venice, The Prodigal Son, Albert Herring, Curlew River, The Burning Fiery Furnace, Noye's Fludde, Oedipus Rex, The War Requiem, St Matthew Passion, St John Passion, Turandot* (as the Emperor).

Notes

[1]Pears' near-contemporaries Richard Lewis (1914–90) and Alexander Young (1920–2000), though their repertoires were coincidentally similar to Pears' in some respects, largely escaped his influence. And both sang several works that Pears either seldom or never sang – e.g. Schönberg's *Gurre-Lieder*.

[2]As a young man, he played cricket and was an accomplished fast bowler.

[3]It might also have meant re-training his voice as a baritone.

[4]This is according to the testimony of people who heard Pears sing 'live'. The author never had that pleasure.

[5]With a few additions and amendments, that LP has now been reissued as a Heritage CD under the title *Great British Tenors*. The additions are Pears himself, Richard Lewis, and Gervase Elwes.

[6]Wendon's voice is more lyric-dramatic than pure lyric, but as his repertoire included such typically lyric roles as Alfredo in *La Traviata*, Rodolfo in *La Bohème*, and Pinkerton in *Madam Butterfly*, it seemed appropriate to include him here. The other tenors featured on that HMV disc, all of whom had more dramatic voices, were John Coates, Tudor Davies, Walter Hyde, James Johnston, Parry Jones, Frank Mullings and Walter Widdop.

20 Jussi Björling:
close to perfection

If there is such a thing as someone who was born to sing, then the Swedish tenor, Jussi Björling (1911–60), is that person.

He was born into a musical family. As a child, he toured with his father and brothers, giving concerts. As a young adult (his first recordings were made when he was nineteen years old), he recorded some dance band numbers under the name Erik Odde and studied voice, first with the Swedish baritone, John Forsell, and later, on Forsell's advice, with the Scottish tenor, Joseph Hislop. It was Hislop who secured Björling's top notes, which, for the rest of his career, possessed an effortless, gleaming brilliance rarely equalled and never surpassed.

The early years of his career saw him established at the Royal Opera in Stockholm, where he sang an impressively varied repertoire ranging from Don Ottavio to Manrico and Radames. He also sang the stratospheric (and terrifying) role of Arnold in *William Tell*, though it did not feature in his subsequent career.

The early recordings reveal a glorious voice, but Italian pronunciation so mangled that some of the time he is literally singing nonsense, or at any rate nothing recognizable as Italian words. Björling's lack of formal schooling might account for his difficulties with other languages (he spoke and sang English well, but neither his Italian nor his French was ever perfect). Another possible reason is suggested by the accompanist, Ivor Newton. According to Newton, Björling was 'difficult, taciturn, and unusually lazy'. The laziness is borne out by an anecdote of Joseph Hislop's. He had once set Björling and another student the task of mastering some very difficult vocal exercises, promising to return in an hour and see how they were getting along. An hour later, he returned to find Björling reclining on a sofa reading a detective story, while his fellow-student was still struggling to master the exercises. Björling, however, was note-perfect. He had learned them simply by listening to the other fellow! And his voice was so easily produced that, once even the trickiest scales were committed to memory, singing them was no problem.

Whatever the reason, Björling's difficulties with languages, though at their most acute in his early years, were never altogether resolved. Even later in his career, he was capable of mispronunciations, in Italian and French. In the 1956 complete *La Bohème*, he sings *piacchia* instead of *piaccia* (a 'k' instead of a 'ch') at the end of '*Che gelida manina*', and in his justly famous recording of the Pearl Fishers duet '*Au fond du temple saint*' with Robert Merrill, he sings *une frère* instead of *un frère*. One can understand why Italians often voice reservations about Björling. How would we English feel if we heard the songs of Dowland or Britten sung by someone obviously imperfectly acquainted with the English language?

At its best, which was most of the time, Björling's voice is a gleaming instrument which fairly glows and never sounds as though it was produced with the slightest effort.[1] Although he had a repertoire of about fifty roles, during his prime he sang only about eleven operatic roles with which he had become closely identified and most of which he recorded. Those he did not record in the studio, such as Faust and Roméo, are available in pirate versions. A few of the records are disappointing: his '*Je crois entendre encore*', for instance, which is loud, inflexible and insensitive throughout. But these are very much the minority. By far the majority of the single arias are worth having, some of them very much so: the '*Salut demeure, Ah fuyez douce image*', a magical '*Au mont Ida trois*

Jon Elsby

déesses' (sung in Swedish), and a '*Cujus animam*' from Rossini's Stabat Mater, beautifully sung and capped with a brilliant top D flat, a note he also produces, to stunning effect, to round off the aria, '*Ich hab' kein Geld, bin vogelfrei*' from Millöcker's operetta, *Der Bettelstudent*.

Of his complete opera recordings, eleven of which were made in the studio, only the *Rigoletto* disappoints, at least as far as Björling's contribution is concerned. His Duca di Mantua lacks charm and, despite the splendour of the voice, does not sound like a credible seducer. In all the others, he is magnificent. His account of the tenor part in Verdi's Requiem is the best on record: in fact the quartet of soloists on this recording is perfectly balanced – they are probably the best available – and this goes a long way to compensating for Fritz Reiner's enervatingly slow tempi and for some rather muddy choral singing. His Des Grieux (Puccini), Rodolfo, Cavaradossi, Pinkerton, Calaf, Radames, Manrico, Canio, and Turiddu are among the very best on record – as are his Riccardo, Faust and Roméo, although these are available only in off-the-air recordings. His *Lieder* recordings are variable, but the best of them, like the early '*Adelaide*', earn a place among the greatest in the genre. At all stages of his career, his recordings of song and operatic arias in his native Swedish are invariably superb: here the inhibitions of which he was sometimes accused are definitely shed, and he sings with glorious abandon and total commitment.

Italian critics are inclined to hesitate over Björling: they admit the splendour of the voice but feel that there is a certain unidiomatic quality – a Nordic *froideur* – about the interpretations. If a single disc could disprove that allegation, it would be Björling's superb late recording of '*Federico's Lament*', '*È la solita storia del pastore*', from Cilea's *L'Arlesiana*. If this isn't the finest and most impassioned account of the aria ever recorded, I don't know what is. Björling's voice changed slightly with age, but it seems never to have deteriorated: even in the last recordings, made just a few months before he died, there are no signs of the surface wear or dryness of tone which mar the later recordings of so many tenors, even the greatest. Björling is one of the few tenors on record who may, without absurdity, be mentioned in the same breath as Caruso. Tragically, a heart attack, probably due to the physical effects of chronic alcoholism, caused his death at the age of only forty-nine.

Anyone who wants to find out more about Björling may be referred to the biography *Jussi* by Anna-Lisa Björling and Andrew Farkas, and to Stephen Hastings' excellent *The Björling Sound* – a detailed analysis of the tenor's recorded legacy. Virtually all of Björling's recordings are covered here except the dance music he recorded under the name of Erik Odde. For the rest, all the *Lieder*, operatic arias, Scandinavian songs, Neapolitan songs, and arias from operettas are critiqued and compared with the recordings of other tenors ranging (chronologically) from Fernando de Lucia to Juan Diego Flórez. This is indispensable.

Björling's complete studio opera recordings are: *Rigoletto, Il Trovatore, Aida, Manon Lescaut, La Bohème, Tosca, Madama Butterfly, Turandot, Cavalleria Rusticana* (two), and *Pagliacci*. He also recorded Verdi's Requiem.

Notes

[1]It doesn't look as though it was produced with any effort either. In video recordings of Björling singing, he appears extraordinarily relaxed. Possibly his exceptional physical strength permitted him to generate sufficient power without the visible (and audible) efforts that most other tenors have to make.

21 Richard Tucker: from Brooklyn cantor to primo tenore

The American tenor Richard Tucker (1913–75) enjoyed one of the most illustrious careers in the history of the Metropolitan Opera. He sang there for thirty uninterrupted seasons, taking thirty-eight roles ranging from Tamino in *The Magic Flute* to Radames in *Aida*.

Tucker, whose real name was Reuben Ticker, was ethnically a Romanian Jew.[1] Like his brother-in-law and fellow-tenor, Jan Peerce (with whom he was famously not on speaking terms), he was religiously devout and orthodox in the observance of his ancestral faith.[2] His career as a singer began as a cantor in the synagogue, where he mastered the demanding art of *chazzanut*, the traditional Jewish cantorial music, with its exotic Eastern melodies and florid decoration. From this background and from his studies with the *Heldentenor* Paul Althouse, Tucker acquired the excellent technique that served him so well throughout his career.

From the first, Tucker had certain advantages. He was a homegrown talent at a time when American singers were sought after at the Met. He had considerable self-confidence. Where other tenors suffered from nerves before every performance, Tucker couldn't wait to get on stage and 'show them' what he could do. His rock-solid technique meant that he was vocally amazingly consistent. He was a highly disciplined performer, always well prepared, hard-working and punctual at rehearsals, dependable in performances, reliable in contractual matters, a peacemaker when disputes arose, and tough but fair in negotiations. These qualities endeared him to the Met management, who otherwise had to deal with a range of tenorial problems such as Björling's alcoholism, di Stefano's utter indifference to contractual obligations, Corelli's nerves and last-minute cancellations, del Monaco's egoism and *machismo*, and Vickers' uncompromising religious beliefs and explosive temper.

But Tucker also had certain disadvantages. Unlike Björling and Bergonzi, he could not read music and had to learn his roles parrot fashion. He lacked the film-star good looks of del Monaco and Corelli, and onstage he cut a less romantic figure than di Stefano or the young Nicolai Gedda. Short and stocky,[3] with the physical build and facial characteristics of a typical tenor, he was not the ideal hero visually, however well he sang. In general, he was a conventional operatic actor – which is to say, no actor at all – but in one role, Canio, late in his career, he gave a performance of a blazing intensity that lingered long in the memory of those fortunate enough to have seen and heard it. And, even later, as Eléazar in Halévy's *La Juive*, the last role sung by Caruso at the Met, he found the part that, in his own estimation, he was born to play. Here his passion for nineteenth-century opera and his profound Jewish faith could both be expressed without reserve.

Tucker was highly regarded at the Met. His appearances in Europe were infrequent, and that may have contributed to the somewhat lower estimate of his talents by non-American critics. British critics, for example, admitted the fine quality of his voice, but had reservations about his artistry. His imperfectly accented Italian was commented on, as were the limits of his expressive range. John Steane, as ever, got to the heart of the matter when he wrote in *The Grand Tradition* (1974)—

Tucker's singing is passionate, commanding, alive, intelligent, firm, resonant and rhythmical, but it is not often charming or tender.

Steane goes on to point to 'something fierce and unyielding in [Tucker's] style' and the lack, in comparison with the greatest lyric tenors, of 'some final gift of art or elegance'. By the time he came to write *Singers of the Century* (1996), Steane had refined and amplified his view of Tucker's voice and art. He writes—

It was the voice itself, the power of expansion, but most of all its timbre, darkly rich in sheen and texture that held attention rapt […] that voice […] will instantly move anyone who loves singing […] the sound is magnificent.

Well, there may be reservations about the interpretative artistry, but about the voice there can be no two opinions: it is quite as magnificent as Steane avers. *Piano* singing is rare, and so is a *mezza voce*. For the most part, Tucker's singing is unsubtle, virile and straightforward; it lacks the elegance of phrasing of a Björling or a Bergonzi. That matters more in some roles than in others. As Rodolfo in *La Bohème*, Tucker misses both the diffident charm of Björling and the seductive appeal of Bergonzi. But as Alvaro in *La Forza del Destino* or Pinkerton in *Butterfly*, he is in his element, finding the right colours for the pain and yearning of the first, and the right manner for the braggadocio and sexual predatoriness of the second. The sincerity of his performances is never in doubt. In general, he is at his best in roles where fervour is at a premium (one is constantly reminded that cantorial music consists largely of petitionary prayer, and that the fervour and conviction with which the prayer is delivered are religiously important aspects of the cantor's art) and charm is not called for.

Tucker's personality was complex. The egoism and considerable *chutzpah* have been much commented on. His feud with Peerce has already been mentioned (although the extent of Peerce's responsibility for that is not clear). But Tucker was also a generous colleague, a devoted family man, and someone whose many acts of kindness (such as his financial support for the impoverished Gigli family) were performed quietly, almost stealthily, without any public advertisement. When rows broke out at rehearsals – a not infrequent occurrence where personalities as volatile as Leonard Warren's were involved – Tucker often acted as a peacemaker. And his down-to-earth sense of humour is attractive. There are many recorded examples of this last quality. My own favourites are two stories about Tucker and Maria Callas, with whom he sang only twice on record, in *La Forza del Destino* and *Aida*. Callas's occasional displays of a *prima donna*'s temperament irritated Tucker, who had a no-nonsense approach to work and was always consummately professional in conduct. He quickly discovered that one way to get his own back was to call the great diva 'Mary', which she hated. Once, in an unusual moment of tenderness, Callas asked him, 'Richard, why is it that, when I sing with you, I feel so good?' Back came the reply: 'That's easy, Mary. When you sing with me, you're in the big leagues!' The second story concerns Tucker's forthright assessment of Callas as a colleague: 'Well, I liked Maria – but she could be a pain in the ass!' – which is surely one of the most honest (and accurate!) assessments of one singer by another.

Another story about Tucker illustrates his generosity as a colleague. He and Franco Corelli were initially rivals, but they became good friends after Corelli diffidently approached Tucker and asked if he could watch him sing the aria '*O dolci mani*' from the last act of *Tosca*. Tucker readily agreed. 'To sing it right, Franco, you have to be Jewish!' he said, to Corelli's amusement.

Vocally, Tucker achieved an astonishing consistency throughout his long career. The voice we hear in the 1974 RCA recording of *La Juive* is recognizably the same as that we hear in the 1947 recording of *Aida* conducted by Toscanini. Over the years, it had darkened slightly and gained in power (though he was no *tenorino* even in

1947), but apart from that it remained unchanged. Tucker's disciplined lifestyle and his careful choice of repertoire undoubtedly had much to do with that. He added the heavier roles – Canio, Manrico, Radames, Alvaro, Samson – to his repertoire gradually, ensuring that he was ready to tackle them before he committed himself to doing so. His studio recordings, mostly made for RCA, are not as numerous as one might expect, or, for that matter, as one would wish. They are of high quality, at least as far as Tucker's own contributions are concerned; but, given the strength of the competition, few would be first choices. Yet any opera lover whose collection allows for multiple recordings of certain works, would want to have some of them. Minimally, the second *Butterfly*, one of the *Forzas*, one of the *Aidas* (the first for Toscanini's conducting, the second for Callas's Aida), and *La Juive* should be in any collection. Tucker sang French well – better than Italian – and it is sad that he was not recorded in *Samson* or *Carmen*, the operas which probably gave him his two best French roles except Eléazar.

Tucker has been called 'the American Caruso'. Well, he wasn't quite that. Caruso's voice remains unique and incomparable in its combination of beauty, power, intensity, technical excellence, and elegance of phrasing. And the deficiencies in Tucker's singing noted by Steane are real. But, in spite of them, he is a great tenor. In an age rich in tenorial talent, he held his own. When he started his Met career in 1945, Björling, Peerce, and del Monaco, all of whom sang some of the same roles as Tucker, were in their prime. A little later, they were joined by di Stefano, then by Corelli, Bergonzi, Gedda, Kraus, Vickers, McCracken, and, finally, by Pavarotti and Domingo. Yet, even in the face of such strong competition, Tucker retained his position as a *primo tenore*. In terms of recordings, his Verdi singing is less elegant and imaginative than that of Bergonzi or Domingo, and his *verismo* singing does not have quite the *squillo* of del Monaco or Corelli. But for sheer quality of sound, his voice is a match for theirs. He was America's greatest tenor, so in that sense at least, the tag 'the American Caruso' may be justified.[4]

The back cover of James Drake's biography of Tucker boasts a series of encomiums by distinguished colleagues from the world of opera. 'One of the most phenomenal voices of the century,' was Dame Joan Sutherland's verdict. Montserrat Caballé opined, 'The most virile tenor voice I have ever heard in opera,' and added, 'No one today has his perfect technique.' Leontyne Price noted 'his ability to sing with total abandon – and to *enjoy* it', adding that he was 'a wonderful colleague'. Perhaps the last word should be left to Robert Merrill, the friend with whom Tucker was on a concert tour when he died of a massive heart attack at Kalamazoo, Michigan. Merrill had one of the longest careers in Metropolitan Opera history. He had sung and recorded with nearly all the great tenors of his day, including, apart from Tucker himself, Peerce, Björling, del Monaco, Bergonzi, Corelli, Vickers, McCracken, Kraus, Cioni, and Valletti. After Tucker's death, Merrill said, 'He was an original, right out of the pages of a Damon Runyon story – and, to me, the greatest tenor in the world'. And who had a better claim to judge?

Tucker made complete studio recordings of *Lucia di Lammermoor, Rigoletto, La Traviata, Il Trovatore, La Forza del Destino* (two), *Aida* (two), *La Bohème, Madama Butterfly* (two), *Cavalleria Rusticana* and *Pagliacci*.

Notes

[1]Throughout Tucker's life, he was known as 'Richard' to most professional colleagues, but intimates called him 'Ruby'.

[2]Peerce and Tucker differed, however, about what was required of an orthodox Jew. When the baritone Leonard Warren converted from Judaism to (Catholic) Christianity, Peerce was reportedly furious and refused to speak to Warren again. But Tucker regarded the conversion as a personal decision and remained friendly with Warren.

³He was also bald, but wore a toupee when appearing in public.

⁴Lest it be thought that this is not much of a recommendation, it should be remembered that American tenors include John Alexander, Lawrence Brownlee, Richard Cassilly, Mario Chamlee, William Cochran, Eugene Conley, Richard Crooks, Charles Hackett, Jerry Hadley, George Hamlin, James King, Gary Lakes, Richard Leech, James McCracken, Chris Merritt, Michele Molese, Barry Morell, Jan Peerce, Neil Shicoff, George Shirley, Robert Dean Smith, Kenneth Tarver, Jess Thomas, and Charles Workman – not a bad line-up by any standards.

22 Mario del Monaco: the brass bull of Milan

M ario del Monaco (1915–82) was never a favourite with British music critics. Idolized by audiences all over the world, he was regularly taken to task by professional reviewers for what, in their view, was coarseness, insensitivity, a lack of taste and musicianship, phrasing unimaginatively, and ignoring the composer's dynamic markings by singing too loudly. Leading the charge was Desmond Shawe-Taylor, the doyen of English music critics and joint author with Edward Sackville-West of *The Record Guide*. In the 1955 edition of *The Record Guide*, he had this to say concerning several recital discs by del Monaco—

Mario del Monaco has probably the finest vocal equipment of any of the younger generation of Italian tenors, and his immense popularity with mass audiences has encouraged him to dispense with anything in the way of nuances or refinements of style.[1] It is rarely that he allows his splendid voice to drop below *forte*, and he prefers *fortissimo*. He is at his best in such frankly rhetorical music as the Improvviso from Giordano's *Andrea Chenier*, and it is not surprising that he should recently have won a triumph in this role at the Metropolitan. On the other hand, he is wholly deficient in elegance or gaiety, and is capable of singing such music as Verdi's '*Questa o quella*' in a ludicrously violent and stentorian manner. In some of his complete opera recordings, there is much to enjoy in the ringing, virile tone and impassioned declamation; but in a miscellaneous

recital the constant all-out style grows unbearably monotonous. Any critic, it may be added, who attempts to tell the truth,
as he sees it, about this idolized tenor is liable to receive abusive
letters from unknown correspondents.

In the 1956 *Supplement*, Shawe-Taylor adds this about del
Monaco's first (1955) recording of what was to become his
signature role, the title part of Verdi's *Otello*—

Mario del Monaco's Otello is the best thing he has yet done for
the gramophone. His voice has the savage ring which the part
demands, and he declaims the text with a fierce energy; but he
fails to convey any notion of pathos, and without pathos Otello
is reduced to the level of a blundering brute. Del Monaco is
exciting in his big scene with Iago in the second act, but he loses
ground in Act 3, making surprisingly little of '*Dio mi potevi
scagliar*' and – to mention one detail characteristic of a general
failure in subtlety – neglecting to modulate his tones, when
reading the letter from the Venetian Senate, in such a way that
the scathing asides to Desdemona shall sound dramatically apt.
His final scene is good, and his sudden cry to Iago '*Ah! discol-
pati*', is memorable; but the total impression of his interpretation is slighter than that made by Ramon Vinay with far less
vocal equipment.[2]

This set the tone for what followed. The authors of *The Stereo
Record Guide*, which, in due course, evolved into *The Penguin
Guide to Compact Discs and DVDs*, adopted a similarly dismissive
attitude towards del Monaco. John Culshaw's memoirs depicted
him in an unflattering light,[3] and even John Steane, a critic who is
a model of fairness and probity, is uncharacteristically severe towards del Monaco in both *The Grand Tradition* and *Singers of the*

Century. On a personal note, I recall a conversation many years ago[4] with the late Roy Douglas, in which he wondered aloud whether 'the fellow [i.e. del Monaco] had a brain at all'. The prevailing view of the British (and, to some extent, the American) critics can be summed up as 'a great voice – but little evidence of artistry'.

The divergence between the critical views and the general opinion of the opera-going (and record-buying) public should give us pause. If del Monaco was really as awful as the critics said he was, why was he so popular with the public? Opera-lovers as a class are not usually devoid of taste, especially in relation to singers, of whom many of them have heard a good number. And del Monaco certainly did not owe his popularity to a dearth of tenorial talent. On the contrary, he belonged to a generation of prodigiously gifted tenors, including Jan Peerce, Mario Filippeschi, Jussi Björling, Richard Tucker, Ferruccio Tagliavini, Giuseppe di Stefano, Franco Corelli, Carlo Bergonzi, Nicolai Gedda, Jon Vickers, and James McCracken. His repertoire, both in the theatre and on record, overlapped with theirs. Yet, even in such distinguished company, he was able to shine. His appearances guaranteed full houses all over the world, and his popularity as a recording artist was matched only by Maria Callas.

Moreover, critical opinion was not unanimous. Italian critics, in particular, took a somewhat different view from their British and American *confrères.* In his *Stars of the Opera: The Great Opera Singers* (1992), Enrico Stinchelli writes—

Mario del Monaco […] was both the last to follow Caruso and the first of a new school, that of the imitators of del Monaco…. […] It must be said that his vocal qualities cannot be copied; any other vocal or respiratory system would be seriously damaged by imitating his techniques. Already rich and powerful by nature, the voice of this Italian tenor was built on the central tenor notes, which were strengthened and thickened, and on the incredible power of his high notes, which were joined to the middle register by an excellent *passaggio*. The result was a declamatory singing, unique in its incisiveness, but sometimes exaggerated, in difficulty in utilizing dynamic effects and *mezza voce*, and with little variety.

Stinchelli here acknowledges what neither Shawe-Taylor nor Steane granted: namely, that del Monaco's lack of dynamic variety and nuance was not the result of trying to appeal to the gallery but a by-product of his vocal technique. It was the price he paid for the exceptional power and intensity of his tone, and its unequalled fitness for the most declamatory passages of the heroic tenor repertoire. Thus in *Aida*, for example, '*Celeste Aida*' may sound more like a call to arms than a love song, but other passages – for example, '*Nel fiero anelito, Si fuggiam da queste mura*' and '*Io son disonorato*' in the Nile Scene – have a fiery, heroic quality that more lyrical voices cannot match.[5]

Helena Matheopoulos, in her *The Tenors*, a lavishly illustrated collection of essays which admittedly borders on hagiography, goes further. She writes—

It was no accident that the role with which [del Monaco] was most identified was Otello […] for which he possessed the ideal temperamental and vocal resources: a manly, thrillingly erotic voice of immense power and volume, with a gleaming, bronze timbre and burnished, 'gladiatorial' colour that instantly bespoke the leader. This impression was strengthened by his broad, generous phrasing and noble declamation, both ideally suited to heroic characters. […]

Del Monaco's prodigious vocal and scenic gifts and film-star good looks were accompanied by intelligence, self-knowledge, and a gift for self-examination. He was equally knowledgeable about singing, forever studying and experimenting with vocal and dramatic possibilities. He probed his characters very deeply and identified with them with every fibre of his being. He burst into prominence after ten years of studying singing, longer than most artists.

Del Monaco owed his vocal technique to his studies with Arturo Melocchi, whose controversial method he made his own. Melocchi's method is sometimes known as the 'low larynx' method, and it has been successfully adopted by other singers, notably the tenors Giovanni Martinelli, Lauritz Melchior, Richard Tucker and Luciano Pavarotti. Jerome Hines explains it like this in *The Four Voices of Man*—

'Laryngeal singers' approach singing with the premise that the voice is produced by the larynx and they make no attempt to place it in the 'mask.' With such an approach, there is a slight sensation of 'pinch' in the larynx. This can be regarded as a form of 'chest voice' since there is no sensation of placement above the vocal folds when employing it. Bear in mind that this refers to the male chest voice, which is the same as the female's 'belting' voice. Such an approach, commonly associated with the Melocchi School of singing, produces a bright, narrow and penetrating sound.

But what made del Monaco unique was the conjunction of the Melocchi method with the colossal amount of breath he used (see Jerome Hines, *The Four Voices of Man*, pp 65–67). This would have been devastating to any singer with a normal physical constitution. But, for some reason, despite the abuse they suffered, del Monaco's vocal cords survived and served him well almost to the end of his career (he was still singing at sixty and his last complete opera recording was made in 1969, when he was fifty-four and had been singing the most strenuous roles in the Italian and French repertoires for over twenty years). The low larynx method and the exceptional amount of breath he was able to use, allied to what was already by nature a potent vocal endowment, combined to make del Monaco the most powerful Italian heroic tenor since Tamagno. Arguably, the only other tenor of any type who could compare with del Monaco in terms of sheer vocal power, was the great Danish *Heldentenor*, Lauritz Melchior.[6]

In del Monaco's centenary year (2015), a thoughtful article by Stephen Hastings, author of *The Björling Sound*, appeared in *Opera* magazine. This suggests that a (long overdue) reassessment may be underway. Certainly, del Monaco's art – or, more precisely, the relation between vocal technique and interpretative art in his particular case – is more complex than the strictures of the majority of British and American music critics suggest.

Mr Hastings' article, entitled 'A Decidedly Modern Tenor', begins by claiming that

Mario del Monaco was, for those who heard him live in the opera house, the most consistently exciting Italian singer of a generation that abounded in vocal talent.

Mr Hastings goes on to compare del Monaco's status, in terms of career duration, popular acclaim, international celebrity, and financial rewards, to that of Beniamino Gigli and Luciano Pavarotti. He points out that del Monaco, like Gigli, 'had direct contact with the last Italian operatic composers of significant stature', including Zandonai, Cilea, Alfano, and Giordano, all of whom admired his art. And he says that del Monaco's recorded legacy – twenty-four complete studio recordings of operas and over ninety live recordings – gives him a place among the most prolific and commercially successful recording artists in history.

Like nearly all singers, del Monaco started his career singing lyric roles. Not surprisingly, he initially modelled himself on Gigli, but he quickly concluded that the lyric tenor repertoire was not for him. In his autobiography, he gives the reason: 'Gigli's voice was a violin, mine was a trumpet,'[7] to which Mr Hastings adds—

The distinction is an apt one, and much of the criticism del Monaco received over the decades could be explained by the fact that most listeners – especially where recordings are concerned – find it easier to listen at length to a solo violin than to a solo trumpet. Del Monaco's phrasing never even remotely possessed the charm of a Kreisler, the flexibility of a Heifetz, the incantatory lyricism of a Huberman, or the structural intelligence of an Adolf Busch.

His was, however, an energizing sound, to a degree that no violin could ever hope to match, capable of sustaining a line with heroic density of tone and of generating an excitement that was eminently theatrical and very much part of the sound-world of nineteenth-century opera: it is no coincidence that accompanying trumpets are strongly associated with such archetypal tenor roles as Verdi's Manrico and Radames.

In fact, del Monaco's voice had a bronze colour and a bell-like clarity which suited the heroic roles of the Italian repertoire perfectly. It is also noteworthy that, more than any other tenor before or since, he was identified with the *verismo* repertoire. Of his twenty roles on record, no fewer than twelve belong to the *verismo* period. For the *veristi*, acting was as important as singing, and del Monaco was a man of the theatre who paid as much attention to the textual, dramatic, and theatrical aspects of his roles as he did to the purely musical aspects. Even in Verdi, he excelled as Otello, which can be regarded as a proto-veristic role, and one of his few French roles was Don Jose in *Carmen*, a part which has strong affinities with the Italian *verismo*. In keeping with their desire for realism, the *veristi* emphasized the importance of words and drama relative to music, and, as we have said (see the article on Aureliano Pertile), developed a grammar of expressive devices (including speech, screams, howls, sobs, groans, shouts, laughter, and other extra-musical vocal effects) significantly different from the purely musical devices favoured by the *bel canto* composers (devices which included *fioriture*, the artistic use of *rubato*, and the skilful use of *portamento* to underpin the *legato*). Del Monaco eschewed all such effects, but made liberal use of the full range of veristic, extra-musical effects in roles where they were appropriate.

In addition to requiring a different, extra-musical range of vocal effects from the *bel canto* composers, the *veristi* demanded more in the way of sheer vocal power. The scores of composers such as Alfano, Boïto, Catalani, Cilea, Giordano, Leoncavallo, Mascagni, Ponchielli, Puccini, and Zandonai, were more thickly orchestrated than those of earlier composers such as Bellini, Donizetti, Mercadante, Pacini, and Rossini. Only in late Verdi do we encounter anything remotely comparable to the orchestral density of the *veristi*. And singers, as always, responded to the demands made of them by the composers. Just as schools of singing evolved to meet the demands placed upon the human voice by the Baroque masters, by Mozart and (later) Beethoven, by the *bel canto* school, by Verdi and Wagner, so too did a school evolve to meet the demands of this new school of Italian composers. The first tenor – perhaps the first singer in any vocal category – to rise to the challenge was Caruso. Caruso retained many of the stylistic characteristics of the *bel canto* school in which he had been originally trained, such as flexibility, dynamic variety, and skill in the execution of *fioriture*. But, as his career progressed, his art and technique became progressively adapted to the needs of the composers who were his contemporaries. Effectively, he founded a new school of singing: the school of *verismo*.

The apotheosis of that school – to an even greater extent than Aureliano Pertile, the tenor on whom, more than any other, he had modelled himself – was Mario del Monaco. It was wittily said that he was an exponent not of *bel canto*, but of *can belto*. There is some truth in the gibe, but it does not tell the whole story. Despite the strictures of some critics, del Monaco was not just a crude shouter and bawler. The best of his recordings (and the best are surprisingly numerous, including *La Forza del Destino*, *Aida*, *Otello*, *La Fanciulla del West*, *Manon Lescaut*, *Tosca*, *Il Tabarro*, *Andrea Chenier*, *Mefistofele*, *Adriana Lecouvreur*, *Cavalleria Rusticana*, *Pagliacci*, and *La Gioconda*, among others) rank among the best versions of those operas available, and his contributions are by no means the least of the reasons for that. He sometimes sings with a subtlety with which he was not often credited. But even when subtlety is lacking, the amazingly 'energizing sound' of which Mr Hastings speaks is much in evidence. When it comes to the ability to communicate the most primal emotions and thereby to generate a visceral sense of excitement, Mario del Monaco was in a class of his own.

Del Monaco's studio recordings included an abridged version of *Norma* and complete recordings of *Rigoletto*, *Il Trovatore*, *La Forza del Destino*, *Aida*, *Otello* (two), *Cavalleria Rusticana* (three), *Pagliacci* (two), *Mefistofele*, *Andrea Chenier*, *Fedora*, *La Wally*, *La Gioconda*, *Carmen*, *Manon Lescaut*, *Tosca*, *La Fanciulla del West*, *Il Tabarro*, *Turandot*, and *Francesca da Rimini*.

Notes

[1]The 'younger generation of Italian tenors' at that time included Ferruccio Tagliavini, Gianni Poggi, Giuseppe Campora, Luigi

Infantino, Giacinto Prandelli, and Giuseppe di Stefano. Despite the fact that Franco Corelli, like di Stefano, was born in 1921, he did not make his mark internationally until somewhat later (after 1960).

[2]Let us leave aside the question whether the huge-voiced Vinay could aptly have been described as having 'far less vocal equipment' than del Monaco – or, indeed, anyone else.

[3]In fairness, it must be added that most tenors emerged from Culshaw's memoirs with their reputations (personal and / or professional) badly tarnished. Corelli and Björling are other examples. In the latter's case, Culshaw's veracity has been called into question by both Anna-Lisa Björling, the tenor's widow, and Birgit Nilsson.

[4]It took place in or about 1975. Roy Douglas (1908–2015) was a composer, arranger, and orchestral musician, who served Vaughan Williams and William Walton as an amanuensis. He was the author of the book, *Working with RVW*.

[5]There is surely, however, much truth in Franco Corelli's assertion, in an interview with Stefan Zucker, that del Monaco 'produced sounds not entirely suitable for his throat and louder than his volume. He exaggerated, striving to produce 110 percent of the sound that he had. The laryngeal method often leads to muscular singing.'

[6]However, whereas Melchior's voice was of a piece with his gigantic physique (he stood six foot three and a half inches tall and weighed over nineteen stones), del Monaco, who was five feet eight and a half inches and sturdily but not massively built, was a man of normal stature gifted with an abnormally large voice.

[7]A perceptive judgment which gives the lie to the idea that del Monaco was either unintelligent or narcissistic. In fact, he was highly self-aware and self-critical.

23 The enigma
of Giuseppe di Stafano

Giuseppe di Stefano (1921–2008) is probably best remembered today as the regular partner, on records and in the opera house, of Maria Callas between 1953 and 1957.

Di Stefano's career had begun a few years earlier. He made his debut in 1946, and was an immediate success, making debuts at La Scala the following year and at the New York Metropolitan Opera in 1948. Unlike many other tenors, he never sang *comprimario* roles – from the first, he was a principal. Listening to his early recordings, one can tell why. The voice is an arrestingly beautiful lyric tenor, with a truly romantic quality, the ideal voice for a young lover in the central Italian and French repertoire. Di Stefano was well suited vocally to French lyric opera, and he sang several French roles, despite having difficulties with the language, like most Italians. His French pronunciation (admittedly much better than Corelli's or del Monaco's) is by no means idiomatic, but his interpretations of Faust, Don Jose, and Wilhelm Meister have been admired by many connoisseurs – and rightly so. In all his roles, his liquid but crystalline diction, velvety *mezza voce*, dramatic involvement, and passionate delivery, are unquestionable assets.

From the first, however, not all was well. Di Stefano lacked discipline, and one suspects that his vocal studies had been pursued half-heartedly. By temperament, he was a playboy, addicted to life in the fast lane. He liked casinos, good cigars, gambling, and sports cars. Rehearsals bored him, and he skipped them whenever he could. Sometimes, performances bored him too. The English tenor,

Nigel Douglas, remembered having spent a hefty part of his meagre income as a student on di Stefano performances, one of which the star withdrew from halfway through, claiming an indisposition (although he was found in a casino in the small hours of the next morning, having lost all his money), while, on another occasion, the great tenor performed perfunctorily for most of the first two acts before switching on and giving an incandescent performance in the third.

This temperamental indiscipline was not confined to rehearsals and the occasional performance. To acquire a sound technique needs constant hard work and commitment. It takes hours of tedious vocal exercises and practice. When di Stefano embarked on a career as a singer, that was not what he had in mind. He wanted fame, applause, adulation, the bright lights, wealth, all the trappings of success. The laborious endeavour which alone can reliably deliver those results in the long term, was not for him. At all events, his technique was unfinished: his vocal method was flawed, and his top notes, unlike Gigli's or Björling's, were not securely poised on the breath. This is apparent even in his earliest recordings. Steane, in *The Grand Tradition*, notes one of the symptoms: above the stave, there was 'an openness of vowel sounds that could nag remorselessly'. Other critics noted a habit of attacking notes from below rather than cleanly, and noted also that his execution of ornaments – for example, the *gruppetto* on the word *punge* in '*Questa o quella*' from Verdi's *Rigoletto* – was far below what one would expect from a lyric tenor of di Stefano's accomplishments. The notes are lunged at rather than sung. Elsewhere he shows himself no master of *bel canto*: recorded in a live performance, his Count Almaviva, even at a slow tempo, is tentative and uncertain in coloratura, and his studio recordings as Arturo in *I Puritani* and Nemorino in *Elisir d'Amore* are inferior, in technical virtuosity, to several competitors, including some who, in terms of purely vocal equipment, were not in di Stefano's league. Even so, the sheer beauty of the voice yields considerable pleasure, compromised in the *Puritani* recording only by the strained and throaty top C sharp in '*Credeasi misera*'.[1]

Di Stefano's short-lived, but prolific, partnership with Callas began in 1953. Over the next four years, they recorded together no fewer than ten operas. By the time the partnership ended in 1957, a decline in di Stefano's voice, a perceptible coarsening of the tone, had already become evident. The 1957 *La Gioconda* and the 1958 *Forza del Destino*, both with Zinka Milanov, show the registers, never correctly blended, starting to separate. The formerly exquisite *mezza voce* is now dangerously close to crooning, which entails taking the voice off support. Yet, in both those recordings, di Stefano gives performances which are more powerfully characterized, and more dramatically compelling, than many better sung versions. But, by 1963, when his second recording of *Tosca* appeared – this one opposite Leontyne Price – di Stefano's vocal degradation was virtually complete. Even in the relatively undemanding role of Cavaradossi, the voice seems but a tattered remnant of its former self. After that, there were to be no more studio recordings of complete operas. His career at the top was over.

The causes of di Stefano's early decline have been disputed. His faulty vocal method has already been alluded to. Others attributed his vocal deterioration to smoking, the unwise and premature assumption of roles too heavy for his essentially lyric voice to tackle, and forcing his moderately sized voice in an effort to compete with the gigantic voices of Mario del Monaco and Franco Corelli. Di Stefano himself blamed allergies. Whatever the truth about the causes,[2] the fact was undeniable: di Stefano's career in the world's premier opera houses ended at an age when most tenors would be coming into their prime.

Despite the brevity of his career, di Stefano left a substantial recorded legacy. So charismatic was he as a performer that he served as a model and inspiration for many of the great tenors who succeeded him, notably Luciano Pavarotti, Plácido Domingo, and Jose Carreras,[3] and it is surely not fanciful to detect his influence today in the timbre and vocal colour of Roberto Alagna and in the passionate declamation of Rolando Villazón. Apart from Callas, Milanov, and Price, his soprano partners on record included Hilde Gueden, Victoria de los Angeles, Antonietta Stella, and Renata Scotto. It is a sign of his stature that he recorded with so many of the greatest lyric and *lirico spinto* sopranos of his day.

How should we evaluate di Stefano's performances on record? The competition in several of the roles he sang is stiff. It includes Gigli, Peerce, Björling, Tucker, Tagliavini, del Monaco, Corelli, Bergonzi, Gedda, Kraus, Aragall, Pavarotti, Domingo, Carreras, and Alagna, among others. Even the 'second string' tenors – Albanese, Campora, Prandelli, Poggi, Infantino, Raimondi, del Monte, and Cioni, for example – pose formidable challenges. Just about any of them would be instantly signed up by any opera house in the world today. Most of them are technically sounder than di Stefano. Many sing more beautifully than he does in any of the recordings made after 1956. But not many sing 'off the words' as expressively. Not many articulate the text as clearly, or provide a total experience as satisfying. As with Callas, I find that, once I have heard di Stefano in a role, his is very often the voice I hear in my mind's ear when I call the role to mind, however many others I may have heard in the meantime. It is difficult to say exactly why this should be, but I know that I am not alone in finding it to be true. In fact, José Carreras went further. In his autobiography, *Singing from the Soul*, he wrote—

The fact that I prefer interpretation over technique probably explains my taste when it comes to tenors. After my [singing] lessons with Ruax, I'd go home and head straight for my record collection. No matter who I started with, I always ended up with Giuseppe di Stefano. Sometimes I'd listen to Enrico Caruso, Beniamino Gigli, Jussi Björling, Richard Tucker, and Franco Corelli, all magnificent tenors. Their recordings were like voice lessons. But when I really wanted to enjoy myself, I took one of Pippo's records from the shelf. To listen to di Stefano is to be enveloped in emotions pouring out with the voice through the music.

Well, perhaps. But not everyone wants to be 'enveloped in emotions', even when listening to music. Some listeners have a more cerebral approach. That is not necessarily to say that they are emotionally dry or frigid. It is merely to say that they are not prepared to give absolute precedence to the heart over the head.

Di Stefano's recordings raise other questions. In timbre, weight, and colour, his voice was not dissimilar to Jussi Björling's. Yet, while Björling was able, from an early stage in his career, to tackle heroic roles like Manrico and Radames, for di Stefano they always seemed a step too far. In his 1957 recording of *Il Trovatore*, he sounds overparted in the declamatory passages, notably '*Di quella pira*', where the final top C is abbreviated and rather desperate-sounding. The same is true of some of the other roles in his recorded repertoire. His Canio lacks both the *squillo* of del Monaco and the tonal concentration of Björling, and his Des Grieux (in Puccini's *Manon Lescaut*) and Cavaradossi are more convincing in the lyric than in the heroic moments. Björling, because of his superior technique, was able to generate a high degree of tension in his tone, and to produce a brilliant and penetrative sound without forcing, in a way di Stefano, with his more limited technical resources, could not.

Surprisingly, in spite of all this, di Stefano is often at his best in the roles to which he was vocally least well suited. As to his lyric roles, his Rodolfo, though lively and personable as ever, is coarsely sung – no match for those of Gigli, Björling and Bergonzi. His Duke of Mantua lacks elegance: he is credible as a seducer but not as an aristocrat. His Pinkerton is, in some respects, more sharply characterized than Björling's or Bergonzi's, but is nothing like so finished in terms of pure vocalization. In *bel canto* roles, his style is anachronistic – more apt to the *verismo* operas that were to follow some fifty to a hundred years later. Del Monaco shrewdly remarked that di Stefano had the temperament of a dramatic tenor but the voice of a lyric tenor. That seems to me profoundly true. And perhaps it explains why this great lyric tenor is best remembered in dramatic roles. Somehow, in many of his performances and recordings, di Stefano manages to transcend considerations of vocal adequacy and make us realize, as very few can, that opera is not just music, but music drama.

Di Stefano's complete studio recordings include *I Puritani*, *L'Elisir d'Amore*, *Lucia di Lammermoor* (two), *Rigoletto*, *La Traviata*, *Il Trovatore*, *Un Ballo in Maschera*, *La Forza del Destino*, *Cavalleria Rusticana*, *Pagliacci*, *Manon Lescaut*, *La Bohème*, *Madama Butterfly*, *Tosca* (two), and *La Gioconda*.

Notes

[1]There are three other top C sharps – one in '*A te o cara*' and two (transposed down a semitone from top Ds) in '*Vieni fra queste braccia*' – but they sound, if not exactly beautiful, at least more secure.

[2]Monocausal explanations of inherently complex phenomena are nearly always oversimplified. Di Stefano's early vocal decline probably resulted from a combination of factors, none of which individually is sufficient to account for it.

[3]Carreras resembled di Stefano in not being content to sing as a lyric tenor. Just as di Stefano tried to compete with del Monaco, Corelli and

Bergonzi, so Carreras tried to compete with Pavarotti and Domingo – and with similar results: after a few years of vocal splendour, the glory departed, never to return.

24 Franco Corelli:
the tenor as matinee idol

It is a moot point whether Franco Corelli (1921–2003) was more notable for his appearance or his voice.

1960 was a mixed year for the Metropolitan Opera. Two of its biggest stars – the American baritone Leonard Warren, and the Swedish tenor Jussi Björling – died in their late forties of heart attacks, the former in March and the latter in September. Warren, in fact, collapsed and died on the stage of the Met in the middle of a performance of *La Forza del Destino*. The Met badly needed some good news.

It came from an unlikely quarter. Two singers made their house debuts in what looked like a routine performance of an old warhorse – Verdi's perennially popular *Il Trovatore*. A young African-American soprano called Leontyne Price was appearing as Leonora, and, in the title role, was an Italian tenor unknown to American audiences: Franco Corelli. Few present could have realized that they were about to witness operatic history in the making. Price and Corelli went on to have two of the biggest operatic careers in the annals of the Met. Price ranks among the greatest Verdian *spinto* sopranos – she is the successor to Ponselle, Destinn, Rethberg, Muzio, Milanov, and Tebaldi.

And Corelli? Well, the audience that night must have pricked up their ears when they first heard his voice in the offstage serenade, '*Deserto sulla terra*'. And they certainly paid attention when he made his entrance. Instead of the stunted, rotund figure they were used to, and probably expected, here was a tall, athletically built man, who looked, in the words of the Met's famously austere General Manager Rudolf Bing, 'like a Roman god'. And the voice! It was a dark, rich, bronze tenor with a stupendous top, as he confirmed in '*La pira*' (sung in the original key, with a pair of thrilling top Cs, the second of which – a long, sustained note – might have sunk a battleship, never mind cracking a wineglass).

For the next sixteen years, Corelli never looked back. He was the Met's undisputed *primo tenore* and its most highly paid star. The competition was stiff. Even without Björling, di Stefano (whose early vocal decline and indifference to contractual obligations had made him *persona non grata* at the Met), and del Monaco (who left in a fit of pique when Corelli was hired), it included Tucker, Bergonzi, Gedda, Vickers, McCracken and Kraus – major talents all. Later, they were joined by Pavarotti, Domingo, and Carreras. Yet, in terms of box office appeal, Corelli was the king. His name in a cast list guaranteed a full house. It wasn't just the voice, of course. The athletic physique and movie-star good looks helped. He received a somewhat back-handed compliment from Leontyne Price, his partner on his debut, who, when asked for her view of Corelli, purred, 'Oh, I just *love* Franco. He has such gorgeous – *legs!*' The reviewers were not slow to notice that the Met's new tenor had acquired a large female following, and their critiques contained frequent sly references to Corelli's passionate (and unmistakably Italian) vocal manner and the fading *pianissimi* which 'made the ladies sigh wistfully'.

Corelli carved out a repertoire which, in some respects, was highly unusual but which reflected the specific properties of his voice. At first, that voice seemed a classic Italian *tenore robusto*, and he was compared with del Monaco and expected to tackle the same repertoire. To some extent, he did. Their repertoires certainly overlapped. But there were significant differences. Del Monaco was essentially a B flat tenor, at home in low-lying roles like Chenier, uncomfortable in a sustained high *tessitura*, and reluctant to attempt top Cs in live performances.[1] Corelli, in contrast, was a high heroic tenor, with a range that extended to a brilliant top D. If del Monaco was the heir to Pertile, Corelli was the heir to Lauri-Volpi. Although he and del Monaco shared several roles,[2] Corelli never tackled Otello, which was del Monaco's signature role. On the other hand, despite his unabashedly Italian style (and accent), he sang several French roles, including some (Faust, Werther, Roméo) which would have been too lyrical for del Monaco, and at least one (Raoul in *Les Huguenots*) which would have lain too high for him.[3] He also sang *bel canto* roles such as the title role in *Poliuto*, Gualtiero in *Il Pirata*, and Pollione in *Norma*, only the last of which featured in del Monaco's repertoire and, if his (abridged) recording of the part is anything to go by, not with conspicuous success. In the latter years of Corelli's career, instead of following the normal practice of adding heavier, more heroic roles to his repertoire, he unexpectedly returned to lighter, more lyrical roles: Roméo in Gounod's *Roméo et Juliette* and Rodolfo in *La Bohème* became particular favourites.

The differences between Corelli and del Monaco are partly a matter of technique. Del Monaco adopted the Melocchi (low larynx) method, which Corelli used only intermittently and with caution because he regarded it as dangerous. For del Monaco, this method, in conjunction with an amount of breath that would be devastating to most singers, permitted him to achieve the bronze colour and *squillo* he aimed at, at least up to a top B. Corelli's freer, less muscular method, allowed him to produce brilliant, and yet cavernous-sounding top notes up to a D flat, and even D natural. This technical difference, to a large extent, accounts for the differences in their respective repertoires: del Monaco sang heroic roles which did not make excessive demands on his top register in terms of either individual high notes or general *tessitura*; Corelli, as we have seen, in his prime, sang the repertoire of a high heroic tenor.

Corelli remains a controversial figure, arousing (sometimes uncritical) admiration and (sometimes hypercritical) condemnation in roughly equal proportions. His detractors point to his lisping diction, his habit of scooping up to notes instead of attacking them cleanly, his exaggerated *portamenti*, and his defective rhythmic sense and tendency to lose the conductor. His admirers point to his grand phrasing, goose-bump *acuti*, ability to fine his tone away to a *pianissimo* on practically any note in his range, and the sheer charisma and bravura of his performances. And, of course, there is the quality of the voice itself, about which there can surely be no argument. Few tenors of any kind on record have possessed such a magnificent instrument.

If Corelli was not as refined an artist as Martinelli, Björling or Bergonzi, neither was he as crude as del Monaco was often accused of being (sometimes with justification). Again, Lauri-Volpi comes to mind. He has similar virtues and defects. On the one hand, playing to the gallery, outrageously flaunted high notes, a tendency to ignore dynamic markings, a certain lack of musicianship; on the other, expressive phrasing, the charisma of the matinee idol, (sometimes) a surprising sensitivity to the meaning of words and to the shape of a musical phrase (consider, for example, the *diminuendo* on the word *trafitto* in '*Ah si ben mio*' from the complete recording of *Il Trovatore*). Examples of his verbal and musical sensitivity are more plentiful than Corelli's critics might want to admit. He is one of the few tenors who treats '*Celeste Aida*' as a love song and not simply as a generalized outpouring of tenorial emotion. In fact, his Radames is one of the finest on record, his voice being one of those rare instruments that possesses both the lyricism for the love music and the *squillo* for the declamatory passages. The role also affords him several opportunities to display his ability – rare among heroic tenors – to float soft high notes, without resorting to crooning.

Corelli never gives the impression of delivering a merely routine performance. Domingo sometimes does – perhaps inevitably, given the vast scope and quantity of his discography. Corelli, whose output of complete opera recordings is surprisingly small (much smaller than those of di Stefano, del Monaco, and Bergonzi, let alone those of Gedda, Pavarotti, Domingo, and Carreras), invariably conveys a vivid immediacy in his characterizations. Even Radames and Manrico emerge not as narcissistic tenors – not even as musicianly tenors! – but as flesh-and-blood creations with real, humanly intelligible emotions. That is no small achievement – even for a star tenor.

Corelli's studio recordings include *Norma*, *Il Trovatore*, *Aida* (two), *Faust*, *Roméo et Juliette*, *Carmen* (two), *Cavalleria Rusticana*, *Pagliacci*, *Andrea Chenier*, *Tosca*, and *Turandot*.

Notes

[1]Although, in his recording of *Rigoletto*, he joins Hilde Gueden at the end of the '*Addio, addio*' duet in a good sustained high D flat. However, notwithstanding his assumption of roles like the Duke (to which he was fundamentally unsuited, vocally and temperamentally) and his almost exclusive focus on the Italian and, to a lesser extent, the French repertoire, del Monaco is probably best thought of as an Italian *Heldentenor* – a Siegfried and Tristan *manqué*.

[2]In studio recordings, they can both be heard as Pollione, Radames, Manrico, Cavaradossi, Calaf, Canio, Turiddu, Andrea Chenier, and Don Jose. And pirated live recordings reveal further overlaps in their repertoires.

[3]Connoisseurs preferred Nicolai Gedda, Albert Lance or Alain Vanzo in the French repertoire, but Met audiences were happy to hear Corelli in any roles he wanted to sing, however atrocious his accent might be. In studio recordings, he sang Don Jose (twice), Faust, and Roméo, but, strangely, abstained from French roles which, it might have been

thought, would have suited his voice better: e.g. Énée, Samson, Jean (in *Le Prophète*), Raoul, Le Cid, Werther.

25 The patrician art of Carlo Bergonzi

Carlo Bergonzi (1924–2014), who died shortly after his nine-tieth birthday, was, by common consent, one of the greatest tenors of the twentieth century. He made his debut as a baritone in 1948 as Figaro in *Il Barbiere di Siviglia*, switching to tenor in 1951 and making a second debut in the title role of *Andrea Chenier*. He never looked back. At no time in his career did Bergonzi sing a *comprimario* role.

But what made Bergonzi great? Unlike many other Italian tenors, he sang practically no French roles,[1] and no German ones either, although Lohengrin had been a favourite with Italian tenors from De Lucia to del Monaco. Bergonzi's repertoire consisted almost exclusively of Italian roles in operas composed between 1830 and 1925. He sang a few *arie antiche* and popular Neapolitan songs, but virtually no art songs, and very few concert works other than Verdi's Requiem. Even within the Italian repertoire in which he specialized, Bergonzi was selective. The only *bel canto* operas he sang regularly were *Elisir d'Amore* and *Lucia di Lammermoor*. For the rest, the high *tessitura* of the *bel canto* roles put them out of his range: wisely, he did not attempt them. And, apart from Puccini, he didn't sing many *verismo* roles either. He recorded Turiddu in *Cavalleria Rusticana* and Canio in *Pagliacci* but neither featured prominently in his roles in the opera house. As to Puccini, Bergonzi sang Rodolfo, Pinkerton, and Cavaradossi fairly frequently, and made outstanding recordings of all three, but rarely essayed the more robust Puccini roles – Des Grieux, Luigi, Dick Johnson, and Calaf – to which he was vocally less well suited.

The truth is that, although his repertoire comprised over fifty roles, Bergonzi's reputation was built almost entirely on his unrivalled prowess as an interpreter of Verdi. Despite living in an era of fine Italianate tenors, Bergonzi quickly established himself as *the* Verdi tenor of his day. When he first appeared on the scene, he faced strong competition from Jussi Björling and Giuseppe di Stefano, but Björling died in 1960 and di Stefano's early vocal decline removed him from contention after 1958. Thereafter Bergonzi still had to compete with the gigantic voices (and movie star looks) of Mario del Monaco and Franco Corelli, with the rich voice and impeccable technique of Richard Tucker, and, latterly, with the rising stars, Luciano Pavarotti, Plácido Domingo, and Jose Carreras. But in Verdi he remained matchless, and was instrumental in the revival of interest in Verdi's early operas (i.e. those composed before *Rigoletto* in 1851).

Which takes us back to the question posed earlier: what made Bergonzi great? Why was he an unrivalled exponent of the Verdi tenor roles, especially given the strength of the competition? What was so special – in fact, unique – about the relationship between Verdi's music and Bergonzi's voice and art?

First, the voice. Bergonzi's was a *lirico spinto* tenor of great beauty of tone, with a rich, velvety timbre, moderate power, and a predominantly dark colour, as befits a tenor who started as a baritone. If he lacked the colossal power and *squillo* of del Monaco and Corelli, there were compensations. His voice was more supple and flexible, and he was able to vary the tone colour to a much greater extent than they. This means that he can lighten his voice to an almost Schipa-like *tenore di grazia* for Edoardo's '*Pietoso al lungo pianto*' from *Un Giorno di Regno* or Fenton's '*Dal labbro il canto estasiato vola*' from *Falstaff*, or darken it to produce the right colours for the heavier roles, such as Ernani, Manrico, and Radames. In *La Traviata*, he finds a delicate, light-lyric sound for

Jon Elsby

the first act, but a much more heroic tone and a darker vocal colour for the *cabaletta*, 'O mio rimorso', in Act Two. Most of Verdi's tenor roles call, ideally, for a dark-voiced *spinto* tenor. Bergonzi fitted the bill to perfection.

Second, the technique. Bergonzi originally trained as a baritone, but, after three years of singing in the lower register and experiencing recurrent problems in the *passaggio*, he withdrew for a period of study on his own, using the recordings of the great Italian tenors as guides. He listened especially to records of Caruso, Pertile, Gigli, and Schipa. From Caruso, he learned how to project a dark voice with 'blade'. From Pertile, he learned the art of declamation and how to shape a phrase. From Gigli, he learned the melting *mezza voce* and immediacy of communication. From Schipa, he learned the importance of a great line and purity of sound. From all, he learned how, and when, to cover his voice so as to protect it as he moved from the chest to the head register. When he first appeared as a tenor, his voice had a fast *vibrato* reminiscent of the young Lauri-Volpi, but this disappeared as he consolidated his technique and refined his vocal method. To the very end of his long career, there was never so much as a suspicion of wobble or unsteadiness in Bergonzi's remarkably even emission of tone.[3]

Third, Bergonzi's diction. This was a model of clarity without ever being obtrusive. Not for Bergonzi the exaggerated rolled r's of Martinelli, or the explosive double consonants of Richard Tucker, or the generally over-emphatic diction of James McCracken. Yet Bergonzi's diction was so clear – the vowels and consonants so cleanly and purely articulated – that every word, every syllable, can be heard. The distinctively Emilian pronunciation was occasionally objected to by native Italian speakers,[4] but few others saw reason to complain. When Bergonzi was singing, there was rarely, if ever, a need for anyone with a knowledge of Italian to resort to a libretto (listen to his crystal-clear articulation, at speed, of the tongue-

150

twisting line, '*il Console della spenta repubblica romana*' from *Tosca*).

Fourth, Bergonzi's phrasing, and especially his mastery of long phrases requiring exceptional breath control. Examples can be found almost anywhere in Bergonzi's discography, but perhaps one of the versions of '*Celeste Aida*' would best demonstrate the breath control, and his glorious interpretation of '*Che gelida manina*' from the complete *Bohème* under Serafin would best demonstrate his ability, by the artistic use of *portamento* to underpin his *legato*, to shape hackneyed phrases in a completely new way and compel the listener to hear them afresh, as if for the first time. And, if other examples of the same qualities are needed, try his majestic '*Cielo e mar*' from *La Gioconda*, or the perfectly poised '*Recondita armonia*' from the 1964 *Tosca*.

Fifth, although Bergonzi, like Jussi Björling, was no actor on stage, he was a fine *vocal* actor. There is no lack of passion in his characterizations, notwithstanding his normally scrupulous regard for note values, dynamics, and other markings in the score, and for the maintenance of a pure vocal line. His Canio, for example, is not just one of the best *sung*; it is also one of the best *acted*. And in Verdian roles which are often treated as mere vehicles for displays of vocal prowess – for instance, Ernani, Manrico and Radames – Bergonzi makes each of them a sympathetic and believable character whose responses to situations and interactions with other *dramatis personae* are humanly intelligible. Perhaps the role in which Bergonzi's ability to act with the voice is most in evidence is the title role of *Don Carlo*, where he gives a magnificent performance, unsurpassed even by such potent competition as Jon Vickers, Plácido Domingo, Jose Carreras, and Roberto Alagna.

Finally, although Bergonzi never possessed the stupendous top notes of, say, Franco Corelli or Luciano Pavarotti, or the sheer *squillo* of Mario del Monaco, his upper register was by no means negligible. At climaxes, he gives generously, as John Steane noted in *The Grand Tradition* (1974), and, in his prime, the top Bs and Cs were produced without effort and with a full, rich tone: they rang out powerfully, as his recordings of *Bohème*, *Butterfly*, and *Trovatore* will witness. Later, as he passed the age of fifty, the top notes (above B flat) became somewhat laboured,[5] but even as late as 1984, when he was sixty, he was still capable of giving a critically acclaimed (and ecstatically applauded) performance as Edgardo in *Lucia di Lammermoor*, a fairly high-lying *bel canto* role, at the Royal Opera House, Covent Garden.

Where does Bergonzi rank among the great tenors in history? Steane gives a clue in *The Grand Tradition*, where he writes—

> More than any other Italian tenor on record, he combines power, beauty, intensity and elegance. Not as powerful as Caruso, not as beautiful as Gigli, less intense than Martinelli, less elegant than Schipa, he nevertheless presents a balance of these attributes that puts him well into the illustrious company, and in case other names from the past are adduced, it might be added that his intonation is reliable, he sings accurately and does not exaggerate. Wild horses might drag him from the straight and narrow of his vocal line, but not even the temptation of three exclamation marks and the directions '*con un grido*' and '*con trasporto di giubilo*' (as in Act Three of *Ernani*) can make him leave the written note and shout something instead.

The first sentence of that paragraph suggests that Bergonzi ranks at the very top; yet this verdict is immediately qualified in the second sentence. A further qualification is suggested by this paragraph, again by Steane, this time from his essay on Bergonzi in *Singers of the Century* (1996)—

Certainly the farewell concert told of something richer and more positive than the merely 'impeccable'. During the course of the evening two memorable voices arose from the audience. One, a resonant bass-baritone in the stalls, cried out: '*Il più grande!*' Bergonzi smiled and made a gesture which meant 'Down a bit'. He was right but the acclaim of 'the greatest' made us think. Then the General Director came out to present a token of our esteem, our appreciation and.... 'And our love' urged a *comprimario* in the upper regions. Mr Isaacs added that he was about to say 'our best wishes'. But 'our love' won the day.

That, too, makes us think. Although great singers are often widely admired, not all of them are loved. And the more cultivated the singer, the less populist his art, and the less likely he will be to inspire love in a wide audience. But Bergonzi did, despite being the most cultivated and aristocratic Italian *lirico spinto* tenor in history. Partly because of his vocal longevity, he was arguably better loved than his great contemporaries, del Monaco, di Stefano, and Corelli. Perhaps the relative narrowness of Bergonzi's repertoire (no French or German or Slavonic roles, no *Lieder* or art song, no oratorio or concert repertoire except Verdi's Requiem, and nothing earlier than 1830 or later than 1925)[6] precludes the accolade of 'the greatest'. But surely a tenor who sang so many Verdian roles (sixteen in all) to such an invariably high standard, and with such patrician art, could justly claim to be the greatest *Verdian* tenor of all? Distinguished predecessors, such as Caruso, Martinelli, Pertile, Lauri-Volpi, Gigli and Björling, had sung a mere handful of Verdi roles in comparison. The only other tenor who has sung as many Verdi roles as Bergonzi is Plácido Domingo, who, not coincidentally, is also the only other tenor to have recorded such an extensive collection of Verdi tenor arias. But, when we come to make detailed comparisons between the two, we almost invariably find that, while Domingo's versions of the arias are intelligently interpreted and musically sung,[7] it is Bergonzi who really shapes the phrases *con amore* and with a truly exceptional degree of interpretative imagination. Domingo's versions are often as good as (almost) any that have been recorded, or even as anyone could imagine. But Bergonzi's are something better. Had they not been recorded, one could not have imagined them.

So, not (perhaps) the greatest tenor, but the greatest *Verdian* tenor – which is rather like being not the greatest actor, but the greatest *Shakespearian* actor. Most tenors – or actors – would be happy to settle for that.

Bergonzi's studio recordings include *Lucia di Lammermoor, Attila, Ernani, I Masnadieri, Macbeth, Luisa Miller, Rigoletto, La Traviata* (two), *Il Trovatore, Simone Boccanegra, Un Ballo in Maschera* (two), *La Forza del Destino, Don Carlo, Aida, La Gioconda, Edgar, La Bohème, Madama Butterfly* (two), *Tosca, Cavalleria Rusticana, Pagliacci,* and *Adriana Lecouvreur.* He also recorded, in 1975, a boxed set of Verdi tenor arias which, in spite of capturing his voice a little past its best, is rightly regarded as an outstanding achievement.

Notes

[1] I believe that, early in his career, he sang some performances of Massenet's *Werther* in Italian. But, so far as I have been able to discover, the only role he sang in French was Don Jose in *Carmen.* This is surprising, given that most Italian tenors, from Caruso onwards, had sung some popular French roles, such as Faust, Nadir, Don Jose, Des Grieux (Massenet), Le Cid, Samson, Roméo, Raoul, and Eléazar.

[2] There were other fine tenors too, whose repertoires overlapped with Bergonzi's, but whose vocal characteristics were sufficiently different to preclude direct competition – e.g. the lyric tenors Alfredo Kraus and

Nicolai Gedda, and the heroic tenors Jon Vickers and James McCracken.

[3]Bergonzi's farewell concert at Covent Garden, fondly remembered by John Steane, was given in 1992, when the tenor was sixty-eight.

[4]Presumably they came from other regions of Italy.

[5]This is noticeable in his masterly three-disc survey of Verdi's tenor arias for Philips, which was first issued in 1975. It does not, however, significantly detract from the pleasure of the performances, all of which are outstanding.

[6]Early in his career, he had sung roles in some modern operas, and in operas with which he was not thereafter associated, including Janáček's *Jenufa*, but he quickly decided that such a repertoire was not suitable to his voice. Between 1948 and 1951, he also sang nearly twenty roles as a baritone.

[7]And, of course, both voices are magnificent.

26 Nicolai Gedda: the tenor as intellectual

The announcement of the death of Nicolai Gedda (1925–2017) prompts a reassessment of his standing among the tenors of the modern era. It was his misfortune to be a countryman of Jussi Björling, and, throughout his career, he was compared to his famous predecessor, nearly always to his disadvantage.

In terms of sheer vocal glamour, Gedda was undoubtedly inferior to Björling. So was almost everyone else. In other respects, it is by no means so obvious that the comparison favours Björling. Gedda was probably the most versatile tenor of the recorded era. Fluent not only in his native languages (Swedish and Russian), but also in German, French, Italian, and English, able to get by in Czech, and thoroughly conversant with Latin, his repertoire ranges from Bach to Barber, from Mozart to Menotti, from Schubert to Shostakovich. And much of it has been committed to disc.

Gedda is something of a musical phenomenon. He has been described, not inaptly, by Nigel Douglas as 'the *beau idéal* of the lyric tenor'; yet his operatic repertoire also includes *spinto* roles like Don Jose in *Carmen*, Arrigo in *I Vespri Siciliani*, and Hermann in *The Queen of Spades*, as well as unequivocally heroic roles ranging from the stratospheric Arnold in *William Tell* and Huon in *Oberon* to the title role of Wagner's *Lohengrin*. With Fritz Wunderlich, he is the most gifted interpreter of Viennese operetta among tenors since the heyday of Richard Tauber and Julius Patzak. Not only is he fluent in several languages, but his diction in all of them is of unimpeachable clarity without ever being obtrusive, and his command of different musical styles is equally impressive. Whether he is singing Baroque oratorio or *verismo* opera, or anything in between, Gedda always sounds entirely at home in the musical and linguistic idiom.

The versatility comes at a price. Because he has recorded so prolifically and in such a varied repertoire, Gedda is not identified with any particular repertoire, as most other tenors are. Mario del Monaco, for example, was identified with the Italian heroic roles, especially those of the *verismo* period. Carlo Bergonzi was identified with the Verdi *spinto* tenor roles, and Juan Diego Flórez with the repertoire of the classic *tenore di grazia*. If there is one area of the tenor repertoire with which Gedda is especially identified by the *cognoscenti*, if not necessarily by the general listener, it is probably nineteenth-century French opera. He made his debut in Adam's *Le Postillon de Longjumeau*, being one of the few tenors who could both sing French like a native and command a secure and effortless top D natural. He has recorded *Faust* and *Carmen* twice each, also *Werther, Manon, Thaïs, Les Pêcheurs de Perles, Les Contes d'Hoffmann, Louise, Benvenuto Cellini, Béatrice et Bénédict, La Damnation de Faust*, and *Guillaume Tell*, in addition to highlights from *Roméo et Juliette* and *Lakmé*. Here he is supreme among tenors since the great Georges Thill. Not even Francophone tenors such as Alain Vanzo, Albert Lance, Henri Legay, Charles Burles, André Turp, Léopold Simoneau, David Poleri, or Roberto Alagna can equal him for his combination of beauty of tone, command of the French style, and perfect enunciation of the French language.

But mention of beauty of tone reminds us that Gedda's glory years, in this respect, were confined to the first phase of his career. He made his debut in 1952, and began his long career in the recording studios the same year, when he sang Dmitri in *Boris Godunov* in the first of Boris Christoff's two recordings of the opera. From then until the middle 1960s, a series of recordings shows him at his vocal best. The voice is a luscious, honeyed lyric tenor with an exquisite *mezza voce* and a beauty of timbre few could equal. But by the end of that decade, some of the bloom had gone; the 1969 recording in French of the rondo '*Mes amis, écoutez l'histoire*' from *Le Postillon de Longjumeau*, though it boasts an impressive top D, is not as exquisitely vocalized as the earlier version in Swedish. And, by 1973, the year when Gedda recorded *Guillaume Tell*, *I Puritani*, and *Così fan Tutte*, although the high notes still ring out freely, the middle of the voice sounds, in comparison with its younger self, tired, occluded, and (surprisingly) effortful.

There are several puzzling features of this relatively early vocal decline. First, why did it affect the middle of the voice but not the top? Second, why did it happen at all to a singer who was so technically accomplished? Was it, perhaps, a consequence of the exceptional breadth of his repertoire? Third, why was it not progressive? Once the symptoms of vocal deterioration have started to appear, they usually multiply, and progress apace. But, in Gedda's case, although the pristine beauty of the voice had largely disappeared by the mid-1970s, the voice itself remained intact for the rest of his very long career.

I would tentatively suggest that one reason for Gedda's vocal problems might have been that his voice naturally had an unusually high placement, but, while some of his roles allowed scope for that, others did not. They had an uncongenially low *tessitura*, which Gedda, thanks to his excellent technique, was able to manage, but which took a toll on his voice, especially in its middle register. Something similar befell Heddle Nash, who complained that his voice liked Donizetti, but that he was obliged to lower its natural *tessitura* in order to sing innumerable performances of Handel's *Messiah*.

Whatever the truth of that, the (partial) loss of tonal beauty was by no means fatal to Gedda, as it would have been to many lyric tenors. His interpretative intelligence, outstanding musicianship, linguistic talents, and stylistic versatility, all remained, and he continued to give excellent performances, even in roles where beauty and purity of tone would seem to be required. In fact, there was a gain in intensity. While some had found his earlier performances, though undeniably beautifully sung, a trifle cool – even uninvolved – dramatically, the same could not be said of the later recordings. In *Guillaume Tell*, for instance, if we compare his performance with Pavarotti's (who sings the Italian version), we find that, while the tonal splendour is all with the Italian, the dramatic involvement favours Gedda. In the aria '*Asile héréditaire* (*O muto asil del pianto*)', Gedda comprehensively out-sings his famous rival, phrasing imaginatively and musically, whereas Pavarotti's singing of the ascending phrases at the words *invan, egli non m'ode più* is clumsy and awkward. And in the ensuing *cabaletta*, '*Amis, amis secondez ma vengeance* (*Corriam, voliam! S'affretti lo scempio*)', it is Gedda who gives much the more exciting account, rounding it off with a sustained top C of clarion brilliance and power. In *I Puritani*, Gedda's lack of vocal bloom is offset by his distinguished phrasing, dynamic variety, and still potent upper register. Top Cs, D flats, D naturals, and even the top F in '*Credeasi misera*', are dispatched brilliantly and without effort, the last in a *voix mixte* without a suspicion of *falsetto*!

Such was Gedda's musicianship that he was able to learn the difficult role of Gerontius in a very short time in order to sing the part in an EMI recording of Elgar's oratorio conducted by Sir Adrian Boult. His English diction, which is *akzentfrei* as they say in Germany, is pellucid as ever. His interpretation has been criticized by some for being 'too operatic', but, bearing in mind Elgar's declared preference for the worldly John Coates over the more spiritual Gervase Elwes in the role, it may well be that Gedda's dramatic and somewhat extravert interpretation would have met with the composer's approval.

Gedda's Mozart singing was highly accomplished early in his career, and his best Mozart recordings date from the years between 1953 and *circa* 1964. Later, as in the *Così fan Tutte*, the vocal unevenness precluded an ideally pure line. Yet, the later performances offer, by way of compensation, a depth of characterization and a richness of interpretative detail missing from the vocally purer early recordings. At no stage of Gedda's career is anything he did lacking in distinction of any kind. There is always a good reason for listening to him.

How, finally, should Gedda be assessed? That is a difficult question to answer. In terms of sheer vocal glamour, of individuality of timbre, and immediate recognizability, he is arguably inferior to several of his great contemporaries – to Björling certainly, and perhaps also to Tucker, del Monaco, di Stefano, Corelli, Bergonzi, Wunderlich, Pavarotti, Domingo, and Carreras, for example. Yet his voice, in its early years, was as beautiful as (almost) any of theirs, and more beautiful than those of Peter Pears, Richard Lewis, Charles Craig, Alfredo Kraus, Alexander Young, Jon Vickers or James McCracken. His artistry was a match for anyone's – more than a match for most. And in terms of versatility and breadth of repertoire, he stands unchallenged, even by Pears.[1] He deserves, it seems to me, a high place among the tenors of the last century.

Gedda is one of the most prolific of all recording artists. His complete opera / operetta / oratorio recordings include: *Requiem (Verdi)*, *Rigoletto*, *La Traviata*, *La Bohème*, *Madama Butterfly*, *Die Entführung aus dem Serail* (two), *Idomeneo*, *Così fan Tutte*, *Don Giovanni* (two), *Die Zauberflöte*, *Der Barbier von Bagdad*, *Martha*, *Der Freischütz*, *Euryanthe*, *Der Zigeunerbaron*, *Die Fledermaus*, *Die Lustige Witwe*, *Das Land des Lächelns*, *Ein Nacht in Venedig*, *Der*

Rosenkavalier, Il Turco in Italia, I Puritani, I Capuleti ed i Montecchi, Elisir d'Amore, Werther, Manon, Faust (two), *Carmen* (two), *Les Pêcheurs de Perles, Vanessa, Louise, Les Contes d'Hoffmann, Boris Godunov* (two), *Eugene Onegin, The Dream of Gerontius, St Matthew Passion, Missa Solemnis, Elijah, La Grande Messe des Morts, Benvenuto Cellini, Béatrice et Bénédict, La Damnation de Faust, Guillaume Tell, Il Barbiere di Siviglia, Palestrina, Alceste, Orphée et Euridice, Die Csárdásfürstin, Das Wunder der Heliane* (Korngold), *Stabat Mater and Petite Messe Solennelle* (Rossini), *Le Devin du Village* (Rousseau), *Cendrillon, Der Bettelstudent, Lady Macbeth of Mtsensk, Messiah, Die Schöne Helena* (*La Belle Hélène*), *Fra Diavolo, Candide, Die Opernprobe* (Lortzing).

Notes

[1]This may seem an extraordinary statement to anyone who judges Pears solely on his operatic repertoire. But, first, even that repertoire is broader than is generally thought, extending from Purcell and Handel to Stravinsky, Britten and Walton, and including roles in operas by Mozart, Rossini, Verdi, Puccini, Offenbach and Smetana. And, second, his concert repertoire, which embraced folksong, art song and large-scale choral works, was enormous and spanned four centuries.

27 Jon Vickers:
the tenor as prophet

Of all the great tenors, the Canadian Jon Vickers (1926–2015) is probably the most idiosyncratic. He didn't even look like a tenor. Of average height, square-jawed, broad-shouldered, and rugged-looking, with the physique of a lumberjack or a rugby prop forward, Vickers was a physically imposing (though hardly a romantic) figure on stage. The voice, too, was not, perhaps, conventionally beautiful in timbre. But it was virile, heroic, and immensely powerful. In some respects, it was the ideal voice for the kind of parts he sang: the dramatic tenor roles of the French and German repertoire, plus a few Italian roles. But even here, Vickers defied expectations. Often thought of as a *Heldentenor*, he sang Erik, Tristan, Siegmund and Parsifal, but no other Wagnerian roles, and, with the exception of Herod in *Salome*, no Richard Strauss tenor roles either. Famously, he withdrew from a projected production of *Tannhäuser* at Covent Garden, claiming that he could find 'no point of personal contact' with the role and that it offended his religious principles. Others speculated that he simply found the role beyond him vocally.[1] In the Verdian repertoire, he sang Radames, Otello, Alvaro, and (early in his career) Gustavo and Don Carlo, but he never sang Manrico, Ernani, or Stiffelio. His only *verismo* roles were Andrea Chenier and Canio; he never sang Turiddu in *Cavalleria Rusticana* or any of the Puccini tenor roles, with the exception of Rinuccio in *Gianni Schicchi*. Yet it would be wrong to imply that the only surprising feature of his repertoire was the lacunae. There were also surprising inclusions: Laca in Janáček's

Jenufa, Vašek in Smetana's *The Bartered Bride*, Giasone in *Medea*, Pollione in *Norma*, Ratan-Sen in Roussel's *Padmavati*, Sergei in *Lady Macbeth of the Mtsensk District*, the title roles in Handel's *Samson*, Berlioz's *Benvenuto Cellini* and Britten's *Peter Grimes*, Elgar's *Gerontius*, Handel's *Messiah*, Schubert's *Winterreise* and Mahler's *Das Lied von der Erde* all formed part of his repertoire.

Although some of his roles had an awkward *tessitura* for a normal tenor, none lay abnormally high in the voice, and the only roles he sang that required a high C were Énée in Berlioz's *Les Troyens* and the title role in *Otello*. Higher-lying roles like Calaf in *Turandot* or Raoul in *Les Huguenots* were off limits as far as Vickers was concerned, and it may have been the requirement for awkwardly placed, difficult high C's that deterred him from singing the otherwise low-lying roles of Manrico in *Il Trovatore* and the *Götterdämmerung* Siegfried.

The adjective that is most commonly used by critics to describe Vickers' stage portrayals is 'intense'. His acting, like his singing, was unconventional, but there was no denying his involvement in the roles he sang. Like a Biblical prophet of old, he exuded authority, on record no less than on stage. The bitter anguish of Florestan or Otello, the burning ardour of Tristan, Siegmund's inner pain and sorrow, the mythic grandeur of Énée, the tormented jealousy of Canio or Don José, the warrior-like nobility of Radames, Samson's penitential grief, the loneliness and isolation of Peter Grimes, were all conveyed both through stagecraft and by purely vocal means.

Vickers's recorded repertoire includes a fair amount of duplication: he recorded Florestan, Otello, and Siegmund twice each, and comparing the earlier recordings with the later is instructive. In all three cases, he is in better voice in the earlier recordings; and, while there is evidence that he continued to think about his roles and develop his interpretations, the evidence also suggests that the results were sometimes not to deepen or strengthen already mightily intense interpretations, but to make them more mannered. For example, in his first Otello, the death scene '*Niun mi tema*' is noble and restrained, and the threefold cry of *morta* is memorable. But in the second version, much of the scene is sung in a head voice that comes perilously close to crooning, and the noble pathos of the first version is lost. The second Otello and Florestan also show significant vocal deterioration, for it seems that in 1973–74 Vickers must have been passing through some sort of vocal crisis. Nevertheless, because Vickers never relied for his effects exclusively, or even primarily, on beauty of tone, the later recordings also have much to offer, even to collectors who already own his first versions of the roles in question.

The actual sound of Vickers' voice has always been controversial. According to Enrico Stinchelli, writing in *Stars of the Opera*,

> With the passing of years, his voice has been marred by a certain hard, woody sound, a fault which an excellent technique has not been able to remedy, and which has not been helped by his timbre, which has always been poor.

'Poor' puts the matter rather strongly, so one returns to the recordings. Now, there is an inescapably subjective element in such judgments, but I have to say that, personally, I do not find Vickers' timbre poor. It is unusual and distinctive. It is utterly unlike the timbre of the great Mediterranean tenors – and that is probably what Stinchelli had in mind. But it is admirably suited to the roles he sings. And, as Steane perceptively observes in *The Grand Tradition*, he often sings most beautifully. His first recorded Otello, for example, is one of the best *sung* on disc, as well as the most dramatically convincing. And, in both that recording and his first Florestan (for Klemperer on HMV), his voice sounds beautiful and noble in timbre – to my ears, at any rate.

It is well-known that Vickers' religious convictions (he was a devout Evangelical Christian) determined his attitude to, and interpretation of, the roles he sang. He studied new roles by thoroughly immersing himself in them dramatically, musically, philosophically and psychologically. Only when he was quite satisfied that he had penetrated to the heart of the character and that nothing in the role offended against his religious sensibilities would he consent to sing it. Of all the great singers, perhaps the only others to share this religious dimension to the same extent were two basses: Jerome Hines and Martti Talvela. Of course, other singers have had equally strong religious beliefs (John McCormack, Jan Peerce, Leonard Warren, and Richard Tucker come to mind) but none of them made his religious convictions normative for his choice of the roles he sang or his interpretations of those roles.

Vickers was not without competition in his chosen repertoire. His contemporaries included Mario del Monaco, Franco Corelli, Richard Tucker, Richard Cassilly, Charles Craig, James King, René Kollo, and James McCracken, all of whom shared multiple roles with him, in the opera house and on record. At the Metropolitan Opera, his rivalry with McCracken in the role of Otello was especially keen. But, all things considered, Vickers is probably the greatest Siegmund and Tristan since the heyday of Lauritz Melchior, and the greatest Otello since Martinelli. I am not overlooking the (not inconsiderable) claims of del Monaco, McCracken and Domingo, but the first is too brutal, the second too exaggerated, and the third lacks the *squillo* ideally required for the role.

Vickers' interpretations were sometimes controversial. Benjamin Britten is known to have disliked his Peter Grimes – but then Britten was, at best, cool towards other tenors who performed the roles he had conceived for Peter Pears. For many opera lovers, Vickers' Grimes, massive, brooding, and exuding a sense of physical danger, incarnated the rough fisherman more credibly than Pears' more cerebral conception. In some of his other roles, Vickers came up against competition from tenors with more conventionally beautiful and sensuous voices. The results were sometimes surprising. As Don José, Otello, Radames, Samson, Florestan, Siegmund and Tristan, he can be compared on disc with Plácido Domingo. And, yes, Domingo's voice has a Mediterranean warmth and richness which Vickers cannot match. Yet, if we call to mind certain key moments from these roles and play them again in our mind's ear, so to speak, it is often Vickers' voice that we hear. This is especially the case where the profoundest and most painful emotions are conveyed – the desolating sense of loss in Samson's '*Ils m'ont ravi la lumière du ciel*', the pained resignation of Florestan's '*Doch gerecht ist Gottes Wille*', or the crushing despair of Otello's '*Dio, mi potevi scagliar tutti mali*', for example. One of the tests of singerly greatness is the ability to express such feelings adequately and to convey them to the listener. Vickers triumphantly meets that criterion – more than almost any other tenor on record.

Vickers' complete recordings of opera and oratorio include: *Messiah*, Verdi's Requiem, *Aida*, *Otello* (two), *Die Walküre* (two), *Tristan und Isolde*, *Parsifal*, *Fidelio* (two), *Carmen*, *Samson et Dalila*, *Les Troyens*, *Peter Grimes*.

Notes

[1]Vickers' fair-minded and balanced biographer, Jeannie Williams, after detailing the evidence and considering what various parties have said about it, concludes that the most probable explanation is that Vickers had moral objections to the opera which he found insuperable, but that he also may have felt that the role would be unsuitable for him vocally at that stage of his career owing to its high *tessitura*. I have some doubts about the second part of this. Vickers' repertoire was more varied than is generally realized, and it included some roles parts of

which lay high in the voice – Énée and Benvenuto Cellini, for example. And he was renowned for finding highly personal ways of singing roles which, at first sight, appeared unsuited to his voice – such as Peter Grimes. If the high *tessitura* of Tannhäuser had been a problem, that would not have prevented Vickers from recording the role. In the course of his career, he recorded for Decca, DG, HMV, Phillips, and RCA, and surely some of those companies would have been happy to record Vickers in *Tannhäuser* had he expressed a wish to record it. Evidently, he did not. The only possible explanation for this is that Vickers did indeed have moral objections to the part, and had no wish to sing it, in the theatre or on record.

28 Luciano Pavarotti: king of the high C's

When most people think of Luciano Pavarotti (1935–2007), their memory probably summons up an image of an enormous figure in evening dress, smiling broadly and waving the trademark white handkerchief, after crowning yet another performance of '*Nessun dorma*' with a dazzling top B.

That image was burned into the public consciousness by a series of 'concerts in the park' which Pavarotti gave in the later stages of his career, and by his appearances alongside Plácido Domingo and José Carreras at the 'Three Tenors' concerts, given in association with successive football World Cup tournaments. Those events cemented the Pavarotti legend in place. But, good clean fun as they were, they are not what makes him of lasting importance. To discover that, we have to go back in time, to the early 1960s.

In 1963, when Giuseppe di Stefano withdrew from a production of *La Bohème* at Covent Garden, his place was taken by Pavarotti, then a young, up-and-coming but comparatively little-known tenor. His early career was marked by steady progress rather than sudden and dramatic success. At that stage of his career, he had not developed either the mannerisms with which he would later be associated, or the enormous bulk that he later assumed. The young Pavarotti, though no sylph, was tall, broad-shouldered and strongly built.

One of those attributes – his height – attracted the attention of the soprano Joan Sutherland and her husband Richard Bonynge. Sutherland, who herself stood six feet two inches in her stockinged feet, was, by her own admission, 'tired of walking around bent at the knees' so that she did not tower over much shorter tenors.[1] Pavarotti was close to her own height. Moreover, their voices were well matched. While many of the great Australian diva's tenor partners, in her preferred *bel canto* repertoire, had smallish voices, Pavarotti's voice was both large and penetrative. His naturally high placement and extensive range, which reached to a top D in full voice,[2] meant that he was particularly well suited to the high-lying *bel canto* tenor roles in the operas of Bellini and Donizetti: repertoire in which Sutherland also excelled. The numerous recordings they made together for Decca established them as one of the greatest and most prolific tenor-soprano partnerships of the recorded era. They recorded *Lucia di Lammermoor*, *La Fille du Régiment*, *L'Elisir d'Amore*, *Maria Stuarda*, *Beatrice di Tenda*, *La Sonnambula*, *Norma*, *I Puritani*, *Ernani*, *Rigoletto*, *La Traviata*, *Il Trovatore*, and *Turandot*. Pavarotti also formed a regular partnership with his childhood friend, Mirella Freni, with whom he recorded *L'Amico Fritz* (his only opera recording for EMI), *La Bohème*, *Madama Butterfly*, *Tosca*, *Manon Lescaut*, *Guglielmo Tell*, *Mefistofele*, and *Pagliacci*. It could be said that these two major partnerships largely defined the trajectory of Pavarotti's career as a recording artist. With Sutherland, he focused predominantly on the *bel canto* repertoire; with Freni, mainly on *verismo*. Pavarotti also recorded several of the Verdi operas, though fewer than either Domingo or Bergonzi. In addition to the four already named that he recorded with Sutherland, he sang in studio recordings of *Macbeth*, *Luisa Miller*, *Un Ballo in Maschera*, and *Aida*, and in live recordings of *Don Carlo* and *Otello*.

In Verdi, Pavarotti, though impressive, is rarely a first recommendation. Less imaginative and stylish than Bergonzi, less elegant than Björling, less powerful or viscerally exciting than del Monaco or Corelli, less tonally beautiful than the young Carreras, less nobly heroic than Domingo, he is defeated by the sheer volume and quality of the competition. There is one Verdi role in which he is arguably to be preferred to all his competitors, and that is the Duke in *Rigoletto*. Here, voice and personality seem ideally suited to the character and he gives a bravura performance, replete with the usual brilliant high notes (a top D flat at the end of the Act One duet with Gilda and a sustained top D natural at the end of his Act Two aria, '*Possente amor mi chiama*'). The high *tessitura* of the part poses no difficulties for him, and he sails triumphantly through '*Parmi veder le lagrime*', one of the most difficult tenor arias in all Verdi, lying, as it does, in the *passaggio* for phrase after phrase. The only possible criticism is that, in the Act Two *cabaletta*, '*Possente amor*', which is taken at a very fast tempo, the *gruppetti* are slurred and we do not hear the individual notes distinctly, as we do in the performances by more agile, lighter-voiced tenors, such as Gedda, Kraus and Flórez.

Critical opinion was divided about Pavarotti's performances of the *bel canto* repertoire. Rodney Milnes, writing in *Opera* magazine, excoriated the 1971 recording of *Lucia di Lammermoor* when it first appeared. And John Steane, normally an admirer of Pavarotti, expressed strong reservations about his first version of '*A te o cara*' from *I Puritani*, contrasting it unfavourably with the celebrated recording by Alessandro Bonci. Other critics have disagreed, responding positively to the effulgent tone, scintillating top notes, and the absence of the bad vocal manners of his predecessors (e.g. di Stefano's open vowels and habit of attacking notes from below, Corelli's scooping, or Poggi's veristic vocalism).

Whether the view taken is positive or negative seems to depend on the standard of comparison. For Milnes and Steane, the standard was set by the tenors schooled in the *bel canto* tradition – De Lucia, Bonci, McCormack. That tradition emphasized grace and accuracy in the execution of ornamentation of the vocal line. In those respects, Pavarotti is demonstrably inferior to several of his great predecessors. But, for other critics, the applicable standard has changed irrevocably as a result of the revolution in singing effected in the twentieth century by artists like Caruso, Chaliapin, and, later, Christoff, Callas, Gobbi, and Fischer-Dieskau. For modern singers, words are as important as the music, and Pavarotti's diction, vivid and crystal-clear, is a vital element in his distinction as a singer. And, in terms of sheer vocal splendour, he leaves De Lucia and Bonci far behind.

When we turn to the *verismo* repertoire, the picture is rather different. Here the word-based aesthetic is more obviously appropriate, and Pavarotti's excellent diction is more advantageous. But it must be admitted that, in comparison with the *bel canto* repertoire, these roles play less to the strengths of his voice. They have a lower *tessitura* and make fewer demands on the upper register, for example – one of the reasons *verismo* was found so congenial by Mario del Monaco, who could sing high but, unlike Pavarotti, could not stay high. They also place a premium less on finesse, artistry, and vocal beauty (Pavarotti's strengths in this repertoire) than on brute force and a full-throated wallop (which is more the forte – no pun intended – of del Monaco and Corelli).

In the final analysis, whether one prefers the brilliant vocalism of Pavarotti, the exceptional stylishness of Bergonzi, or the sheer thrills of del Monaco and Corelli in *verismo*, is a matter of personal taste. But for many listeners, considerations of style and idiom are secondary. What is of primary importance is the voice itself. Like all truly great tenors, Pavarotti is immediately recognizable. Even people unused to operatic voices have little difficulty in distinguishing him from other tenors. The tone, bright and tense (if somewhat monochrome), with its forward production and distinctively Italian vibrancy, is attractive, but detailed comparisons show that, judged by the very highest standards, it lacks something.

Jon Elsby

It does not quite have the luscious beauty of Gigli's voice, for instance, or the gleaming splendour of Björling's. Pavarotti, like del Monaco, used the Melocchi method (albeit with far less breath than his celebrated predecessor) and the result is that the tone is narrow and somewhat tightly produced. He rarely produces an authentic *mezza voce* (though a notable, and ravishing, exception occurs at the start of the short solo '*Era d'amor l'imagine*' from *Maria Stuarda*). He is not able to float soft high notes in the head voice as effortlessly as Gigli, Björling, Gedda, Alagna, or Kaufmann, to cite a few examples, because his less flexible technique does not allow it. The most apt comparison that Pavarotti's voice suggests is Martinelli. The vocal method is similar. The only difference is that Martinelli used more breath and assumed the more heroic roles in the repertoire prematurely,[3] whereas Pavarotti wisely eschewed them until he felt ready to tackle them.

The best of Pavarotti is probably to be found in his interpretations of the tenor roles of Donizetti and Bellini. The high *tessitura* of these parts suits his voice, and he brings to them not only the brilliant top notes they demand, but also a vocal weight which they ideally need, but don't often get. Roles such as Arturo in *I Puritani* and Leicester in *Maria Stuarda* are often sung by *tenori di grazia*, but they benefit from the extra power that Pavarotti can offer. The singing may not be in the *bel canto* tradition, but it represents the best of the modern school in its clean line, clear diction, impeccable intonation, alert rhythmic sense, and inherent musicality. And, in addition to these virtues, there is a glorious voice. That is much to be thankful for.

Pavarotti's complete opera and oratorio recordings are: *Guglielmo Tell, Maria Stuarda, Lucia di Lammermoor, La Favorita, La Fille du Régiment, Elisir d'Amore, Norma, I Puritani, Beatrice di Tenda, La Sonnambula, Ernani, Macbeth, Rigoletto* (two), *Il Trovatore, La Traviata, Luisa Miller, Un Ballo in Maschera, Don*

Heroes and Lovers

Carlo, Aida, Otello, L'Amico Fritz, Cavalleria Rusticana, Pagliacci, Manon Lescaut, La Bohème, Madama Butterfly, Tosca, Turandot, Andrea Chenier, Mefistofele, La Gioconda, Idomeneo, Der Rosenkavalier, Verdi's Requiem, La Grande Messe des Morts (Berlioz), and the Stabat Mater and La Petite Messe Solennelle (Rossini).

Notes

[1] Of her other tenor partners, only Franco Corelli, Nicolai Gedda, Franco Bonisolli, and Plácido Domingo equalled or exceeded her in height. But Corelli retired when Sutherland was still in her prime, Gedda was under contract to EMI while Sutherland was contracted to Decca, Bonisolli was too unreliable, and Domingo, being unable to manage the high *tessitura* of the *bel canto* roles, did not sing the same repertoire. Only Pavarotti was able to partner her satisfactorily on stage *and* on disc.

[2] On disc, he also sings two top E flats in a *voix mixte* (in the aria 'Si lo sento Iddio mi chiama' from Verdi's I Due Foscari) and a top F in *falsetto* (in the ensemble 'Credeasi misera' from Bellini's I Puritani).

[3] To be fair, this was forced on Martinelli. After Caruso's death in 1921, his lyric roles went to Gigli at the Metropolitan Opera, while Martinelli, still only thirty-six years old, was obliged to take on the heroic roles before he was ready for them. Thanks to his excellent technique, his voice was not ruined. But it was somewhat impaired, in certain respects.

29 Plácido Domingo:
the tenor as polymath

A distant memory: many years ago – it was, I think, in 1968 – I was sitting in a car parked outside a shopping mall in Fairfax, Virginia. It was a Saturday, and the matinee broadcast from the Metropolitan Opera was about to start. The opera was *Tosca* and the mouth-watering cast was headed by Birgit Nilsson and Franco Corelli, with William Dooley as Scarpia. Nilsson and Corelli were one of the most combustible partnerships in the history of the Met, and I had been looking forward to the performance all week. But then came the announcement I had been dreading. Milton Cross, the veteran broadcaster who presented the Texaco-sponsored broadcasts from the Met in those days, said that Corelli was 'indisposed' (a fairly common occurrence where that most temperamental of tenors was concerned). His place would be taken by a young Mexican (*sic*) tenor making his broadcast debut. His name was Plácido Domingo (born 1941).

To say I was disappointed would be an understatement. But the disappointment was short-lived. It lasted until the opening bars of '*Recondita armonia*'. By the end of the aria, I knew that I had just heard something exceptional – a voice of thrilling quality with a rich, dark timbre, allied to ample power. Of course, I didn't realize back then what an extraordinary career Domingo would go on to have, but I knew he was not destined for a career as an understudy, and the enthusiastic and prolonged applause at the end of the performance confirmed it.

Two years later, in 1970, the first of an unprecedented series of complete opera recordings appeared – a *Trovatore* in which Domingo was joined by Leontyne Price, singing the second of her three recorded Leonoras, Fiorenza Cossotto, singing her second recorded Azucena, and Sherrill Milnes as di Luna, under the baton of Zubin Mehta. The reviews were polite, but not effusive – the *Gramophone*'s critic thought the new version inferior to the 1952 RCA set with Björling and Milanov and the 1957 HMV set with di Stefano and Callas (the latter conducted by Herbert von Karajan): judgments which few would endorse today.

The RCA *Trovatore* was followed by a steady stream of operatic recordings – a stream which, at times, became almost torrential. A number of Verdi tenor roles equalled only by Carlo Bergonzi, a number of *verismo* roles equalled only by Mario del Monaco, more French roles than any other tenor on record except Nicolai Gedda, much of the German repertoire including several of the major Wagner roles and a couple by Richard Strauss, some Slavonic roles such as Hermann in Tchaikovsky's *Queen of Spades*, several *zarzuela* recordings, and a prodigious number of recital discs embracing repertoire ranging from opera to popular songs and ballads – Domingo's recorded repertoire is probably unexampled in its combination of diversity, quality and quantity. He is generally thought of as a 'B flat tenor' – i.e. one who was not comfortable with the higher notes; yet his recorded repertoire includes quite a few top C's (e.g. in *Bohème*, *Manon Lescaut*, *Turandot*, and *Faust*, as well as in his three recordings each of *Trovatore* and *Otello*), a top D flat (in *Giovanna d'Arco*) and a top D (in *I Vespri Siciliani*). Among his early operatic recordings was a complete version of Weber's *Oberon* in which Domingo tackled the hair-raisingly difficult role of Huon, which is both high-lying and fearsomely florid. It is hard to imagine it better sung.

It is said that familiarity breeds contempt, which may be a slight overstatement; but it certainly breeds indifference and boredom.

Domingo came to be taken for granted. Like the poor, he was always with us. Minor cavils crept into the critical encomiums. His performances sounded much alike; characters were insufficiently differentiated; the interpretations were somewhat generalized; he was not equally well suited vocally to all the roles he sang; his pronunciation of French and German was imperfect – and so on. Some critics even expressed a nostalgia for the good old days of Mario del Monaco and Franco Corelli, when voices were *really* heroic! In light of what they had said about del Monaco and Corelli when both were still active, one can only wonder at their nerve. But then it has been a perennial pastime of critics to use the great of the past as sticks with which to beat the great of their own day. It sometimes seems that they are constitutionally incapable of appreciating anything except in retrospect.

It would be idle to pretend that all of Domingo's recordings are automatic first choices. For one thing, in many of his roles, the competition is stiff. For another, the choice of a complete operatic recording does not depend on the performance of one singer, but on the performance as a whole. However, Domingo's work never falls below a certain naturally high level of distinction. His musicianship is outstanding, and has been much commented on. But the detailed consideration given to Domingo's musicality, intelligence, versatility, and unflagging industry, has to some extent obscured the heart of the matter: namely, his voice and his interpretative artistry as a singer.

First, the voice: in its early years, it was a rich, lustrous *lirico spinto* tenor with a predominantly dark, chocolatey, almost baritonal colour and plenty of 'blade'. Domingo's diction was a model of clarity, although some of the vowel sounds, especially the Italian e's, could be somewhat extreme (compare, for example, Domingo's delivery of the phrase *la morte è men crudel del tuo disprezzo* from Arrigo's aria '*Giorno di pianto*' in *I Vespri Siciliani* with the renditions of the same passage by Richard Tucker or Carlo Bergonzi). The technique was unimpeachable, the registers perfectly blended up to a fine top C. That top C was not, however, effortless or totally reliable. Early in his career especially, it was apt to crack. We know, from Sherrill Milnes' account, how many attempts it took for Domingo to land a perfect top C in that 1970 *Trovatore*. And Domingo himself has admitted that, even in his prime as a tenor, he found the note problematic, and would sing it in public only when the musical context made it relatively easy. Later in his career, the top notes became more secure, and, after 1975, when he added the title role of *Otello* to his repertoire, the voice itself began subtly to change. Some of the early velvet disappeared to reveal the gleaming metal underneath. In this phase of his career, Domingo was ideally suited to the Verdian *spinto* repertoire and to some of the more heroic French roles, notably Samson and Don Jose. Such was his technical skill, however, that, even in these years, he was able successfully to lighten his voice so as to take on lyric roles like Nemorino in *Elisir d'Amore*, in which the fluency of his *fioriture* eclipses that of lighter-voiced tenors like Giuseppe di Stefano and Luigi Alva. He even released, as late as 1991, a disc of Mozart arias; and, while it cannot be claimed that his is the ideal voice for this repertoire, the skill involved in the execution of (for example) the runs in '*Il mio tesoro*', and his idiomatic command of Mozartean style throughout, are undeniable and impressive. So is the way he scales down his voice for a delicious performance of Basilio's aria from *Le Nozze di Figaro* – a triumph of comic characterization.

As the years went on, the repertoire expanded. Domingo began to assume some of the heavier German roles: Lohengrin, Walther von Stolzing, Tannhäuser, Florestan, Parsifal and Siegmund. His accounts of these roles are among the most musical on record. No other tenor – not even Ben Heppner or Johan Botha – has *sung*

Walther as beautifully as Domingo does, and his Lohengrin and Tannhäuser are truly knightly creations. The approach to high notes in the Wagnerian *Fach* is quite different from that in Italian and French opera. So much of them lies in the upper middle part of the voice that top A's feel like top C's. Typically, Italianate tenors who sing Wagner lose their top notes (the top B and C) and, in consequence, are obliged, at some point, to give up most, if not all, of their Italian and French roles. Whether this happened to Domingo, or the sacrifice of those roles was planned, either in order to take account of vocal and physiological changes, or because he felt he was too old to act them convincingly, is hard to say. In any case, Domingo first gradually gave up most of his Italian and French repertoire, confining himself to a few German and other lower-lying roles, and then reverted to baritone roles. It is a wonder that, in spite of his punishing workload and strenuous repertoire, so much of the voice has survived unimpaired into his seventies. Yet he is far from ideal as a Verdi baritone. It is true that he has the range, and the voice has remained rock-steady: a testimony to his iron constitution as well as to the soundness of his technique. But it does not have the dark, almost basso-like colour, tonal resonance, or the penetrating timbre of the genuine Verdi baritone. In the days of Warren, Merrill, MacNeil, Gobbi, Sereni, Lisitsian, Bastianini, Panerai, and Taddei, he would probably not have been able to undertake the baritone repertoire, at least not in houses as prestigious as the Met and Covent Garden. But times have changed. Authentic Verdi baritones are rare[1] today, and Domingo has stepped into the breach.

Interpretatively, Domingo has developed since his early days. He has recorded many of his roles more than once, and the later recordings usually show that he has thought further about them, musically and textually, and penetrated more deeply into them. After seeing Domingo as Otello at Covent Garden, Laurence

Olivier is said to have remarked, 'My God, he acts the role as well as I do – and he *sings* as well!' That said, it must be admitted that, vocally, Domingo's interpretations rarely have the intensity of a Vickers or a Martinelli, or the utterly beguiling quality of, say, a Gigli or a Bergonzi. His singing is invariably sensitive, intelligent, musical, and thoughtful – but, interpretatively, it often seems to lack some final quality of spontaneity, imagination, or insight. In 'live' performances on DVD, this lack is compensated for by the excellence of his stagecraft. But, in aural recordings, a certain sameness does obtrude and it provokes in listeners a reaction, if not of boredom, then of careless inattention. 'Oh, it's Domingo,' they say, and somehow cease to listen as alertly as they would if the tenor were someone else – someone less familiar.

The reasons for this lack of interpretative variety when compared with the very best of his competitors, are partly technical and partly stylistic. Technically, as Stephen Hastings has observed, Domingo 'never really developed his head voice', which limits his dynamic range, especially in high-lying phrases. He deserves credit for singing '*Je crois entendre encore*' from Bizet's *Les Pêcheurs de Perles* in the original key, despite its awkwardly high *tessitura*, but his performance sounds laboured – it has nothing like the effortlessness, the tonal variety, or the sheer heady beauty of sound we find in the accounts by Nicolai Gedda and Roberto Alagna. Stylistically, to quote Hastings again, Domingo's singing sometimes seems 'clean to the point of blandness, a style much favoured in those years'. The late John Steane probably had something similar in mind when he noted, in *The Grand Tradition*, a certain deficit in intensity in Domingo's portrayals as compared with Martinelli's.

However, it would be ungrateful to end on a negative note. Such is the diversity, magnitude, and scope of Domingo's achievement that it is probably too soon to assess it. A balanced appraisal will have to await a certain perspective, which only comes with the passage of time. The patina of over-familiarity must be given time to wear off. A discography so enormous, so varied, compiled over a career so long, presents problems of critical judgment to those who have, as it were, lived with and through it. What can be asserted with confidence is this: no tenor in recorded history has matched Domingo's versatility in opera; and no other tenor (with the exception of the great Jewish cantor, Gershon Sirota) has come so close to equalling Caruso in terms of vocal timbre and quality as Domingo in his prime.

If that is to stand as the last word on Domingo's career, few tenors have had a better one.

Domingo's discography as a tenor includes: *Lucia di Lammermoor, Elisir d'Amore, Norma, Il Giuramento, I Lombardi alla Prima Crocciata, Ernani, Nabucco, Macbeth*, and the Requiem (Verdi), *Giovanna d'Arco, Simone Boccanegra, Un Ballo in Maschera* (three), *Don Carlo* (three), *La Forza del Destino* (two), *Aida* (four), *Otello* (three), *Rigoletto, La Traviata, Il Trovatore* (three), *I Vespri Siciliani, Luisa Miller* (two), *Le Villi, Edgar, La Fanciulla del West* (two), *La Bohème, Madama Butterfly, Tosca* (two), *Turandot, Il Tabarro, Gianni Schicchi, Mefistofele* (two), *Cavalleria Rusticana* (two), *Iris, Pagliacci* (two), *I Medici, Adriana Lecouvreur, La Gioconda, Andrea Chenier, Fedora, L'Amore dei Tre Re, Il Guarany, Faust, Roméo et Juliette, Carmen* (three), *Le Cid, Hérodiade, Werther, La Navarraise, Louise, Samson et Dalila* (two), *L'Africaine, Les Contes d'Hoffmann* (two), *La Damnation de Faust, Béatrice et Bénédict, Fidelio, Der Fliegende Holländer, Tannhäuser, Lohengrin, Die Meistersinger, Die Walküre, Tristan und Isolde, Parsifal, Oberon, Der Rosenkavalier, Die Frau ohne Schatten, Idomeneo, Merlin, Pepita Jiménez* (Albéniz), *Luisa Fernanda* (Federico Moreno Torroba), *La Verbena de la Paloma, La Dolores* (Tomás Bretón), *La Tabernera del Puerto* (Pablo Sorozábal), *Doña*

Francisquita (Amadeo Vives), *El Gato Montes* (Manuel Penella), *Christ on the Mount of Olives, La Grande Messe des Morts, Das Lied von der Erde.*

Notes

[1]The current dearth of Verdian baritones makes it surprising that the possessor of one of the most stupendous voices of recent years – the Mongolian baritone, Amartüvshin Enkhbat – was denied the first prize in the 2015 Cardiff Singer of the World competition.

30 José Carreras:
passion and pride

When José Carreras (born 1946) first appeared on the scene – it was, I think, in the mid-1970s – the effect was electrifying. Here was a potent rival to Pavarotti and Domingo, and he seemed to have a more beautiful voice than either. It was, according to Pavarotti, 'a goosebump voice', and one knows what he meant. Moreover, the new Spanish tenor, though not tall, was slim, handsome, a good actor, and had a charismatic stage presence.

The voice, though darker in colour, had a clarity and a velvety sheen that recalled the young di Stefano, as did the ardent manner and expressive way with the words. But he had a more finished technique than di Stefano (listen to the accomplished way Carreras sings the florid passages in Rossini's *Otello* or the same composer's *Elisabetta Regina d'Inghilterra*, and compare di Stefano's tentative negotiation of the runs in Almaviva's serenade in a live recording of *Il Barbiere di Siviglia*) and a cleaner style (he does not attack notes from below, as di Stefano did persistently).

Carreras, in the short years of his prime, made many recordings of superlative quality which will assure him of an enduring place among the greatest lyric tenors on disc. Unfortunately, as with di Stefano, vocal decline set in early. And he did his reputation no service by continuing to record prolifically when his voice was well past its best.

What were the reasons for Carreras's early decline? Unlike his idol di Stefano, he does not suffer from obvious technical imperfections. Some have blamed the onset of the leukaemia which so nearly killed him, but that is implausible – a marked vocal deterioration had already occurred before leukaemia was diagnosed. I suspect the real reason is that Carreras's voice was a pure lyric tenor, lacking the *spinto* capacity of Domingo (whose voice was larger and had metal underneath the velvet) or Pavarotti (whose voice was brighter and more penetrative). Nevertheless, he wanted to compete with them, and unwisely assumed too soon heavy roles to which he was vocally ill suited – Don Carlo, Radames, Manrico, Samson, Canio, Calaf, and the like. If he had waited a few years, his voice might have developed into a *spinto tenore* that could have tackled those roles safely. But he didn't. The result was that, in order to cope with sometimes declamatory vocal lines and dense orchestration, he was obliged to use too much breath in the middle register. This is a form of forcing. Over time, the middle register spread and the top notes atrophied. The lyric tenor who, early in his career, had sung a top E flat without audible strain in his recording of *Lucia di Lammermoor*, now struggled with mere B flats.

Fortunately, in the short years of his prime, Carreras recorded enough in the way of complete operas and recitals to assure him of a place in history. His fine performances in two Rossini operas have already been noted. Equally fine are his recordings of four early Verdi operas for Phillips – *Stiffelio*, *Un Giorno di Regno*, *La Battaglia di Legnano*, and *I Due Foscari*. There was much else to admire: other recordings of the Italian repertoire and some excellent performances of French opera, notably *Werther*, *Carmen*, and *La Juive*, in which his impassioned manner and outpouring of limpid, opulent tone yielded satisfaction to even the most crabbed and determined golden-agers. His French pronunciation, though not perfect, was better than that of most non-French tenors.

Best of all, in my opinion, was an early recital disc which featured arias from a number of little known operas – Mercadante's *Il*

Giuramento, Donizetti's *Il Duca d'Alba* and *Maria di Rohan*, Bellini's *Adelson e Salvini*, Verdi's *Jérusalem*, and Ponchielli's *Il Figliuol Prodigo* – alongside better known pieces. In all of these, the voice was glorious and easily produced, and the singing combined passion and refinement in a way close to ideal. One aria especially deserves to be singled out: '*Angelo casto e bel*' from *Il Duca d'Alba*. This is one of the most romantic pieces of singing on record, and Carreras's gorgeous *legato* in the phrase '*a lei le gioie, a me i dolor*', once heard, haunts the memory. The liquid beauty of the Italian language is a gift to the singer at this point, and Carreras makes the most of it.

Another aspect of Carreras's art in his prime which has not been much commented on is his exceptional breath control. This is best exemplified by his singing of the opening phrase of the final scene of *Lucia di Lammermoor* – '*Tu che a Dio spiegasti l'ali, o bell' alma innamorata*' – which he sings on one breath: the only tenor on record, so far as I am aware, to do so.

Carreras also showed himself capable of mastering non-operatic styles when he recorded, with Kiri Te Kanawa, Bernstein's *West Side Story* and Rodgers and Hammerstein's *South Pacific*. Not everyone thought essentially operatic voices best suited to these works, but it is undeniable that they have never been better sung, even if the style is not always entirely appropriate.

Carreras's complete studio recordings include *Elisabetta Regina d'Inghilterra*, *Otello* (Rossini), *Lucia di Lammermoor*, *Elisir d'Amore*, *Un Giorno di Regno*, *Stiffelio*, *La Battaglia di Legnano*, *I due Foscari*, *Macbeth*, *Il Trovatore*, *Un Ballo in Maschera*, *Simone Boccanegra*, *La Forza del Destino*, *Don Carlo*, *Aida*, *La Juive*, *Carmen*, *Werther*, *Samson et Dalila*, *Cavalleria Rusticana*, *Pagliacci*, *Manon Lescaut*, *La Bohème*, *Madama Butterfly*, *Tosca*, and *Turandot*.

31 Alfredo Kraus and Juan Diego Flórez: the revival of the tenore di grazia

The *tenore di grazia*, for whom so many of the *bel canto* tenor roles were written, has undergone a revival in recent years, following an eclipse which lasted for most of the preceding century, for these agile, light-voiced tenors could not, it was thought, compete with the magnificent outpourings of Caruso and his successors. The difference this revival made can be seen in a comparison of the repertoires of the two preëminent *tenori di grazia* since the days of Tito Schipa and Heddle Nash. I refer to Alfredo Kraus (1927–99) and Juan Diego Flórez (born 1973).

In the years of Kraus's prime, the repertoire of the *tenore di grazia* had fallen out of favour. With few exceptions, the operas of the *bel canto* period, and especially the florid works of Rossini, were seldom, if ever, performed. Pragmatically, Kraus adapted himself to the realities of the situation and sang the repertoire of the high light-lyric tenor – the few *bel canto* roles that retained a foothold in the repertoire of the world's opera houses, the lyric French repertoire, and a handful of other roles (Alfredo in *La Traviata*, the Duke in *Rigoletto*, Fenton in *Falstaff*). Perhaps it was not ideal. Perhaps those roles did not exhibit his greatest qualities – or not all of them, at any rate. But he was able to bring to them a refined taste, a perfectly placed light-lyric voice, effortless top notes, and an elegance of vocal line, gesture and bearing that they did not get from most of his contemporaries.

The actual sound of Kraus's was, for some, an acquired taste. John Steane evidently changed his mind about it. Having described

Kraus's timbre as 'uningratiating' in *The Grand Tradition*, he wrote this some twenty years later in *Singers of the Century*—

> These [qualities – refinement, elegance, feeling for style] are found […] consistently in […] the period 1830 to 1860. In Bellini, Kraus's Arturo in *I Puritani* is finely caught on records, one of its great assets being the placing of the voice, so wonderfully matching the high tessitura. His Donizetti is still better, and among my own most cherished memories of opera at Covent Garden is his aria in Lucrezia Borgia, performed with Sutherland in 1980. Then, in any assessment of him, the sheer longevity of his career must have a place – it testifies to the soundness of his method.

And, one might add, to the soundness of his judgment. Unlike some other light-voiced tenors, Kraus was never tempted into an unsuitable repertoire. He had a clear sense of his vocal possibilities (and their limits), and therefore knew precisely which roles lay within his compass and which did not. His extensive upward range (up to a top E flat) meant that, even in his late sixties, he was comfortable and secure in high-lying roles which most other tenors either preferred to avoid because they were risky, or had to avoid because they were impossible. He wisely confined himself to a repertoire of about twenty-four operatic roles which were suited to his voice.

My own recollections of Kraus on stage (in *Faust* and *Lucrezia Borgia*) are that the elegance of his singing was matched by that of gesture and deportment. There was a certain aristocratic quality in his manner and bearing. The trim figure – so unlike that of the usual rotund tenor – was also an asset, and gave him, even in later years, a youthful appearance appropriate to the roles he sang. The voice, slender and penetrative, was so well projected that, even with huge-voiced colleagues like Joan Sutherland and Montserrat Caballé, he was able easily to hold his own.

Kraus's vocal control was exceptional. He seemed able to execute a *diminuendo* on practically any note in his range, and his breath control was such that, in the *I Puritani* recording praised by John Steane, he sings the long phrase '*ogni gioia gli par duol*' (which is repeated) on a single, enormous span of breath – a remarkable feat otherwise unexampled on record. To an unusual extent (probably uniquely among the tenors of his generation), conductors permitted him the freedom to shape phrases and use *rubato* in a way that recalled the singers of an earlier era. This was not always to everyone's taste. Steane, though usually the first to applaud the artistic use of *rubato*, found Kraus's use of it in *Werther* excessive: he criticized the tenor's interpretation as 'exaggeratedly self-pitying and emphatic'. For others, Kraus's Werther is definitive – a profoundly personal realization of Goethe's and Massenet's conception.

Another gifted *tenore di grazia* is the Peruvian Juan Diego Flórez (born 1973). He is the natural successor to Alfredo Kraus, but he has had the good fortune that his career has coincided with a revival of interest in the *bel canto* repertoire, especially the works of Rossini and Donizetti, to which his voice is best suited. The result is that, whereas Kraus was obliged to undertake French and Italian lyric roles, such as Werther and (on disc) Rodolfo in *La Bohème* (to which he was not ideally suited), and never sang in, say, *La donna del lago* or *Semiramide* (which would have suited him to perfection), Flórez has been able to concentrate on the light-lyric, florid roles of Rossini, Donizetti and Bellini, which allow him to display his brilliance and fluency in the execution of runs and ornaments and his extensive upward range (up to top E flat in full voice).

His recital discs and complete opera recordings show him to be a sensitive and musical artist as well as a prodigiously talented one. The voice is not large, but its tone is bright, virile and penetrative, and he is capable of softening it when necessary. His repertoire extends from the *bel canto* operas backwards to Baroque works and forwards to such Verdian roles as Edoardo in *Un giorno di regno*, the Duca di Mantua in *Rigoletto* and Fenton in *Falstaff*. And he now has options of adding to that repertoire by exploring Baroque and early music or by continuing to revive neglected works from the *bel canto* period: works by composers such as Pacini and Mercadante, for example, have scarcely yet been touched.

His recital discs confirm that, even in an age where the competition includes such skilful and accomplished tenors as William Matteuzzi, Bruce Ford, Salvatore Fisichella, Rockwell Blake, Raoul Gimenez, Lawrence Brownlee and Barry Banks, he stands in a class of his own. For his combination of beauty of tone, elegance of line, upward range, dazzling high notes, ability to cope with a stratospheric *tessitura*, fluency and precision in the execution of the most difficult embellishments, dynamic and colouristic variety, flawless musicianship, subtle interpretative skills both musically and dramatically, and the vividness and individuality of his characterizations, there is no one to match him today.

Kraus's opera recordings include *Così fan tutte*, *Lucia di Lammermoor*, *Lucrezia Borgia*, *La Fille du Régiment*, *I Puritani*, *La Jolie Fille de Perth*, *Werther*, *Roméo et Juliette*, *Manon*, *Rigoletto* (two), *La Traviata*, *Falstaff*, *La Bohème*. There are also many live recordings on CD and DVD of his appearances in these and other roles.

Flórez has recorded several recital discs in the studio, of which those devoted to the *bel canto* repertoire are especially rewarding. He can also be heard on numerous CDs / DVDs of live performances of complete operas.

The Great Tenors
Part Three

32 Short notes

We know from written records of many great tenors of whom we have no aural recordings, tenors like Rubini, Mario, Nourrit, Donzelli, Duprez and Tamberlik. We have some idea, from the very detailed accounts of their contemporaries, of what they sounded like. But having some idea is a long way from knowing; and the earliest outstanding tenor of whom we have enough reliable recordings to form a reasonably accurate idea of what he sounded like, is Tamagno. We shall therefore start with him.

Francesco Tamagno (1850–1905) was a dramatic tenor of an unusual – perhaps even a unique – kind. The voice, which is enormously powerful, appears to be uncovered throughout its range. Its timbre is bright and slightly nasal, the upper range exceptionally brilliant, and the low notes full and well supported. Interpretatively he is sometimes moving, as in his remarkable version of '*O muto asil*', with its softly floated B flats, and often exciting, as in his martial accounts of '*Re del ciel*' from *Il Profeta*, the *improvviso* from *Andrea Chenier*, the *corriam* from *Guglielmo Tell* and the excerpts he recorded from Verdi's *Otello*, the role he famously created. The only other Verdian role to feature in his discography is Manrico in *Il Trovatore*: his version of '*Di quella pira*' – taken, like Caruso's, at a slow tempo – ranks with the best, being viscerally exciting with ringing high C's, yet also unusually accurate, with the semi-quavers precisely articulated without recourse to aspirates. All his records are impressive but they do not

191

suggest an artist of great subtlety. He favours slow tempi and takes frequent liberties with notes, tempo and rhythm but, despite this musical latitude and the dynamic variety already noted, his phrasing lacks breadth and plasticity, perhaps because his health was failing (he died of heart failure only two years after the recordings were made, and heart trouble had caused his retirement some years earlier). If we compare his versions of the *Otello* solos with those of Martinelli, we find that, while the vocal splendour is all with Tamagno, the interpretative insight is Martinelli's. Interestingly, while his voice has the power of a *Heldentenor*, it does not have the baritonal timbre or upwardly limited range which are characteristic of voices of that type. The brilliance and ease of his upper register, which extended to a top C sharp, allowed him to sing high tenor roles such as Raoul, Arnold and Poliuto, as well as roles with a lower *tessitura* such as Andrea Chenier, Alvaro and Manrico. The latter three roles, but not the first three, were in the repertoire of Mario del Monaco (*q.v.*), the modern Italian tenor whose voice perhaps most resembles Tamagno's in colour, timbre and type. However, it is noteworthy that, whereas del Monaco specialized in *verismo* rather than in the works of Verdi or earlier composers, Tamagno refused to sing the *verismo* repertoire (with the exception of Chenier), feeling that such roles were not suited to his voice and method of voice production, and might prove injurious. The vocal similarities between Tamagno and del Monaco notwithstanding, there were also significant vocal, technical and stylistic differences. The most obvious of these are del Monaco's adoption of the laryngeal Melocchi method, which eschews vocal placement; and the fact (not unrelated to his vocal method) that he sometimes produced a covered tone as low as D natural.

Léon Escalaïs (1859–1941) was a French heroic tenor, gifted with a voice of exceptional power and brilliance, especially in the upper register. Escalaïs is an unusual example of an heroic tenor who has a mastery of the graces and techniques of the lyric tenor. He can sing trills, and execute mordents and *gruppetti* accurately and gracefully. The voice itself has a clarity, a force, and a trumpet-like brilliance reminiscent of Tamagno. In music that calls for these qualities, he is unsurpassed. In the *Sicilienne* from Meyerbeer's *Robert le Diable*, which calls for extreme vocal agility, or in '*Je veux entendre*' from Verdi's *Jérusalem* with its top C sharps, to cite two examples, he is superb. But there is more to Escalaïs than this. For instance, in Eléazar's '*Dio m'ispira*' from Halévy's *La Juive* (which is sung, inexplicably, in Italian) and in Otello's '*Dio mi potevi*', he sings with fervour, nobility and conviction. The clarity of his diction, whether he is singing in French or Italian, is exemplary. Escalaïs was barely five feet tall – he was once unkindly described as having the head of a bull and the legs of a basset hound – and his lack of height would have limited his career in the opera house today. Fortunately, in his own day, when the average height was less than it is now, and the standard of dramatic verisimilitude expected of opera singers was more modest, it does not seem to have affected his career at all. One of the most exciting tenors on record.

The problems with **Fernando De Lucia** (1861–1925) are different. The voice was a lyric tenor but evidently one capable of *spinto* development since his repertoire included roles in operas by Bizet, Verdi, Puccini, Mascagni and Leoncavallo, and even the title role of Wagner's *Lohengrin*. Ironically, his posthumous reputation rests largely on his recordings of a very different repertoire: the *bel canto* roles of Rossini and Bellini. In particular, his execution of the ornaments in the tenor arias from Rossini's *Barbiere di Siviglia*, especially the opening serenade, '*Ecco ridente in cielo*', is considered exemplary by his admirers. And, as his admirers include such discriminating judges as John Steane and Michael Henstock, their views should not be lightly dismissed. It is possible, however, to share their admiration while noting that the extreme agility is attained by adopting a blanched tone and a very light delivery which contrasts with his full voice. One cannot therefore compare his performances with those of later *tenori di grazia* such as Heddle Nash or Juan Diego Flórez,[1] who sing the runs and execute the *fioriture* in full voice, because one simply would not be comparing like with like. It is also possible to note that the voice, as recorded, has a pronounced *vibrato*, that the tone is not especially attractive, that the range is short with no top notes to speak of, and that arias which require them are excessively transposed. He takes other liberties which, to modern listeners, will seem unwarrantable. For example, in his recording of '*Recondita armonia*', he alters the final words from *sei tu* to *sei te*, despite thereby committing a grammatical solecism, evidently because the *e* vowel was easier to sing. He sings quite expressively, but his good interpretative intentions are somewhat vitiated by a tendency to abuse effects such as *rubato* and ornamentation which, if used more judiciously, would not draw attention to themselves and would be all the more effective for it. It is only fair to add that the *vibrato* which is such a prominent feature of his recordings, was said by his pupil, Georges Thill, not to be a noticeable feature of his singing in the flesh.[2] The chief interest of de Lucia's recordings is in the glimpse they afford us of the style, technique, and vocal method of a lost age: the age of Rubini, Mario, and Nourrit. That age came to an end with the advent of Domenico Donzelli (1790–1873) and Gilbert-Louis Duprez (1806–96), with his famous (or infamous, according to taste) '*ut de poitrine*'. But its influence lingered until the vocal amplitude and splendour of Caruso made audiences intolerant of the small-scale but, in some respects, more refined, art of his immediate predecessors, of whom de Lucia and Bonci were the most eminent. This should not be taken to imply that de Lucia possessed a small voice, however. As Canio, Turiddu, Don Jose, and Lohengrin, he must have had considerable reserves of power at his command, even if they were sparingly used and did not measure up to the seemingly inexhaustible resources of Caruso.

The English tenor, **John Coates** (1865–1941), has already been referred to as an example of a great singer who lacked a great voice. Yet too much can be made of this. Coates was no voiceless marvel. His voice, as Michael Scott remarked, was 'a sound instrument of good quality': it was sturdy and serviceable. But such adjectives suggest damning with faint praise, and that would be far from the truth. Scott himself (no easy critic to please) goes on to refer to Coates' perfect taste, imagination, clarity of diction, and technical skill, and concludes that he was 'one of the finest English singers on record'. Few would argue with this. What made Coates remarkable was not the voice itself, but what he did with it. Gerald Moore, who, at the outset of his career, worked with Coates for many years, said that Coates had taught him everything he knew about the art of accompanying, and described him as 'the finest and most imaginative of tenors'. The operative words are 'most imaginative'. Coates sang an astonishingly wide repertoire and to everything he sang he brought a vivid imagination, a luminous intelligence, a flawless technique, consummate musicianship, and exemplary diction. For a tenor, his voice had a low centre of gravity. He was more comfortable with the *tessitura* of Wagner than with that of Verdi. Nevertheless, his operatic repertoire embraced Italian and French roles as well as German. His operatic roles ranged from Faust and Hoffmann to Tristan and Siegfried. Don Jose in *Carmen*, Pedro in *Tiefland* (by d'Albert), and the title roles in *Lohengrin* and *Parsifal* also formed part of his repertoire. His Italian roles included Dick Johnson (in *The Girl of the Golden West*) and Radames. He sang an enormous concert repertoire of song, ranging from the

Elizabethans to the moderns, including Max Reger; and oratorio, ranging from Bach and Handel to Saint-Saëns and Elgar. He had a command of several languages rare among singers of his day. His recording of '*Dai campi, dai prati*', for example, apart from being a masterly interpretation which penetrates to the heart of this meditative aria rather than treating it as just another conventional tenorial outpouring with a climactic top note, is also sung in perfect Italian. Although this aria has a rather high *tessitura*, he sings it without forcing – a testimony to the excellence of his technique. Certainly, Coates's recordings, although some were made when he was past his prime, give ample evidence of his splendid musicianship, impeccable technique, clear diction whatever the language, and exceptional interpretative intelligence.

Another English tenor, **Gervase Elwes** (1866–1921) made his career entirely on the concert platform. This decision was probably enforced: a career as a singer was considered unsuitable for a gentleman of Elwes' class (he belonged to the minor aristocracy), and a career on the stage would have been regarded as beyond the pale. In order to avoid a permanent rift with his family, Elwes probably had to agree to limiting himself to concert appearances. The decision had other consequences: according to Elwes himself, he was told by his voice teacher that he could train as a tenor if he intended to confine himself to the concert repertoire, but, if he wanted a career in the opera house, he would have to train as a baritone. This fact, combined with his repertoire, suggests a voice with a low range for a tenor, but one capable of extending its range upwards by the artful use of falsettones. That would have been possible in concert works like the Bach Passions (in which Elwes sang the high-lying parts of the Evangelists), but not in the standard operatic repertoire of the day: Elwes was, after all, a contemporary of de Lucia and Caruso, and opera audiences would have expected a more ringing and robust approach to top notes. Elwes was an exceptional artist, lauded and admired by many English composers, including Elgar, Vaughan Williams and Quilter. He gave the first performance of Vaughan Williams's Housman song-cycle, *On Wenlock Edge*, of which he also made the first recording. He and Coates were the two most admired interpreters of Elgar's Gerontius of their day, and he made something of a speciality of the attractive songs of Roger Quilter. He also introduced many of the *Lieder* of Brahms (another speciality of his) to the British musical public. On record, the voice sounds surprisingly dark, virile and baritonal in timbre, and the higher notes have more weight and body than one might expect.

The gigantic Moravian tenor, **Leo Slezak** (1873–1946), ranked together with Zenatello as Tamagno's successor as Otello, and his preëminence in certain European houses, especially Vienna, made him one of the few tenors of his day who could, without absurdity, be mentioned in the same breath as Caruso. At six feet four inches tall and over 280 lbs (twenty stones) in weight in his vocal prime, he certainly cut an imposing – not to say Chestertonian – figure on stage. But there was more to him than a Gargantuan physique. He sang a huge repertoire, ranging from Mozart roles such as Belmonte and Tamino, to Wagnerian roles such as Lohengrin and Tannhäuser. He also sang the high-lying heroic roles of Arnold in *Guillaume Tell* and Raoul in *Les Huguenots*. Nor was he limited to opera; he was also a highly regarded *Lieder* singer, and some of his recordings show why. This breadth of repertoire was not as exceptional in Slezak's day as it has become since: English tenors like John Coates and Walter Hyde were comparably versatile, though more judicious in their choice of operatic roles especially. For no one could sing a repertoire quite as varied and strenuous as Slezak's without paying a price. The *vibrato* loosened, the voice acquired an unsteadiness which verged on a wobble, and the top notes at full volume became hard and strained: in consequence, some of his later recordings do not make pleasant listening. At his best, however, he fully deserves his place here, the voice plangent and penetrative without hardness, the style subtle and sensitive. His exquisite version of the little-known aria, '*Magische Töne*', from Goldmark's *Die Königin von Saba* stands comparison with Caruso's; and the final high-lying phrases culminating in a seraphic top C, headily beautiful and easily produced, are a considerable improvement on the Master's thin *falsetto* at that point. Slezak's trumpet-toned version of '*Ora e per sempre*' also suggests that he was one of the finest Otellos of the recorded era and a worthy successor to Tamagno (although singing the role may have taken a toll on his voice and been a factor in his comparatively early vocal decline).

Giovanni Zenatello (1876–1949), a contemporary of Caruso, created the role of Pinkerton in *Madama Butterfly* but, in his subsequent career, was noted chiefly as an exponent of more heroic roles such as Canio, Manrico, Radames and, especially, Otello, the role in which he succeeded Tamagno. His recordings mostly suggest that he had a powerful, metallic voice of no great beauty of tone, though the earlier recordings tell a slightly different story. His acoustic recording of the *Miserere* from *Trovatore* with Emmy Destinn, for example, compares favourably with Destinn's later recording with Martinelli: here Zenatello's voice does sound tonally appealing, which, in many of his later recordings, it does not. It may be that a premature assumption of heroic roles took its toll on his voice. By the time of the 1928 Covent Garden *Otello*, excerpts of which were recorded live, the voice is certainly not a thing of beauty, although the interpretation, anguished and forceful, is memorable. Of course, by 1928 he was fifty-two years old, an age at which a good many singers, especially heroic tenors, are showing signs of wear and tear. As Boito's Faust, he is urgent, dramatic and exciting. In some later recordings, his intonation is unreliable but in the *Otello* excerpts there is no sign of the tendency to sing flat that is evident elsewhere. Throughout his recorded output, there is little indication of the baritone he originally was. He sounds always like a clarion-voiced, trumpet-toned heroic tenor, having more in common with Tamagno, Martinelli or del Monaco, than with such baritonal tenors as Zanelli,[3] Vinay or McCracken.

Hermann Jadlowker (1877–1953), the Latvian-born Russian (later Israeli) tenor, also trained as a cantor, which accounts for the throaty and plaintive timbre of his voice, his facility in *falsetto*, and the exceptional flexibility of his technique. These qualities serve him well in '*Meine Freunde, sind hier ganz im Stillen versteckt*' from Auber's *Fra Diavolo* and in '*Fuor del mar*' from Mozart's *Idomeneo*, of which he gives an astonishing account: this version sets the standard for other tenors much as John McCormack's '*Il mio tesoro*' does. In Rossini's '*Ecco ridente in cielo*', the fluency of the coloratura rivals de Lucia, and is achieved in full voice, which de Lucia's is not. His vocal timbre is strongly reminiscent of other cantors, notably Berele Chagy. The throatiness is by no means unattractive, and his account, in German, of the Tomb Scene from *Lucia di Lammermoor* is most affecting. In Manrico's '*Ah si ben mio*', unlike the majority of tenors, he supplies genuine semitone trills where required by the score. Wherever flexibility is called for, whether it be in Mozart or Rossini, he supplies it to a degree unsurpassed by any other tenor, and matched by very few. His repertoire ranged from Mozart to Wagner, and embraced *Lieder* as well as opera. But, as with Slezak, he paid a price for his versatility: later in his career, the registers tended to separate and the voice showed signs of wear. At his best, he remains one of the most amazing singers on record, and an affecting and conscientious artist.

Joseph Hislop (1884–1977) was a Scottish (later naturalized Swedish) tenor who might today have been much better known if he had not had the temerity to say 'no' to La Scala. As it is, he enjoyed a distinguished career instead of the stellar one that beckoned when he became the first British tenor to sing a principal tenor role in an Italian opera at La Scala, where he took over the role of Edgardo from Pertile and made an excellent impression on critics and the opera house management. Hislop possessed a mellifluous lyric tenor of fine quality, sang well and stylishly in both French and Italian as well as English, and was among the best lyric tenors of his day, despite strong competition. His recordings are well worth investigating. His '*Salut demeure*' is near perfection, one of the best versions on record and crowned with a really fine top C. His '*Che gelida manina*' reminds us that he was described by Puccini himself as '*mio Rodolfo ideale*', an accolade he surely deserved to judge from this recording. The timbre of the voice – rich, mellow and youthful – suits the music to a marvel and the interpretation too entitles this version to rank with the very best. Perhaps surprisingly, he makes a fine impression in two Wagner items, the *Preislied* from *Meistersinger* and Lohengrin's '*In fernem Land*', repertoire with which he was not generally associated, and which would certainly have been too heavy for him to sing in the opera house. Operetta and Scottish folksongs also find in Hislop a stylish and sympathetic interpreter. A tenor who deserves much wider fame (and many more recordings) than he achieved.

Alfred Piccaver (1884–1958) was an English-born tenor who made his career mainly at the Vienna State Opera, where he was idolized. He seems to have occupied the same position in the affections of the Viennese public as Caruso in those of the opera lovers of New York. Indeed he returned to Vienna in the last years of his life and, when he died, was granted a state funeral, which was so well attended that the city came to a virtual standstill. His recordings show a fine *lirico spinto* voice without really confirming his reputation with the Viennese. Steane notes a certain stolidity, a phlegmatic quality in the interpretations, and notes too that Puccini had a word for it: *squadrato*, square. Yet it is only fair to point out that Nigel Douglas, himself an accomplished tenor and one who studied with Piccaver, has a higher view of his art (see his *Legendary Voices* for a touching memoir of his teacher). Piccaver may have been one of those singers who make a greater impression in live performances than they are able to in the very different, and infinitely less stimulating, environment of the recording studio. He was also an example of an authentic British *spinto* tenor (his contemporaries Tom Burke and Tudor Davies were others) and was thus the musical progenitor of such distinguished later artists as James Johnston, Henry Wendon, Tom Swift, Charles Craig, Kenneth Collins, David Rendall, Dennis O'Neill, Edmund Barham, John Hudson, Rhys Meirion, Peter Auty and the Australian-born but British-naturalized Julian Gavin.

Tudor Davies (1892–1958), along with Parry Jones, was the most distinguished Welsh tenor of his day. Of the two, Davies had the more beautiful voice. His career took him to the British National Opera Company, the Carl Rosa, Sadler's Wells and Covent Garden, where he sang Rodolfo opposite Melba. Records reveal a fine *spinto* tenor with a sound technique and a passionate interpretative style. Like Walter Widdop (*q.v.*), he sings a splendid version of Handel's 'Sound an alarm'. He is also admirable in such varied operatic fare as Max's '*Durch die Wälder, durch die Auen*' from Weber's *Der Freischütz* and Cavaradossi's '*Recondita armonia*' (both sung in English). Fragments of his Gerontius can be heard – enough to suggest that we have missed a great deal by the absence of a complete recording. He does feature in a complete recording of *Madama Butterfly* as an ardent and powerful Pinkerton. Indeed, his operatic repertoire seems, from the recorded evidence, to have been unusually extensive: he makes an impassioned Turiddu opposite the rather sedate-sounding Santuzza of Florence Austral in the duet '*Tu qui Santuzza?*' (in English) and sings a splendid '*Bildnisarie*' from *The Magic Flute*. Best of all are his recordings of two pieces by Coleridge-Taylor: 'Onaway! Awake, beloved' from *Hiawatha*, and the song 'Eleanore', of which he gives a magnificent reading with orchestral accompaniment, one full of passion and yearning, quite eclipsing a good version (with piano accompaniment by Gerald Moore) by Henry Wendon. Davies's skilful use of *portamento* and *rubato*, the generous, full-throated Italianate sound, the passionate manner, and the exemplary clarity of his English diction (very typical of his period with its rolled r's and distinctive pronunciation of words such as 'here', which is pronounced as 'heerr'), all combine to create an ineffable effect: one of the most powerfully moving interpretations of an English song on record. Sadly, he later undertook such unsuitably heavy roles as Siegmund,[4] and that, as well as heavy drinking,[5] may have precipitated a premature vocal decline. In his prime, however, he was justly described as a kind of British Pertile.

Tudor Davies featured in a complete recording of *Madama Butterfly* (in English).

The English tenor, **Walter Widdop** (1892–1949), is generally thought of as a *Heldentenor* and he did indeed make some excellent recordings of Wagner, notably a version in English of '*In fernem Land*' ('In distant land') from *Lohengrin* which is one of the most outstanding examples of Wagnerian singing on disc.[6] Nevertheless, it diminishes Widdop's achievement to see him purely as a *Heldentenor*. He was also a superb Handelian and a fine interpreter of Bach. The conjunction of Handelian and Wagnerian roles, not uncommon with British singers but virtually unknown elsewhere, is remarkable: one does not expect a Siegmund and a Tristan to be capable of negotiating the fearsome runs and plentiful top B flats of 'Sound an alarm' or the melismatic vocal line and high *tessitura* of the tenor arias from Bach's B minor Mass or *St Matthew Passion*. Yet Widdop does both – and magnificently. In another Handel aria – 'Waft her, angels, through the skies' from *Jephtha* – he sings nobly and expressively. He is also very fine (albeit at an unfashionably slow tempo) in the aria 'If with all your hearts' from Mendelssohn's *Elijah*. In two contrasting arias by Gounod, we get an idea of the range of Widdop's art. In 'All hail thou dwelling' (*'Salut demeure'*) from *Faust*, he is lyrical and tender, producing a heady and effortless top C and then achieving a melting *diminuendo* on the word *fare* in the next phrase before rounding off the aria with a perfect *messa di voce* on the middle syllable of the word *excelling*. In 'Lend me your aid' (*'Inspirez-moi race divine'*) from *La Reine de Saba*, he is thrillingly heroic. This is a version worthy to stand beside Caruso's. In Vladimir's aria from Borodin's *Prince Igor* – not, perhaps, the sort of repertoire with which he was generally associated – he compares well with the young Jussi Björling. He sings 'Yes! let me like a soldier fall' from Wallace's *Maritana* with a fine swagger and ringing top notes. Finally, his recording of Dibdin's song 'Tom Bowling' is the most moving version on record. It has been alleged by some critics that Widdop is temperamentally phlegmatic, and a stolid, inexpressive singer. The present writer can make no sense of this whatsoever. It is contradicted by all the recorded evidence. The inescapable conclusion, from an impartial and attentive hearing of the recordings, is that he was not only one of the greatest heroic tenors on record, but one of the most underrated.[7] Though tall and burly in physique, he was no actor (Beecham likened his unhurried and deliberate movements on stage to those of 'that estimable quadruped, the hedgehog'), and his effectiveness in the Wagnerian and other operatic roles was entirely due to his splendid voice. If only the vocal attributes of Widdop could have been combined with the histrionic skill of that other fine English Wagnerian, Frank Mullings! We might then have had a *Heldentenor* who would have eclipsed all rivals.

The Danish-born tenor, **Helge Roswaenge** (1897–1972), made his career mainly in Germany, becoming a fixture in Berlin, where he sang a wide repertoire ranging from Mozart through Verdi and Puccini to Wagner and Richard Strauss. His Mozart, probably most famously represented on record by his Tamino in Beecham's 1938 recording of *Die Zauberflöte*, lacks the charm and elegance of Tauber and notes in the middle of his range sound surprisingly effortful for a tenor who possessed so virile a top D. He is better heard in the aria '*Hier soll ich dich denn sehen*' from *Die Entführung aus dem Serail*, of which he gives a strenuous but typically characterful account. His version of Hugo Wolf's song, '*Der Feuerreiter*', is rhythmically energetic and hair-raising in its intensity, as is his version of '*Gott! Welch Dunkel hier*' from Beethoven's *Fidelio*. But best of all is his matchless recording of the rondo, '*Freunde vernehmet die Geschichte*', from Adolphe Adam's *Der Postillon von Longjumeau*. The exuberance and sheer *élan* of this account are irresistible. No other version comes near it, not even the young Nicolai Gedda's early recording in Swedish, which, though beautifully sung, is less characterful and vividly animated than Roswaenge's performance. As for the top D, Roswaenge simply nails it, hitting the note smack in the middle with clarion force, brilliance and complete freedom from strain; the attack is clean without any aspirate or lifting: an astonishing feat for any singer, especially for one endowed with a voice of such heroic weight and size. Elsewhere, in arias from Glinka's *A Life for the Tsar*, Verdi's *Il Trovatore*, Richard Strauss's *Der Rosenkavalier*, and Weber's *Oberon*, he displays the tireless brilliance of his upper register to impressive effect. In more lyrical music, the strenuous vocal method and sometimes exaggerated diction can seem obtrusive, and they tend to deprive his singing of the relaxed and easy-going charm of Tauber or Gedda. But he is a sensitive and intelligent artist. His recordings of Italian arias, like '*Das nur für mich dein Herz erbebt*' ('*Ah si ben mio*' from *Il Trovatore* – complete with the trills shown in the score, but rarely attempted), '*Holde Aida*' ('*Celeste Aida*' – tenderly sung, with the final B flat sung *pianissimo e morendo*, as marked), and '*Wie sich die Bilder gleichen*' ('*Recondita armonia*' from *Tosca* – for once, really sounding like a love song, rather than just another opportunity for a narcissistic star tenor to show off his top notes), show a conscientious attention to the composer's dynamic markings, and an acute interpretative intelligence and imagination. Later in his career, the effects of singing so varied and demanding a repertoire became apparent as the registers began to separate, but he kept the clarion top notes to the end. Amazingly, he was still singing principal roles at the time of his death at the age of seventy-five.

Roswaenge recorded *Die Zauberflöte* complete (under Beecham).

The Viennese tenor, **Julius Patzak** (1898–1974) shows how far a singer can go without a first-class voice provided he has intelligence, musicianship and a capacity for hard work. Patzak had all three in abundance. The voice, plangent and distinctive, was instantly recognizable but not an instrument of any sensuous beauty. It was, however, responsive to every demand made on it by a keen and discriminating musical intellect. Patzak's Florestan was rightly famed and his account of the role is second to none, but he is also superb in other, very different repertoire: in operatic roles as diverse as Radames, Palestrina and Hoffmann; in Viennese operetta, notably Johann Strauss's *Die Fledermaus* and *Der Zigeunerbaron*, in which he displays a deftness and lightness of touch of which very few opera singers are capable; and in the taxing tenor songs in Mahler's *Das Lied von der Erde* – though it must be admitted that, by 1952, when he made the famous Decca recording with Kathleen Ferrier and Bruno Walter, his voice was drier than it had been in his prime. He was also an outstanding interpreter of Mozart, especially of the roles of Belmonte in *Die Entführung aus dem Serail* and Tamino in *Die Zauberflöte*. In Janos Ferencsik's memorable 1968 recording of Schönberg's *Gurre-Lieder*, he appears as the Narrator, a spoken role, in which his interpretative intelligence and sensitivity to words are clearly evident. (Incidentally, his speaking voice is instantly recognizable to anyone who is familiar with his singing). He was also one of a very small number of non-Anglophone tenors to sing and record (in German) the title role of Elgar's *Gerontius*. Patzak was an artist of exceptional versatility and musicianship, whose medium-sized and essentially lyric voice proved capable of withstanding considerable pressure and tackling repertoire which would ordinarily have been thought outside its compass.

Patzak's recordings include complete versions of *Fidelio, Die Fledermaus, Der Zigeunerbaron* and Mahler's *Das Lied von der Erde*. He also recorded Elgar's *The Dream of Gerontius* in German.

The German tenor, **Marcel Wittrisch** (1901–55), matured from a Tauber epigone (in Steane's words, 'though less individual in style [than Tauber], he was certainly comparable in timbre and less restricted in the upper register') into an heroic tenor capable of tackling roles such as Lohengrin, Siegmund and Parsifal. His recordings do suggest similarities in timbre and colour to both Tauber and Roswaenge. Like the latter but unlike the former, he has a ringing upper register: in a deservedly famous recording (with the fine *lirico spinto* soprano, Margarete Teschemacher, in German) of a duet from Meyerbeer's *Les Huguenots*, he rises to a superb and unforced top D flat: a note certainly outside Tauber's modest compass. In this recording also, he displays his fine *legato*, musical use of *portamento* rather than crude sliding, and the sweep and breadth of his phrasing. A complete recording of the opera with Wittrisch in the demanding role of Raoul (and a suitable supporting cast) might have stood unchallenged to this day. In common with most German-trained tenors of his era (Völker, Schmidt, Tauber, Patzak, Roswaenge, and Anders, are other examples), he excelled in the Viennese operetta repertoire, showing that it is possible to combine a voice of genuinely heroic weight and power with the grace and lyricism required to tackle a lighter *Fach*. In modern times, the German *lirico spinto* tenor, Jonas Kaufmann, has similar qualities, though he does not appear to share Wittrisch's extensive upward range. Wittrisch's voice is a distinctively Germanic tenor, which combines the grace of the lyric tenor with the ringing power of the heroic, and which possesses the (not unattractive) slightly throaty quality characteristic of the breed.[8]

Hugues Cuénod (1902–2010) is something of a freak among tenors, even apart from the fact that he lived to be 108, and was still performing (well) in his nineties. Quite unclassifiable, he had a breadth of repertoire that beggars belief, ranging from Monteverdi to Stravinsky to Noël Coward. He made his Metropolitan Opera debut at eighty-four, as the Emperor in *Turandot*, becoming the oldest singer to debut at the Met. His career lasted from 1928 to 1994. He preferred to sing *comprimario* roles, and several of these became his specialities: Basilio in *Le Nozze di Figaro*, Sellem in *The Rake's Progress*, and M. Triquet in *Eugene Onegin*. With characteristic modesty, he attributed this preference to laziness. But he also sang the demanding high tenor part of the Astrologer in Rimsky-Korsakov's *Le Coq d'Or*, being one of the few tenors who could manage the stratospheric *tessitura*, including the sustained top E natural. His repertoire included early music (Machaut and Monteverdi), which he sang with great distinction, and the whole range of the French *mélodie* – from Gounod, Fauré, and Duparc, to Honegger, Roussel, Auric and Poulenc – of which he was an unrivalled exponent. He was also rightly renowned as an interpreter of Bach, especially as the Evangelist in the *St Matthew Passion*. In Richard Bonynge's stellar-cast recording of *Les Contes d'Hoffmann*, Cuénod contributes scene-stealing performances in no fewer than four roles: Andrès, Cochenille, Pitichinaccio and Frantz. There is no more brilliant example of comic acting on record. On stage, his gangling six-foot-five frame was an asset, particularly in roles like the Dancing Master in Strauss's *Ariadne auf Naxos* or Linfea (a travesty role) in Cavalli's *La Calisto*. Cuénod's modesty and humour are inseparable from his distinction as an artist. He once joked that he was hired not because of the beauty of his voice but because of the strangeness of his repertoire. And, when asked about his extraordinary vocal longevity, Cuénod is said to have replied that he had never lost his voice because he had never had one to lose. This should be taken with a pinch of salt. In fact, his exquisitely light, dry tenor is perfectly suited to his catholic, but carefully chosen, repertoire. In later life, he gave master classes at the Britten-Pears school in Aldeburgh and elsewhere. He encouraged his students not to concentrate overmuch on the physiology of singing but to acquire a broad general culture by visiting museums, art galleries, theatres and ballet, studying languages (he himself was almost equally fluent in German, Italian and English as in his native French), and reading widely – then, he said, they would have something to sing about. A superb sight-reader and an immaculate musician, Cuénod is a shining example of how much can be accomplished by intelligence, imagination, musicianship, and artistry in the absence of a voice of outstanding quality. He is one of the most fascinating singers on record – and entirely *sui generis*.

Joseph Schmidt (1904–42), an Austro-Hungarian-Romanian-Jewish tenor, is, in many ways, a tragic case. His diminutive stature (he was approximately four feet nine tall) precluded a stage career, and he died of a heart attack, aged only thirty-eight, while trying to escape the Nazis. Nevertheless, the career he did have was far from negligible. He was much in demand on radio, and he became a prolific – and very popular – recording artist. One can see why. The timbre of the voice is very attractive, despite a weak and breathy lower register. The middle register is adequately powerful and the top notes are brilliant and secure. His cantorial training gave him an excellent technique and unusual facility in *coloratura* (as happened with other Jewish tenors, notably Hermann Jadlowker, Jan Peerce and Richard Tucker). He is also a vividly communicative singer, whether in opera, operetta or song. Top C's, D flats and D naturals abound in his recorded output and are invariably dispatched with ease and *élan*. His operetta recordings may be mentioned in the same breath as those of Tauber, Patzak, Gedda and Wunderlich – a rare accolade. In opera, he possesses that delicate quality known as *morbidezza* (perhaps the nearest English equivalent is 'tenderness'): something he shares with Tito Schipa. In this, he is unique among tenors with cantorial training, most of whom are more notable for the fervour and fiercely petitionary power of their singing than for any gentler qualities: see what is said elsewhere about Jan Peerce and Richard Tucker, for example. In popular songs (such as '*Ein Lied geht um die Welt*') and some of the better-known *Lieder* (such as Schubert's '*Ständchen*'), he is superb. All his recordings are causes for gratitude and for poignant regret that he was denied the long, stellar career that he deserved. Lyric tenors who can survive comparison with the likes of Tauber, Schipa, Heddle Nash and Wunderlich, and emerge not only unscathed, but with distinction, are rare. Schmidt is certainly one of them.

The American-Jewish tenor, **Jan Peerce** (1904–84), began as a radio performer singing popular songs and numbers from the musicals. He struggled to establish himself against strong competition at the New York Metropolitan until he came to the attention of Toscanini, whose advocacy made his career, especially as a recording artist. He sang in the maestro's recordings of *Fidelio*, *Traviata*, *Ballo in Maschera* and *La Bohème* as well as in Act Four of *Rigoletto* and in Beethoven's Choral Symphony. He also sang in a complete *Rigoletto* under the baton of Renato Cellini and in a *Carmen* conducted by Fritz Reiner. There were other recordings too, including a *Lucia di Lammermoor* and, surprisingly, an *Ariadne auf Naxos*, an opera which generally attracts more heroic tenors. Later in his career, he reverted to popular music, singing Tevye in *Fiddler on the Roof* on Broadway with great success. He was also a prolific recorder of *chazzanut* – Jewish cantorial music. Peerce's voice is a sturdy, virile lyric tenor, not notable for any romantic quality or for sensuous beauty of tone, but having many of the virtues, as well as the drawbacks, rightly ascribed by John Steane to Peerce's brother-in-law, Richard Tucker (*q.v.*). He is a fine musician with an excellent rhythmic sense, a good line, and the ability to shape a phrase suavely and elegantly: qualities which doubtless helped to endear him to Toscanini and which stand him in good stead in his operatic performances. Everything is done with a high degree of professionalism. The technique is sound and the upper register strong and secure up to a splendid top C. In terms of phrasing, virility of sound, and musical discipline, one can see that he shared qualities with Pertile, who had been Toscanini's tenor of choice at La Scala, just as Peerce was in the NBC recording studio. He is a stylish, strong-voiced and accomplished lyric tenor who has often been given less credit than he deserves. Steane, for example, sums up Peerce's recordings as 'unloveable marvels', though he grants them certain virtues, praising the tenor's intensity and devotion to the score, but noting a certain nasality of tone. This, though as ever a defensible view, seems (unusually for Steane) slightly ungenerous. Peerce's combination of rhythmic accuracy, tonal virility, technical proficiency, physical energy, and interpretative vitality, seems to call for more gratitude than this. His voice may be less glamorous, less powerful, and less sensuously beautiful than that of his brother-in-law, Richard Tucker, but his phrasing is commonly smoother, broader and more imaginative. His interpretations of the Italian lyric repertoire strike this listener as more idiomatic than Tucker's, though it must be admitted that Tucker sings the French language better, and seems more at home in the French repertoire and its characteristic musical idiom than Peerce does.

Peerce made complete recordings of *Rigoletto*, *La Traviata*, *Un Ballo in Maschera*, *La Bohème*, *Fidelio*, *Lucia di Lammermoor*, *Ariadne auf Naxos*, and *Carmen*.

The Chilean baritone-turned-tenor-turned-baritone **Ramòn Vinay** (1911–96) had a chequered career. His enormous voice clearly had a hybrid quality, not unambiguously either tenor or baritone, but, in range and timbre, partaking of some of the qualities of each. Like Slezak and Melchior, he was a big man, six foot two tall and weighing 220 lbs (fifteen stone ten pounds). For the twenty or so years of his tenorial career, he was ideally suited both physically and vocally to the repertoire of the true *tenore di forza*: the Wagner roles, Otello, Radames, Samson, Canio and Don Jose. Of these, he is chiefly associated with the title role of *Otello*, partly because the celebrated 1947 Toscanini broadcast of the opera gave him his one and only studio recording, and partly because there are several other pirate recordings in which he is equally splendid in the role. Bergonzi considered him the only tenor who had the right colours in his voice for Otello, and one can see why.

To a greater extent than anyone else, Vinay captures all the facets of the role, thrilling in the *Esultate*, commanding in '*Abbasso le spade*', tender in the love duet, stupendous in the duet with Iago, and terrifying in his Act Three recriminations. His death scene is also among the best on record, restrained, noble and deeply moving. In the light of all this, it is difficult to make sense of the comments in the old *Record Guide* (1951–55) by Desmond Shawe-Taylor and Edward Sackville-West to the effect that Vinay lacked the heroic ring proper to a great Otello, or that he had 'far less vocal equipment' than his only contemporary rival in the role, Mario del Monaco. He was a superb actor, vocally and physically, and this too contributed to the unforgettable effect he made in the great heroic roles, especially Otello. The voice itself is a remarkable instrument, very dark in colour (his is one of the few recordings of *Otello* where the protagonist is actually darker-voiced than the Iago, Giuseppe Valdengo) and immensely powerful. But one can see why he didn't have the high notes for long. A vocal method which carries the baritone fullness up to a top B is too prodigal to last. The tenor top notes need a narrower, more focused sound, if they are to endure. Melchior was criticized by some, notably Walter Legge, for 'xylophonic' top notes early in his career as a tenor, but this was precisely because he recognized the need to produce a narrower sound in the upper reaches of the voice than in the middle. Later he was able to integrate and equalize the registers more successfully. Vinay's failure to achieve this ultimately cost him his career as a tenor. In 1962, he reverted to baritone, singing Telramund, Iago, and Falstaff, among other roles, but with limited success. He retired from singing in 1969.

Vinay's only complete studio recording (but a magnificent one) is the 1947 *Otello* under Toscanini. There are also pirate recordings of the same opera conducted by Busch, Furtwängler, Cleva, Beecham and Kubelik, as well as pirates of *Carmen*, *Pagliacci*,

Samson et Dalila, and several Wagner operas. He is most successful as Otello and in the Wagnerian *Fach*. In other Italian and French roles, the huge, dark voice lacks the necessary plasticity in phrasing and dynamics: it can seem awkward and musclebound.

Richard Lewis (1914–90), who was born in Manchester of Welsh parents, was the foremost British lyric tenor of his day, the successor to Heddle Nash. Like Nash, he sang Italian and French lyric roles, including Pinkerton, Rodolfo and Don Jose, but, unlike Nash, he quickly dropped them from his repertoire, feeling that they were best left to tenors with a more naturally Latinate sound. His core repertoire consisted of Mozart and Baroque roles, which he sang extensively at Glyndebourne and the Royal Opera House, Covent Garden, and modern roles, such as those in operas by Schönberg, Walton, Britten and Tippett. He was also a masterly interpreter of Elgar's *Gerontius*, a role he recorded twice, and of Mahler's *Das Lied von der Erde*, which he recorded no fewer than four times. The voice is a fine lyric tenor with a distinctive, rather melancholy quality, an easy upper register (ranging up to a top D natural), a sound technique, and sufficient power to tackle some dramatic repertoire, such as Walton's Troilus, Bacchus, Aegistheus, Florestan, Gerontius, Mark in *A Midsummer Marriage*, Waldemar in the *Gurre-Lieder* or Hermann in *The Queen of Spades*. In a BBC recording of Bizet's *The Fair Maid of Perth* under Beecham, he sings superbly, producing an effortless high C in the serenade, making one regret that he did not record more of the French lyric repertoire – roles such as Faust, Werther, Gerald in *Lakmé*, Nadir in *Les Pêcheurs de Perles* or Vincent in *Mireille* – to which his voice, with its naturally high placement and pure, slightly melancholy timbre, seems ideally suited. The Slavonic repertoire, too, would have suited him, one feels, and one can only imagine what he would have made of such roles as the Prince in *Rusalka* or Jenik in *The*

Bartered Bride. His repertoire included some unexpected roles: he
sang Paco in Falla's *La vida breve* opposite Victoria de los Angeles,
and Licinius in *La Vestale* opposite Kyra Vayne. He was a good
vocal actor and his Herod[9] in *Salome* is one of the best, despite the
fact that the role does not require anything in the way of vocal
beauty. He roughens his voice effectively, but one longs to hear him
in music where he does not have to. Fortunately, there is plenty on
disc to choose from. In a wide and varied repertoire encompassing
works as diverse as the Britten's *Spring Symphony*, Tippett's *A Child
of Our Time*, Gilbert and Sullivan operettas, Coleridge-Taylor's
Hiawatha's Wedding Feast, Mozart's *Idomeneo*, Monteverdi's
Incoronazione di Poppaea, Schönberg's *Gurre-Lieder*, Handel's
Messiah, Mendelssohn's *Elijah*, Brahms' *Liebeslieder-Walzer*,
Walton's *Troilus and Cressida*, Busoni's *Doktor Faust* (in which he
sings the cruelly high-lying role of Mephistopheles), and the works
by Elgar and Mahler already mentioned, he is magnificent, perhaps
even peerless. A burly six-footer, he also cut an impressive figure on
stage, making a suitably regal Idomeneo, an imposing Troilus, a
commanding Nero, and a physically menacing Peter Grimes. It is a
great pity that his Grimes and Captain Vere were not recorded.
What he did record enables one to say with absolute confidence
that, in purely vocal terms, he was the best British lyric tenor
between Heddle Nash and Stuart Burrows. Given that his rivals
included such fine tenors as Peter Pears, Walter Midgley and
Alexander Young, that is no small claim. Yet it can be
substantiated. His voice is more beautiful and more extensive in
upward range than Pears', richer and warmer in quality than
Midgley's, and more individual than Young's. Despite the (wholly
unjustified) complaints of die-hard 'golden agers' to which Steane
alludes in his *Singers of the Century*, he ranks with the best lyric
tenors on record.

Lewis made complete recordings of *L'Incoronazione di Poppaea*,

Idomeneo, Der Fliegende Holländer (as the Steersman), *Salome* (as Herod), *Hiawatha's Wedding Feast, Elijah, A Child of Our Time, Messiah, Gurrelieder, HMS Pinafore, The Mikado, The Pirates of Penzance, Trial by Jury, Yeomen of the Guard, The Gondoliers, Ruddigore, The Dream of Gerontius* (two), *Doktor Faust, The Fair Maid of Perth* (BBC radio recording, not released commercially), and Sir John Stainer's *The Crucifixion.*

Not even his most fervent admirers would claim that the American tenor, **James McCracken** (1926–88), was one of the most musical tenors on record. Like Jon Vickers, he was a heroic tenor; indeed they were rivals, especially in the role of Otello. They also shared several other roles: Florestan, Radames, Canio and Don Jose. Also like Vickers, he had a bull-like physique (he stood six feet tall and weighed a burly 250 lbs – nearly eighteen stone) and great physical strength. But there is very little vocal resemblance between them. McCracken has a bronze, baritonal timbre. He continues the tradition of dark-voiced heroic tenors, the tradition of Zanelli and Vinay which went on to include Hopf, Cossutta, Domingo, Galouzine and Cura. Vickers' huge voice, on the other hand, has a trumpet-toned, unmistakably tenorial timbre and colour. He belongs to the tradition of bright-voiced heroic tenors, the tradition of Tamagno and Zenatello which went on to include Pertile, Martinelli, del Monaco, Heppner, and Botha. McCracken's chief asset is neither tonal beauty nor musicality, but dramatic intensity. Indeed this can sometimes be carried too far: his Canio over-emotes embarrassingly and, despite his usual sincerity and commitment, is one of the worst on record. His Otello, greatly admired by many good judges, including the authors of the Penguin Guide and the late John Steane, is powerful and intense, but not always beautifully sung: he delivers the Act Three monologue '*Dio mi potevi scagliar*' with its repeated A flats in a *parlando* style which some will defend as a dramatically justifiable, if musically free, interpretation (analogous to, say, Alexander Kipnis's similarly free declamation in *Boris Godunov*), but others will criticize as an unwarrantable musical liberty. Also his exaggerated diction with its explosive consonants contrasts oddly with the impeccably liquid Italian of his Iago, Dietrich Fischer-Dieskau. Perhaps less controversial might be McCracken's performance in Meyerbeer's *Le Prophète*, where he sings in good French and employs a head voice to good effect. He also gives an exciting and suitably martial account of '*Roi des cieux*'. In his two other arias – '*Oui, pour Berthe moi je soupire*' and the '*Brindisi, Versez que tout respire*' – he makes a fine impression, singing more continently than usual, and all the better for it. His Don José, in Bernstein's recording opposite the feisty Carmen of Marilyn Horne, is also good. And he is one of the few tenors on record to have the full measure of the exacting part of Waldemar in Schönberg's *Gurre-Lieder*. It is unfortunate that he was not recorded in some of his best roles: Calaf, Manrico, Radames, Samson, or – his one and only Wagnerian role, of which he was said to have given a superlative account at the Met – Tannhäuser. But enough has been said to show that he was not the 'one-trick pony' that some claim. His comparatively early death, at a time when he was still singing well, was the result of a stroke.

McCracken's complete opera / song recordings are: *Otello*, *Pagliacci*, *Fidelio*, *Carmen*, *Le Prophète*, *Gurre-Lieder*.

The German lyric tenor, **Fritz Wunderlich** (1930–66), died at the age of thirty-five after a tragic accident. He and Gedda were the supreme Mozart tenors of their day,[10] and the supreme interpreters of Viennese operetta. But Wunderlich's repertoire also embraced lyric tenor roles in the French, Italian, German, Czech and Russian operatic *Fach*, *Lieder* and folksong, oratorios and liturgical works. He sang everything from Bach to Berg, and all of it superbly. The golden voice, unimpeachable technique, and flawless style whatever the repertoire, all made Wunderlich one of the greatest lyric tenors of the century. It is hard to over-praise his records, and harder still to withhold the highest praise from any of them. Whether he is singing Bach or Haydn, Verdi or Wagner, Strauss or Puccini, Schubert or Mahler, Wunderlich sings with a vivid imagination, keen intelligence, athletic vigour, clarity of diction, an alert sense of rhythm, beauty of tone, and impeccable taste. All of his recordings are desirable and many are indispensable. His Tamino is unsurpassed, as is his singing of the tenor solos in Bach's *St Matthew Passion*. His Jenik in Smetana's *The Bartered Bride*, Nemorino's cleverer Czech cousin, is not only beautifully sung, as one would expect, but also full of fun and humour, a delightful performance. His *Lieder* performances, which include two recordings of Schubert's *Die Schöne Müllerin* – one with Kurt-Heinz Stolze and one with Hubert Giesen – and the Klemperer version of Mahler's *Das Lied von der Erde*, in which he partners Christa Ludwig, are full of interest: rarely can these songs have been sung by a voice of such gorgeous quality. Like Tauber and Gedda, he brings to Viennese operetta the same musicianship and refinement that he lavishes on Mozart. Had he lived longer, he might well have grown into a more dramatic repertoire and become a successor not only to Tauber, but to Björling. Despite his prodigious talent and many accomplishments, Wunderlich remained a humble, unaffected man who described himself as a student and eagerly seized every opportunity to learn from the experience of colleagues. It may well be that his natural modesty and simplicity of nature were the greatest of all his gifts, since they enabled him to make the most of all the others in the short time that was granted him.

Wunderlich's complete opera / oratorio recordings include: *St Matthew Passion, Die Schöpfung, Die Zauberflöte, The Bartered Bride*.

The Welsh tenor, **Stuart Burrows** (born 1933), succeeded Wunderlich in the Mozart roles, his Tamino being one of the very few to bear comparison with his predecessor's magisterial performance. But there is more to Burrows than this. His operatic repertoire on disc includes Hoffmann, Leicester in *Maria Stuarda*, Percy in *Anna Bolena*, and Faust in Berlioz's *La Damnation de Faust*, as well as several Mozart roles: and in all of these, he sings lyrically and stylishly. He has also almost single-handedly attempted to rehabilitate the Victorian drawing-room ballad. (Robert Tear (*q.v.*) also recorded some of these with the baritone Benjamin Luxon, but his approach was decidedly tongue-in-cheek, whereas Burrows sings them 'straight'). His unaffected and direct yet sensitively sung versions of such songs as '*Macushla*', 'Bonnie Mary of Argyll', 'The Rose of Tralee' and 'I Hear You Calling Me' are comparable to versions by such distinguished competitors as McCormack and Heddle Nash. John Steane's point that Burrows' expressive range is somewhat limited – that he lacks, in Steane's words, 'the Geddan art of smiling with the voice' – is well made, but, within those limits, Burrows' singing is by no means inexpressive or lacking in charm. *Fioriture* are executed with great skill – for once they really sound like 'flowerings' of the vocal line that emerge from it, and are sung, naturally, rather than being grafted on and carefully negotiated by the singer. In this respect, he is more accomplished even than Nash. Listen, for example, to Burrows' turn on the word 'Eden' in 'Bonnie Mary of Argyll' and compare Nash's (or, surprisingly, even McCormack's) less fluent delivery of the same ornament. And, astonishingly, at Solti's slow tempo, he not only sings the long central run in '*Il mio tesoro*' fluently and in a single breath, but also phrases smoothly over into the recapitulation: a feat otherwise unexampled. In *Idomeneo* at Covent Garden, he showed his command of coloratura by singing the longer (and more demanding) version of '*Fuor del mar*' and giving a bravura performance. The voice is darker and richer than that of many light tenors. It is of unfailingly beautiful quality, and he has a wider palette of colours at his disposal than many of his rivals. The upward range in full voice was somewhat short – at Covent Garden, he sang the high C in Faust's '*Salut, demeure*' in a *voix mixte*, rather than producing the usual stentorian *ut de poitrine*. This seemed to me entirely acceptable (after all, the great French tenor Georges Thill did the same in his recording), though not all critics agreed. Burrows' reputation has probably suffered for his devotion to Victorian drawing-room ballads (which tend to be despised by highbrows) rather than *Lieder* and art song, but he remains one of the best British lyric tenors – and one of the most accomplished Mozarteans – on record.

Burrow's complete opera recordings include: *Die Entführung aus dem Serail, Die Zauberflöte, Don Giovanni, La Clemenza di Tito, Anna Bolena, Maria Stuarda, Les Contes d'Hoffmann, La Damnation de Faust, Eugene Onegin, A Midsummer Marriage* (as Jack). His other recordings include Handel's *Messiah*, Beethoven's Choral Symphony, and Mahler's *Das Klagende Lied*, as well as several discs of drawing-room ballads and other popular songs.

Franco Bonisolli (1937–2003) was the leading Italian high heroic tenor after Franco Corelli. Somewhat improbably, this very tall (he was well over six feet in height) and athletically built man, who later achieved deserved renown in a similar repertoire to Lauri-Volpi, Filippeschi, and Corelli, began his career as a light-lyric tenor. His Metropolitan debut was as Count Almaviva in *Barbiere di Siviglia*, and his other roles at this stage included Nemorino, Alfredo and Pinkerton. But he soon began to assume heavier roles, and the parts with which he was chiefly associated later in his career included Manrico, Arnoldo, Carlo in *I Masnadieri*, Don Jose, Radames, Otello, and Calaf. Bonisolli made few studio recordings: apart from a Decca recording of *I Masnadieri* and an EMI version of *Il Trova-*

tore, there are recordings of *Rigoletto*, *La Traviata* and *Tosca*, and of Leoncavallo's *La Bohème*. And these are the only studio recordings of complete operas he made. In part, the reason might be his well-founded reputation for eccentric and undisciplined behaviour. He was cruelly nicknamed *il pazzo* – the madman – and the nickname stuck, doing nothing to enhance his prospects of employment by either record companies or opera houses. But even the meagre evidence available confirms that Bonisolli fully deserves his place among the great Italian tenors. The voice is remarkable, darkly baritonal and weighty but with an astonishing upward extension to a top D natural, a note which he displays and sustains to stunning effect in a studio recording of *Rigoletto* and in a live performance of *I Vespri Siciliani*. The voice is unremarkable for beauty of tone compared with many of the other tenors we have considered, but it is undeniably exciting, and the top notes have a cavernous quality which is reminiscent of Corelli. His Carlo in *Masnadieri* is stylish, romantic and virile, less elegant than Bergonzi's, but highly impressive, and replete with interpolated high C's and D flats of a clarion force and brilliance quite beyond Bergonzi's, or most tenors', resources. His Manrico is among the best on disc and certainly one of the most exciting, ranking in this respect with del Monaco and Corelli, even if he cannot quite match them in terms of vocal timbre. However, Bonisolli's performance is more musical and stylishly sung than theirs. Needless to say, the top C's are superb.

Bonisolli's complete opera recordings are: *I Masnadieri*, *Rigoletto*, *Il Trovatore*, *La Traviata*, *Tosca*, *La Bohème* (Leoncavallo).

The Welshman, **Robert Tear** (1939–2011), earns a place in this essay by virtue of his prodigious versatility as much as anything else. His operatic repertoire includes both principal roles, ranging from Jupiter in Handel's *Semele* to Lensky in *Eugene Onegin* to the title role in Vaughan Williams' *Hugh the Drover* to Aschenbach in *Death in Venice* to Dov in *The Knot Garden*, and character roles as varied as Basilio in *Nozze di Figaro*, Pitichinaccio in *Les Contes d'Hoffmann*, Edmondo in *Manon Lescaut* and Loge in *Das Rheingold*. In the concert repertoire, he has recorded songs and song cycles by Schubert, Chopin, Rachmaninov, Jánàček, Parry, Vaughan Williams, Finzi, Butterworth, Copland, Britten and Tippett. His enormous discography (which amounts to some 250 recordings) also includes cantatas, oratorios and liturgical works by Monteverdi, Bach, Handel, Haydn, Mozart, Mendelssohn, Berlioz, Bruckner, Elgar, Dyson, Britten and Tippett, and many operas by British composers including Delius, Holst, Vaughan Williams, Tippett and Britten. From the point of view of sheer beauty of tone, it must be admitted that Tear's voice is not especially ingratiating. He is, in many ways, untypical of the Welsh tenor tradition, which includes such fine singers as Ben Davies, Dan Beddoe, Evan Williams, Edward Lloyd, Tudor Davies, Parry Jones, David Lloyd, Edgar Evans, Stuart Burrows, Kenneth Bowen, Arthur Davies, Dennis O'Neill, Geraint Dodd and Rhys Meirion. Tear strikes one as perhaps more representative of the typical English tenor. Indeed, in a Decca recording of Britten's *The Prodigal Son* he appears with Peter Pears, and strikingly resembles the older tenor in tonal quality: the timbre is somewhat reedy and the high notes, though stronger than those of Pears, lack ring. But he is a subtle and sensitive interpreter, good at languages (at least phonetically: he sings Rachmaninov in what sounds like idiomatic Russian and Chopin in Polish), and with a complete command of a considerable range of musical styles. His technical skill is in evidence in his fine account of Britten's Serenade for Tenor, Horn and Strings where the melismatic vocal line is sung with accuracy and assurance, and in the confident way he handles the hair-raising challenges of the Monteverdi Vespers or the role of the Evangelist in Bach's *St*

Matthew Passion. He began his career as a member of the Deller Consort, where he gained experience of the early music repertoire which stood him in good stead. At the other end of the chronological continuum, he has mastered many difficult modern scores, notably the late works of Michael Tippett. Like Ian Bostridge (*q.v.*), he is a published author with two books to his credit: *Tear Here* and *Singer, Beware*, a pair of idiosyncratic but intelligent and insightful books about singing and the singer's life. Tear is one of the most musicianly and intelligent singers on record.

Tear's extensive discography includes some works in which he sings *comprimario* roles, e.g. Edmondo in *Manon Lescaut*. The recordings in which he features more prominently include: *Fennimore and Gerda, A Village Romeo and Juliet, Hugh the Drover, The Canterbury Pilgrims, The War Requiem, The Dream of Gerontius, St Matthew Passion, Béatrice et Bénédict, The Creation, Messiah, The Knot Garden, The Mask of Time, The Turn of the Screw, The Prodigal Son, The Wandering Scholar, The Cunning Little Vixen*, and the Monteverdi Vespers.

Another musicianly and highly intelligent singer is the English tenor, **Philip Langridge** (1939–2010). Langridge's repertoire is similar to Tear's in both its breadth and its content, although, where Tear is especially associated with the works of Michael Tippett, Langridge has been chiefly associated with those of Harrison Birtwistle. Both are fine interpreters of Britten. Both are physically wiry and good actors. Both have an excellent phonetic command of other languages. Both are equally distinguished in the operatic and the concert repertoire. Both have a first-rate vocal technique. Langridge has the more beautiful voice. Indeed, he represents an English tenorial tradition which includes in modern times such distinguished artists as Eric Greene, René Soames, Peter Pears, Richard Lewis, Alexander Young, Ian Partridge, Ian

Bostridge, Anthony Rolfe Johnson, Martyn Hill, Neil Jenkins, Nigel Douglas, Adrian Thompson, John Mark Ainsley, James Gilchrist, Mark Padmore, Andrew Kennedy and Toby Spence.[11] These tenors have much in common in terms of range, timbre, colour, vocal type, and repertoire. If Langridge has been chosen in preference to many of the others, it is because he is the most versatile and has probably the most extensive discography. He exemplifies all that is best in the English tenor tradition. He has recorded songs by Schubert, Dowland, Dvořàk, Jánàček, Holst, Britten and Maw, among others. His operatic roles range from the title role in Mozart's *Idomeneo* to Shuisky in *Boris Godunov* to Rossini's *Otello* to Loge in *Das Rheingold* to the Witch in *Hänsel und Gretel* to many of the Britten tenor roles and several in operas by Birtwistle. His vast concert repertoire includes *Lieder* and art songs, liturgical works, Handel's *Messiah*, Elgar's *The Dream of Gerontius* and Britten's *War Requiem*. To everything he sings, he brings the same total commitment, tireless energy, good taste, technical excellence, interpretative skill, and an exceptionally high degree of musical and dramatic intelligence. The voice is a typically English lyric tenor. Langridge himself has said that he considers his voice similar in colour and weight to that of Richard Lewis (although he modestly added that Lewis's voice was more beautiful), and that, when offered a new role, he considers whether or not it would have been suitable for Lewis before deciding whether to accept it (Pavarotti used Björling as his standard for the same purpose). It is worth adding that, although his voice was not large, it was projected with such clarity and consummate skill that, even in the vast spaces and unhelpful acoustics of the London Coliseum, where many singers with much larger voices struggle to make themselves heard, his every word was audible in such demanding roles as Captain Vere in *Billy Budd* and the title roles in *Peter Grimes* and Stravinsky's *Oedipus Rex*.

Langridge's complete opera / oratorio recordings include: *The Turn of the Screw*, *Peter Grimes*, *The Dream of Gerontius*, *Boris Godunov*, *Messiah*, *Punch and Judy*, *Gurre-Lieder*, *At The Boar's Head*.

The Canadian tenor, **Ben Heppner** (born 1956), has made a name for himself chiefly as a Wagnerian, although his repertoire also includes such non-Wagnerian roles as Otello, Calaf, Énée, the Prince in Dvořák's *Rusalka*, Peter Grimes and Andrea Chenier. His discography, which is less extensive than one might wish, includes a disc of arias from the French heroic operatic repertoire, which he sings more lyrically and romantically than anyone since Georges Thill. Unlike predecessors such as Melchior, his voice has nothing of the baritone about it. It is a pure lyric tenor which has gradually developed heroic size and strength without losing any of its lyric quality. Heppner's stamina is also equal to the demands of the heroic tenor *Fach*, even roles such as Tristan and Otello. He is a musical singer and a vivid interpreter whose recordings consistently give pleasure and offer one the rare experience of hearing a genuinely beautiful voice in roles where tonal beauty has often seemed to be the last consideration. By alternating between Italian / French roles and Wagner, Heppner has made the transition to *Heldentenor* without losing his lyrical qualities or his top notes, which remain clear, unforced and brilliant. Like Leo Slezak, Lauritz Melchior, Johan Botha (*qq.v.*), William Cochran and several other *Heldentenors*, he has a massive physique which, while it may undermine dramatic credibility in romantic roles, probably helps to provide the necessary power and stamina to sustain his very demanding repertoire. He comes nearer to fulfilling the Herculean demands of the role of Énée in *Les Troyens* than anyone else on disc (Vickers' towering 1969 performance, which, like Heppner's is conducted by Colin Davis, is slightly marred by his lack of a sensuously beautiful tone). Wagnerian roles such as Walther, Lohengrin, and Tristan can rarely have been more beautifully sung than they are by Heppner at his best. In April 2014, he announced his retirement from singing, citing the difficulty of maintaining a satisfactory standard of singing, and occasional vocal unreliability, as his reasons.

Heppner's recordings include *Oberon*, *Rusalka*, *Die Meistersinger von Nürnberg* (two), *Der Fliegende Holländer*, *Lohengrin*, *Turandot*, *Les Troyens*, *Hérodiade*, *Fidelio*, *Die Frau ohne Schatten* and *Ariadne auf Naxos*. His other recordings include Beethoven's Choral Symphony, Mahler's Symphony Number 8 and *Das Lied von der Erde*, and Schönberg's *Gurre-Lieder*.

The Argentinian tenor, **Jose Cura** (born 1962), is a dark-voiced heroic tenor whose repertoire is similar to Mario del Monaco's in years gone by – that is, it embraces the Italian and French heroic roles but excludes the German and Slavonic. Cura's reputation rests on such roles as Canio, Otello, Radames, Cavaradossi, Calaf, Samson and Don Jose. Vocally he resembles Zanelli or Vinay, though his voice is probably less massive than theirs. However, it is large enough to do justice to his chosen repertoire, as his recordings amply confirm, and his upper register is probably more extensive and more secure than his Chilean predecessors', both of whom started as baritones and neither of whom would have cared, at any stage of his career, to undertake the high-lying role of Calaf. He has also sung Manrico – again not a role that lower-voiced tenors care to tackle, not on account of its general *tessitura*, but because of the two top C's in '*Di quella pira*'. Cura's recordings of the roles of Samson and Canio rank with the best on disc. In the former, this powerfully built sometime rugby player is one of the very few tenors in history who actually looks the part. His recital disc of Puccini arias contains some surprises. '*Nessun dorma*' is disappointing, interpretatively dull and with a persistent tendency to attack notes from below. Also, the aria seems to call for a more brilliant voice with a brighter colour and more penetrative sound. The well-known arias from *Bohème*, *Tosca* and *Madama Butterfly*, though strongly sung, are not especially individual. The surprises come in the less familiar items. He scales down his big voice very effectively for two arias from *La Rondine*, which he sings with elegance, tenderness and charm, and the high *tessitura* of Rinuccio's '*Firenze è come un albero fiorito*' from *Gianni Schicchi* seems to hold no terrors for him – and here, again, his singing is lyrical and stylish. Best of all are the two arias from *Il Tabarro*, which are given fiery and passionate readings of great power, intensity and conviction. In this music, he appears a worthy successor to del Monaco and Domingo.

Cura's only complete opera recordings made in the studio (both highly regarded) are *Samson et Dalila* and *Pagliacci*. He can also be seen and heard to advantage in DVDs of *Otello*.

The Franco-Sicilian tenor, **Roberto Alagna** (born 1963), is one of the most exciting lyric tenors to have emerged in the period since the dominance of the 'Three Tenors'. Though his repertoire overlaps with that of Juan Diego Flórez (*q.v.*), his voice is heavier, with a *spinto* capacity. His numerous recital discs for EMI and Deutsche Grammophon and his complete opera recordings (he may well prove to be the last great tenor to make a respectable number of studio recordings of complete operas, thus ending a line which began with Gigli and Pertile) give a fair conspectus of his art. The voice is a lyric tenor of excellent quality, slightly dry (in the French manner) compared with Carreras or di Stefano, for instance, but technically superior to either. He sings within his means, never forcing his voice. Breath control is exceptional, as is shown by his recording of '*Celeste Aida*', where the phrasing has a breadth Martinelli might have envied. Also exceptional is his ability to float high notes in the head voice: his top C at the end of a fine version of Nadir's '*Je crois entendre encore*' and the top D flat in a rare French version of Donizetti's '*Un ange, une femme inconnue*' from *La Favorite* are examples of this. The range is extensive, reaching a stunning top E flat in his recording of *Lucie de Lammermoor*, the French version of Donizetti's opera. Elsewhere he proves capable of ringing top D's and D flats. On the DG recordings, the voice sounds warmer, fuller and more rounded than it does in EMI's drier acoustic. The DG recital discs devoted to *bel canto* and *verismo* arias respectively both show the voice at its most attractive and suggest a depth to his artistry not always apparent in the earlier EMI discs. They also show a greater dynamic variety, exemplified by a melting, almost Gigli-like *mezza voce* and a willingness to sing *piano* (or even *pianissimo*) and to execute perfect *diminuendos*, none of which was a conspicuous feature of his earlier recitals for EMI. His complete opera recordings compare favourably with the competition – and it must be remembered that the competition, especially in the standard repertoire, has been getting steadily stiffer. All of his French opera recordings are superb. French is Alagna's first language and no one since the heyday of Vanzo, Lance and Gedda has sung and pronounced French so well. In Italian opera, he is especially good as Nemorino, a role he has recorded twice. He is also a fine Rodolfo in *Bohème* and a stylish Ruggiero in *La Rondine*. In recent years, he has undertaken heavier roles such as Manrico, Radames and Canio, with considerable success, albeit inevitably with a loss of some of the lyric grace and refinement of his earlier recordings. His approach to the more dramatic repertoire appears to be modelled on that of Jussi Björling – sensibly so, since their voices are similar in colour, weight, and power.

Alagna's complete opera recordings include: *Elisir d'Amore* (two), *La Bohème, Tosca, La Rondine, Lucie di Lammermoor, Don*

Carlo, *Rigoletto*, *La Traviata*, *Il Trovatore*, *Aida*, Verdi's Requiem (Verdi), *Werther, Manon, Carmen, Roméo et Juliette, Les Contes d'Hoffmann*. There are also several DVDs of 'live' performances.

The English tenor, **Ian Bostridge** (born 1964) is another in the long line of outstanding English lyric tenors which stretches back as far as Gervase Elwes. Like others in this line, Bostridge sings a varied repertoire comprising opera (Baroque, classical and modern), and concert works (songs, song cycles, cantatas, oratorios and liturgical compositions), ranging from early to contemporary music. Steane suggests that what makes Bostridge stand out in a distinguished company is the vividness with which he presents the *ich*, the self or narrator's voice at the heart of so many *Lieder* and song cycles, perhaps especially those by Schubert. It is no accident that Bostridge is a particularly fine interpreter of *Die Schöne Müllerin* and *Winterreise*, two song cycles in which the personality of the narrator is essential to the interpretation of the songs. But Bostridge's art has developed over the years in both depth and variety. He was always a good Peter Quint, but now he has added Captain Vere and Aschenbach to his Britten roles. He has also sung roles in operas by Monteverdi, Purcell, Handel, Mozart, Smetana and Stravinsky. His height (six foot three and half inches) and slim physique give him a certain credibility and presence on stage or concert platform. He was a fine Tamino in the English National Opera's production of *The Magic Flute* (the slender, silvery sound carrying, without apparent effort, to the further reaches of the London Coliseum) and has also proved highly successful in the title role of *Idomeneo*, and as Belmonte in *Die Entführung aus dem Serail*, Tom Rakewell in Stravinsky's *The Rake's Progress*, and Lysander in Britten's *A Midsummer Night's Dream*. Conspicuously absent from his repertoire, as from that of most other members of the English lyric tenor line, with the prominent exceptions of

Heddle Nash and (to a lesser extent) Richard Lewis, are nineteenth-century French and Italian opera. He feels, probably rightly, that the timbre of his voice is ill-suited to the demands of the Romantic French and Italian operatic repertoire. In song, he has tackled, in addition to *Lieder* by Schubert, Schumann and Wolf, the complete range of English song from the Elizabethans to the moderns (including Noël Coward), and songs by Jánàček and Henze. His concert repertoire also includes the part of the Evangelist in the Bach Passions, cantatas by Bach and Handel, the Britten Canticles, and the part of Uriel in Haydn's *The Creation*. He is also a published writer: his critical and autobiographical work, *A Singer's Notebook*, published by Faber & Faber in September 2011, is a rare, perhaps even unique, example of a genuinely scholarly and luminously intelligent collection of essays of cultural exegesis by a tenor. And his book on Schubert's *Winterreise*, entitled *Schubert's Winter Journey: Anatomy of an Obsession*, is outstanding – lucid, insightful, culturally informed. In all his recordings and performances, he displays a light-lyric tenor voice of silvery beauty and tonal purity, a penetrating intellect, breadth of culture, unmistakable evidence of assiduous preparation, and innate musicality. He is often referred to as the successor to Peter Pears. Despite some similarities in outlook and repertoire, this is misleading. Vocally, Robert Tear was closer to Pears. So, arguably, were Philip Langridge and Anthony Rolfe Johnson. Bostridge's voice is more tonally beautiful than Pears' ever was. It also sounds younger; and perhaps for that reason, one can't quite imagine Bostridge ever making a convincing Peter Grimes. He is rather the successor to Ian Partridge, with a less rounded and beautiful voice, but a more extensive and varied operatic repertoire.

The South African *Heldentenor*, **Johan Botha** (1965–2016), like Ben Heppner, his Canadian counterpart, was physically enormous, reputedly weighing around 400 pounds (twenty-eight and a half stone). This was a disadvantage in dramatic terms, though not as great a one as might be thought, for Botha was a surprisingly agile figure on stage. In a 2009 *Lohengrin* at Covent Garden, he moved well during the swordfight and, in a flowing robe which disguised his bulk, made a dramatically convincing hero. As for the voice, this was quite simply the Lohengrin of one's dreams: a bright, gleaming blade of a tenor, secure throughout its range, hitting every note in the middle, never sliding or lifting, never sounding fatigued, of ample power and of really beautiful quality. It was also capable of dynamic variety, and his *piano* singing was well supported and tonally beautiful. The studio recording and his recital disc of Wagner excerpts confirm the impression, as does a BBC recording of Mahler's *Das Lied von der Erde*: here is a truly outstanding *Heldentenor*, and one gifted with interpretative intelligence as well. Like Heppner, he graduated from lyric to heroic roles and, also like Heppner, he was able to make the transition to the Wagnerian *Fach* without abandoning his roles in the Italian repertoire. A further resemblance to the Canadian tenor is that Botha's voice, too, has nothing of the baritone in its timbre: it is a pure, bright-toned tenor, which is surprising, as he began his career as a bass-baritone. He continued to sing such parts as Calaf, Chenier, and Otello alongside his Wagnerian roles. In 2015, he sang a superb Tannhäuser at the Met. A deeply religious man, he brought a spiritual intensity to his portrayals which recalled Jon Vickers. He considered adding Tristan to his repertoire, while conceding that, were he to do so, he would have to sacrifice Lohengrin and his Italian roles, which lie much higher in the voice. Notwithstanding such variously gifted Wagnerian singers as Hans Hopf, Set Svanholm, Hans Beirer, Ludwig Suthaus, Wolfgang Windgassen, Jess Thomas, Karl Liebl, Ernst Kozub, Fritz Uhl, René Kollo, Jon Vickers, James King, Klaus König, Alberto Remedios, Siegfried Jerusalem, Peter Hofmann,

John Mitchinson, John Treleaven, Ian Storey and Peter Seiffert, Botha and Heppner were the most exciting new arrivals among *Heldentenors* since the heyday of Lorenz, Völker, Widdop and Melchior. Their voices were exceptionally beautiful and technically secure, and they sang better than any of their contemporary rivals. Tragically, this gifted tenor died of liver cancer at the early age of fifty-one.

The German *lirico spinto* tenor, **Jonas Kaufmann** (born 1969), slim and athletic-looking, is possibly the handsomest tenor since Franco Corelli. Indeed, he cites Corelli and Wunderlich – a rather improbable combination – as the chief influences on his art and career. Kaufmann is also a good actor and a highly intelligent singer with a fine voice, a virtually accent-free command of several languages, and an unusually wide repertoire which ranges across German, French and Italian roles and embraces *Lieder*. His most recent recordings include much-lauded, if somewhat unorthodox, versions of Schubert's *Die Schöne Müllerin* and *Winterreise*: one does not normally associate *Lieder* with his type of voice. He has also released a disc of romantic arias, from Weber's '*Durch die Wälder, durch die Auen*' to Verdi's '*Io la vidi*' and Bizet's '*La fleur que tu m'avais jetée*'. The voice has a hint of baritone in the timbre and enough power to do justice to the *spinto* repertoire without sacrificing his lyric roles. The range extends to a good top C, yet is solid enough in the lower and middle parts register to suggest that he will one day become a fine exponent of the *junger Held* Wagnerian roles, such as Lohengrin and Walther. He has also recently – and perhaps surprisingly – undertaken the low-lying *Heldentenor* role of Siegmund in *Die Walküre* and the all-but-impossible role of Énée in *Les Troyens*[12] with success. Whether he will be able to venture any further into this very demanding repertoire and retain the essentially lyrical quality of his voice and his range into the high notes above B flat, remains to be seen. For the time being, he is one of the few tenors in history who have managed to be equally effective in both Verdi and Wagner roles at the same time. (Several tenors have graduated from Verdi to Wagner as their voices grew darker and larger, but most dropped their Verdi roles when they did so). Unafraid of controversy, he has also become the first tenor to record (and record very well) Wagner's *Wesendonck Lieder*, a work more generally associated with the soprano voice. His recent recording of Radames in *Aida* was a revelation: unusually, '*Celeste Aida*' was really sung and phrased as a love song, and the final top B flat, customarily belted out at a solid *fortissimo*, was sung *pianissimo e morendo*, as marked in the score. This is one of the rare occasions when a tenor succeeds in making the listener hear an old warhorse as if for the first time. Recently he has sung the title role in *Andrea Chenier* with great success at Covent Garden, and announced that he intends to concentrate on Italian and French roles for the foreseeable future. This is welcome news, as that decision will probably prolong his career. However, it must be admitted that his voice, though beautiful and individual in timbre, lacks something in terms of sheer tonal glamour, when judged by the highest standards – in comparison with, say, Björling, Pavarotti, Domingo, or the young José Carreras.

The Mexican-born French-naturalized (since 2007) tenor, **Rolando Villazón** (born 1972) is one of the most gifted, but also one of the most controversial, artists in opera today. As to the gifts, he has a *lirico spinto* tenor, predominantly dark in colour, sufficient but not overwhelming in power, with ringing top notes which extend up to a good high C. As to the controversy, he has recently been plagued by vocal problems which he has blamed on a congenital cyst on his vocal cords, but which some others have attributed to a defective technique. The latter claim seems doubtful. At the outset of his career, Villazón impressed Plácido Domingo, no less, who knows a thing or two about vocal technique; and it is not obvious, as it was with di Stefano, for example, that his technique is deficient in any way. It may be the case that he forces his voice, as José Carreras did his, by using too much breath and pushing for more volume than it naturally possesses, and that this has caused the vocal difficulties he has experienced. For the present, the jury is out, and only time will tell. As to the timbre, several listeners have noted a similarity to Domingo, although Villazón's voice is neither as rich nor as powerful as Domingo's. In his early recital discs, we heard not only a beautiful voice but also an intelligent interpreter, willing to sing quietly when the occasion demanded it, and able to execute a melting *diminuendo*. He even attempted the difficult feat of the *messa di voce*, and nearly brought it off. His interpretations of French and Italian arias were impassioned in the Latin manner, but also musical and imaginative. They had that elusive, but instantly recognizable, quality – a sort of vocal charisma – that characterizes the greatest singers and separates them from the rest. Sadly, those good impressions have not been confirmed by Villazón's more recent appearances. At a 2012 gala at the Royal Opera House, Covent Garden, given in honour of Plácido Domingo, he gave a disappointingly loud and monochromatic rendition of '*La Légende de Kleinzach*' from Offenbach's *Contes d'Hoffmann*. His voice seemed to have lost much of its early bloom and tonal variety, and the singing was dull, coarse and unstylish. His previously excellent diction, too, seemed to have suffered, for the vowels, especially the French diphthongs, had become indistinct and undifferentiated. Whatever the cause of his current vocal problems, it is to be hoped that he will soon recover the vocal form of his early career. Recent portents are not encouraging, however.

The last entry in our cavalcade of tenors is the Maltese tenor, **Joseph Calleja** (born 1978). Calleja has the most arrestingly beautiful lyric tenor voice since the young José Carreras first appeared on the scene in the mid-1970s. To judge from his tall, broad-shouldered physique, it seems likely that, in the fullness of time and provided he chooses his repertoire carefully, Calleja will develop into a *lirico spinto* tenor with dramatic possibilities. That is to say, he will one day be able to sing roles such as Ernani, Manrico, Alvaro, Radames, Calaf, Canio, and perhaps even Otello. For the present, we have an outstanding lyric tenor with a big, generous sound and golden tone, ideal for the more lyrical Verdi and Puccini roles and for the French lyric repertoire. He is a good linguist and has stage presence and a pleasing personality. It is too soon to say whether he will develop into an interpreter of the calibre of Bergonzi or Domingo, but his interpretations are musical, sensitive, and intelligent, if not yet quite as imaginative or original as those of the very greatest tenors. However, it is indicative of what Calleja has already accomplished that he invites comparison with them.

Notes

[1] Let alone the astonishing Hermann Jadlowker, who possessed a voice capable of tackling all but the heaviest Wagnerian roles, but executed the runs in '*Ecco ridente*' and in Idomeneo's '*Fuor del mar*' with unrivalled fluency and brilliance.

[2] It is only fair to add that, in more recent CD transfers made at the correct speed, de Lucia's *vibrato* is much less evident.

[3] Tamagno, Martinelli, del Monaco, Vinay and McCracken are covered elsewhere in this essay. Renato Zanelli (1892–1935), like Vinay, was a Chilean who started his career as a baritone and retained a dark, baritonal colouring after re-training as a tenor. His few recordings confirm that he was among the greatest exponents of the role of Otello.

Had it not been for his tragically early death, he might have merited a place in this essay.

[4]On record, however, he makes a fine impression in the role, singing both more passionately and more lyrically than most Wagnerians.

[5]When he sang at the Sadler's Wells theatre in Rosebery Avenue, he often had to be retrieved from a neighbouring pub, where he had repaired, in full costume, for a drink (or several) while he was offstage.

[6]It is also noteworthy that the great Wagnerian soprano, Frida Leider, declared that he was her favourite Tristan.

[7]It is worth noting that Walter Widdop, Tudor Davies, and Heddle Nash belonged to an extraordinary generation of tenorial talent in Britain. Their contemporaries and competitors included Frank Mullings, John McCormack, Joseph Hislop, Parry Jones, Frank Titterton, Browning Mummery (Australian but based in Britain), Henry Wendon and James Johnston.

[8]This is a characteristic German tenors share with Jewish cantors. This throat-centred method of voice production seems to facilitate the exceptional flexibility and fluency in the execution of runs and ornaments that are typically required by *chazzanut*. The same qualities are also required by early, Baroque, and classical music (e.g. Haydn and Mozart).

[9]Interestingly, this was a role also sung by the huge-voiced Ramòn Vinay, a tenor as far removed from a lyric tenor such as Lewis as could readily be imagined.

[10]The greatest, that is, to follow the generation dominated by two stylish but sharply contrasting tenors: the Slovene, Anton Dermota (1910–89) and the French Canadian, Léopold Simoneau (1916–2006). According to Dame Elisabeth Schwarzkopf, who sang with both of them, Dermota possessed a 'Mediterranean' timbre while Simoneau had a 'Björling' sound. The distinction is well made. Dermota does indeed possess the warmth and richness of the typical Mediterranean tenor, while Simoneau has the bright, forward sound and pinpoint definition of tone characteristic of Jussi Björling. Pursuing this

distinction a little further, one could say that Wunderlich inherited the mantle of Simoneau, and Burrows that of Dermota.

[11]See the entry on Alfred Piccaver and note 7 above for reference to somewhat different British, rather than English, tenor traditions. The tenors named in the Piccaver entry were Italianate lyric or *lirico spinto* tenors. Those named in note 7 are more heterogeneous in nature, though none belongs in the distinctively English tenorial tradition.

[12]A role which, according to Jon Vickers, who sang and recorded it, required a combination of a Gigli-like lyric tenor, a dramatic tenor, and a lyric baritone!

Part Four

33 Future prospects

What of the future? Some of the tenors mentioned above are still in their prime, and (God willing) have many more years of good singing ahead of them. In addition, there are such artists as Ramón Vargas, Marcelo Alvarez, James Gilchrist, Toby Spence, Mark Padmore, Andrew Kennedy, Ben Johnson, Robin Tritschler, Stuart Skelton and Simon O'Neill – all of them fine tenors who are currently singing magnificently and giving much pleasure in live performances and recordings alike. On this evidence, there seems no reason to fear for the future of the classical operatic or concert tenor.

Yet there is. The reputation of singers (to say nothing of their income) and the continuing popularity of opera as an art form have depended for many decades on recordings, which have brought the names and voices of singers to a wider public than could have heard them in the opera house or concert hall. Yet now the record companies have withdrawn almost entirely from the operatic field. The availability of pirate recordings and downloads have made studio recordings – especially of such an inherently expensive art form as opera – commercially unattractive, or even non-viable. Instead, we are offered DVD recordings of live performances. Modern singers can thus not reach as wide a public, or be heard by them in as advantageous conditions, as their predecessors. It is harder now for a tenor – or indeed any classical singer – to forge a major reputation: almost impossible for him to achieve the worldwide fame of a del Monaco or a Corelli, let alone that of a Caruso, a Gigli, a Pavarotti or a Domingo.

Consider this: between 1934 and 1946, Gigli made nine studio recordings of complete operas;[1] Tucker made fourteen between 1947 and 1975; between 1952 and 1960, Björling made twelve; del Monaco made twenty-six between 1952 and 1970, and di Stefano eighteen between 1953 and 1967; Corelli made thirteen between 1954 and 1970; Bergonzi twenty-four between 1958 and 1980; Carreras twenty-six between 1976 and 1990; and Gedda, Pavarotti and Domingo in their respective long careers, goodness knows how many. There is a picture of steady growth in the number of complete opera recordings per tenor from 1935 to 1995. Yet, since 1995, the picture is one of abrupt and rapid decline. The leading tenors of the post-Domingo / Pavarotti generation have made pitifully few studio recordings of complete operas. Lyric or dramatic tenors of anything like comparable eminence in the generations between Gigli and Domingo would have achieved a far larger recorded output, and therefore much greater renown. Because of the enormous expense of recording operas with stellar casts,[2] and the relatively meagre financial returns to the record companies, tenors today are likely to be recorded only live, whether on DVD or CD, and their recordings will therefore probably suffer from the well-known limitations of live recordings: poor sound, stage and audience noise, imbalances between voices and orchestra, and the impossibility of correcting errors. The only advantages live recordings enjoy over their studio counterparts is that some of them – the best – are more spontaneous, more natural-sounding, and more dramatically involved. Do these advantages compensate for the drawbacks? Not in the present writer's view. On repeated hearings, the flaws of live performances become more obtrusive and more irritating, and the virtues are subject to the law of diminishing returns in a way that the more considered, carefully constructed virtues of studio recordings are not.

If this were not enough, there are other musical problems for the aspiring young singer, especially if he happens to be a tenor. Orchestral pitch is now significantly higher than it was in Rossini's day, and the high notes that he and the other *bel canto* composers wrote for tenors, which, even in their day, were stratospheric enough, have now become all but unreachable. And the tenor is no longer allowed to use the head voice or the *voix mixte* to negotiate such perilous high notes safely. Not only the *ut de poitrine* is expected, but also the C sharp, D, E flat, E, and even F, without *falsetto*. And the tenor has to contend with the increasingly boisterous playing of modern orchestras, who are equipped with powerful modern instruments and encouraged to play as loudly as possible by egocentric superstar conductors. It is small wonder that singers are accused of sacrificing delicacy to sheer volume. If they want to be heard at all above the orchestral din, what choice do they have?

And there are five other phenomena, unique to our time, which may militate against the survival not only of classical singing as we know it, but also of classical music. The first is cultural democracy. No longer is democracy confined to the political sphere. There is a widespread assumption that questions of taste and the allocation of public funds should also be determined by democratic means. According to this view, whatever is popular deserves governmental support. Minority interests are not, and do not. This is a consequence of the collapse in belief in objective goods. If goods are not objective, then all that remains is the market. It is not for politicians or other putative authorities to set goals, establish spending priorities, or determine the ends to which policy will be directed. Only the free market can determine which, among the plethora of choices on offer, is optimal and will therefore survive. It is the logic of the market that has dictated that studio recordings of operas will no longer be made. They are not cost-effective. They do not maximize the return on investment. How long will it be before that same inexorable logic leads governments to withdraw subsidies from opera houses and orchestras, condemning them to bankruptcy and extinction?

The second phenomenon is the emergence of a class of highly intelligent people who see no reason to apply their intelligence to any cultural pursuits or questions. Uninterested in the arts, philosophy, or any purely intellectual matters, they devote themselves exclusively to the pursuit of wealth, socio-economic status and pleasure. Their tastes are no different from those of the unintelligent majority. Trashy novels, witless films, video games, vacuous television programmes, and popular music, are the cultural staples of their lives. Anything that requires a severe effort at comprehension but is unrelated to the utilitarian goals mentioned above, is dismissed out of hand. Such things are 'boring', 'irrelevant', 'elitist', or just 'uncool'. Politicians – quick, as ever, to detect the rumble of an approaching bandwagon and jump on board – will dissociate themselves from any art forms and activities deemed 'elitist' and, conversely, associate themselves with whatever captures the current mood of the public and reflects existing trends. In this climate, the art form that is loosely referred to as 'classical music' cannot prosper. It is too hard and exacting, too much of an intellectual challenge. Its practitioners will find it increasingly difficult to win financial support, attract audiences, or make a living.

The third phenomenon is the commercialization of publishing. Not very long ago, it was possible for a mainstream publisher to issue highly specialized works, such as John Steane's *Singers of the Century* (three volumes) or Michael Scott's *The Record of Singing* (two volumes) or *Opera on Record* (edited by Alan Blyth – three volumes). It is doubtful whether such books, let alone more esoteric works such as *Herman Klein and the Gramophone* or Tuggle's *The Golden Age of Opera*, would ever see the light of day in the profit-obsessed, cutthroat, market-driven environment of modern publishing. With fewer recordings, a more meagre literature, less publicity, and fewer patrons, how can the art of the classical singer, which has been celebrated in these pages, continue to survive and prosper? How can classical music itself, as we know it, and the performance traditions with which it is associated, long remain in existence?

The fourth phenomenon is the commercialization of broadcasting. The BBC, once the bastion of high quality programming, has virtually abandoned all pretence of aiming at quality. Radio 3, which was formerly devoted almost exclusively to classical music and drama of high quality, has declined into a dumping ground for programmes that do not obviously belong anywhere else. The casual listener, if he tunes in at random, is more likely to hear trivial conversation, or anything from film scores to world music, jazz or rock, than anything properly describable as classical music. BBC 2, which used to be the television equivalent of Radio 3, is now indistinguishable from BBC 1; which is to say, it broadcasts programmes intended to have a popular appeal, but of no artistic or intellectual merit whatsoever. BBC 4, the digital channel which supposedly replaced BBC 2 as the 'culture' channel, broadcasts about ten programmes of popular music (repeats of *Top of the Pops*, *The Old Grey Whistle Test*, etc.) for every one it devotes to classical music. There are very few opportunities for lovers of classical singing (or, for that matter, newcomers to the art) to hear examples of the best – the greatest voices and interpreters – that the long history of singing on record has to offer. As for the independent broadcasters, whether on radio or television, the less said of their offerings, the better.

The fifth phenomenon is the confusion that currently surrounds education policy in the UK. On the one hand stands the academic establishment, which has long considered the principal purpose of education to be the personal development of the child, rather than the transmission to posterity of cultural and moral knowledge. On the other hand stands the business and political establishment, which regards education simply as a branch of vocational training. Neither the academics nor the businessmen and politicians seem to have much time for musical education – or for arts education in general, for that matter – and standards in this area, in all but a handful of private specialist schools, are lamentably low.

The future for opera – for classical music generally – is uncertain. High culture in general is imperilled by the prevalence of an aggressive low culture, coupled with a vulgar attitude of either hostility (owing to inverted snobbery) or indifference (owing to laziness) towards the artefacts and mentefacts of high culture. Not only classical music but classical literature, philosophy, art, theology, religion, and much else besides, are in danger. A time when a tenor voice, for many people, is typified by Russell Watson or Paul Potts, or at best by the half-trained Andrea Bocelli, is not an auspicious one for classical music[3] in general or vocal music in particular. To sing with the technical and interpretative accomplishment of the operatic and concert tenors we have been discussing, requires years of total dedication to study: the study of voice and vocal method; of music, musical styles and idioms; of languages and texts; of acting and stagecraft; of repertoire in opera, oratorio and song. And fully to appreciate the art of such singers requires an educated ear, a certain breadth of culture, and some understanding of the vocal, technical, and interpretative skills which they have mastered. Fewer and fewer people are willing to invest the time and effort required to become a genuine classical singer,[4] or even to grasp enough of the singer's art to appreciate it properly. This does not bode well for the future.

For, after all, where might this noxious cocktail of philistinism, cultural democracy, celebrity worship, technology, and marketing, lead? Is it possible to imagine a future in which all singing, even in opera, will rely on the microphone? In which no one will study voice anymore? In which the 'natural' voice of the pop singer will be the voice we hear in the opera house and the concert hall, assisted by electronic amplification and other artificial enhancements? In which orchestras will be replaced by pre-recorded soundtracks? In which the glorious voices of the past will sound merely 'weird' or 'funny' to audiences inured to pop music and the very different (some would say 'degenerate') method of singing which it fosters? In which mass marketing will determine the audience for classical music, and performance styles and standards will be based on what yields the highest returns? In which opera singers will not be trained professionals, but the winners of *The X-Factor* and *Britain's Got Talent*? In which even the historic recordings of the great singers of the past will not be valued, and may perhaps be destroyed by people who have no sense of their artistic and historical importance?

But I would rather end on a celebratory than a monitory note. Whatever the future holds – and we must beware of over-estimating the predictive possibilities of our present perspectives – the past is rich in achievement; and the history of tenors on record is not over yet. The glories of Caruso and Sirota, Gigli and Björling, Melchior and Widdop, Schipa and Flórez, Tauber and Wunderlich, Patzak and Pears, and all the other tenors whose voices and art have been celebrated in these pages, remain as a monument to a particular stage in the history of vocal culture. Unlikely as it seems, it may be that their achievements will be matched in the future – but probably in ways that we do not expect and cannot yet foresee. For example, we may see a growth in authentic performance practice, extending from early and Baroque music to music of the classical, romantic, and early modern periods. That would create opportunities for a new school of singing; one more culturally aware, technically sophisticated, musically alert, and historically informed, than any that has existed up to now. Recurrent accusations which have been levelled over the years against the tenors who have excelled in the Italian repertoire especially, include vulgarity of taste and lack of musicianship. The extension of authentic performance practice, based on musicological research and scholarly criteria, to the nineteenth-century French and Italian operatic repertoire might address those objections. And, if, as part of such a scholarly recovery of the past, both the lower orchestral pitch of Rossini's day and the mastery of the *voix mixte* were reintroduced, then some of the stratospherically high *bel canto* roles might be brought within the reach of the generality of tenors instead of remaining the province of a few exceptionally endowed specialists. As ever, there is reason to hope, as well as cause for concern.

Notes

[1]For the purposes of these statistics, I have treated the Verdi Requiem as equivalent to an opera.

[2]There is also the difficulty of scheduling recordings, given the jet-set lifestyles of most modern singers. However, that is probably a relatively minor consideration. It would certainly not be advanced as an insuperable objection if the financial case for opera recordings made sense.

[3]Of course, for an earlier generation, Mario Lanza (1921–59) was the archetypal operatic tenor. Lanza lacked the self-discipline to become a well-schooled singer, and, while his recordings in his prime reveal a splendid voice and a certain natural spontaneity and *élan*, his vocal technique, his musicianship, and his interpretative skills, were never of the front rank.

[4]'Genuine' as opposed to an *ersatz* product like Bocelli or Katherine Jenkins.

Acknowledgements

I am indebted to Alan Bilgora and Stephen Hastings, who not only reviewed this book kindly in *The Record Collector* and *Opera* respectively, but also pointed out a couple of mistakes and some unacknowledged lacunae in my selection.

The mistakes have now been rectified – at least, I hope so. As to the lacunae, while the task of writing further articles is, for the present, beyond my competence (apart from trying the patience of my publisher), I feel that I should at least mention by name some of the outstanding tenors who were omitted through no fault of their own, but chiefly because of the constraints involved in producing a book which could retail at an affordable price.

First, then, the Spanish school. The only Spanish tenors covered in my text are Alfredo Kraus, Plácido Domingo and José Carreras. Such distinguished predecessors as Miguel Fleta (who created the part of Calaf in Puccini's *Turandot*), Hipólito Lázaro, and Antonio Cortis are unmentioned – a particularly grievous omission. Contemporaries of Domingo and Carreras include two more gifted Spanish tenors: Giacomo (Jaime) Aragall and Francisco Araiza.

Some members of the French school are alluded to in the essay on Georges Thill, but others equally eminent include Émile Scaremberg, Fernand Ansseau, André d'Arkor (in fact Ansseau and d'Arkor were both Belgian, but they sang extensively in the French repertoire and exemplify the French school at its best), José Luccioni, Georges Noré, Henri Legay, Jean Giraudeau,

Acknowledgements

Charles Burles, the Australian-born Albert Lance (Lance Ingram), Alain Vanzo, Gilbert Py, and Guy Chauvet. The accomplished Swiss tenor Libero de Luca also made his name chiefly as an interpreter of French opera.

The omission of the Russian school was especially regrettable as the style and technique of the nineteenth-century school of singing was preserved in Russia for much longer than it was in the West. In the early Russian tenors of the recorded era we gain what is perhaps our most accurate impression of what the tenors of the bel canto period really sounded like. Fortunately, the archives have been opened up in recent years and now we can study the achievements of the remarkable artists who flourished behind the Iron Curtain, although the earliest of them also made careers in Imperial Russia. Prominent among them were Alexander Bogdanovich, Vasili Damaev, Alexander Davidov, Ivan Ershov (the only one of whom I did make mention), Nicolai Figner, David Juzhin, Andrey Labinsky, Gavriil Morskoy, Dmitri Smirnov, and Leonid Sobinov. All these tenors were featured on two CDs – *Tenors of Imperial Russia* vols 1 and 2 – released on the Pearl label.

The Italians omitted are too numerous to mention individually – Mr Bilgora kindly wrote to me mentioning the *lirico spinto* tenors Giulio Crimi, Francesco Merli, Antonio Melandri, Giuseppe Taccani, Luigi Marini, Piero Menescaldi, Galliano Masini, and Alessandro Ziliani, and the lyric tenors Dino Borgioli, Enzo de Muro Lomanto, Roberto D'Alessio, Giovanni Manuritta, and Luigi Fort, to which I would add the names of the later Mario Filippeschi, Bruno Prevedi, and Flaviano Labò, all of whom I have admired on record – and these will have to serve as a representative sample. Italy's magnificent contributions to all the creative and performing arts are rightly celebrated, and not the least of them is her extraordinary profusion of world-class tenors.

Select Bibliography

Further Reading, General

Blyth, Alan (1992), Opera on CD: *The Essential Guide to the Best CD Recordings of 100 Operas*, London: Kyle Cathie Limited

—— (1995), *Opera on Video: The Essential Guide*, London: Kyle Cathie Limited

Blyth, Alan (ed.) (1979, 1983, 1984), *Opera on Record* (3 volumes), London: Hutchinson

—— (ed.) (1986, 1988), *Song on Record* (2 volumes), Cambridge: Cambridge University Press

—— (ed.) (1991), *Choral Music on Record*, Cambridge: Cambridge University Press

Bostridge, Ian (2011), *A Singer's Notebook*, London: Faber

Boyden, Matthew (2001), *Icons of Opera*, San Diego, California: Thunder Bay Press

Brook, Donald (1949), *Singers of Today*, London: Rockliff

Douglas, Nigel (1992), *Legendary Voices*, London: André Deutsch

—— (1994), *More Legendary Voices*, London: André Deutsch

—— (1996), *The Joy of Opera*, London: André Deutsch

Frisell, Anthony (1964), *The Tenor Voice*, Somerville, Massachusetts: Bruce Humphries Publishers

Gammond, Peter (1979), *The Illustrated Encyclopedia of Recorded Opera*, New York: Harmony Books

Greenfield, Edward *et al* (1993), *The Penguin Guide to Opera on Compact Discs*, London: Penguin Books

Select Bibliography

Gruber, Paul (ed.) (1993), *The Metropolitan Opera Guide to Recorded Opera*, London: Thames & Hudson

Hahn, Reynaldo (1990), *On Singers and Singing*, Portland, Oregon: Amadeus Press

Harris, Kenn (1973), *Opera Recordings: A Critical Guide*, Newton Abbot: David & Charles

Herbert-Caesari, E. (1951), *The Voice of the Mind*, London: Robert Hale

—— (1958), *Tradition and Gigli*, London: Robert Hale

Hines, Jerome (1982), *Great Singers on Great Singing*, London: Victor Gollancz

—— (1997), *The Four Voices of Man*, New York: Proscenium Publishers

Hurst, P. G. (1958), *The Age of Jean De Reszke: Forty Years of Opera 1874–1914*, London: Christopher Johnson

—— (1963), *The Golden Age Recorded*, Lingfield: Oakwood Press

Klein, Herman (1933), *The Golden Age of Opera*, London: Routledge

Macy, Laura (ed.) (2008), *The Grove Book of Opera Singers*, New York: Oxford University Press

Matheopoulos, Helena (1986), *Bravo*, London: Weidenfeld & Nicolson

—— (1999), *The Great Tenors*, London: Laurence King Publishing

Moran, William R. (ed.) (1990), *Herman Klein and the Gramophone*, Portland, Oregon: Amadeus Press

Mordden, Ethan (1987), *A Guide to Opera Recordings*, Oxford: Oxford University Press

Necula, Maria-Cristina (2009), *Life in Opera*, Wisconsin, USA: Hal Leonard Corporation

Pahlen, Kurt (1973), *Great Singers from the 17th Century to the Present Day*, London: W. H. Allen

Pleasants, Henry (1966), *The Great Singers*, London: Gollancz

Potter, John (2009), *Tenor: The History of a Voice*, London: Yale University Press

Rushmore, Robert (1971), *The Singing Voice*, London: Hamish Hamilton

Scott, Michael (1977, 1979), *The Record of Singing* (2 volumes), London: Duckworth

Shawe-Taylor, Desmond & Sackville-West, Edward (1951), *The Record Guide*, London: Collins [an updated edition was published in 1955 and thereafter various supplements appeared]

Simpson, Harold (1972), *Singers to Remember*, Lingfield: The Oakwood Press

Steane, J. B. (1974), *The Grand Tradition*, London: Duckworth

—— (1992), *Voices, Singers and Critics*, London: Duckworth

—— (1996, 1998, 2000), *Singers of the Century* (3 volumes), London: Duckworth

—— (1999), *The Gramophone and the Voice*, Harrow: Gramophone Publications Limited

Stinchelli, Enrico (1992), *Stars of the Opera: The Great Opera Singers*, Rome: Gremese International

Tear, Robert (1990), *Tear Here*, London: André Deutsch

—— (1995), *Singer, Beware*, London: Hodder & Stoughton

Tuggle, Norman (1983), *The Golden Age of Opera*, New York: Holt, Rinehart & Winston

Studies in Interpretation

Bernac, Pierre (1970), *The Interpretation of French Song*, London: Cassell

Bostridge, Ian (2014), *Schubert's Winter's Journey: Anatomy of an Obsession*, London: Faber & Faber

Bannerman, Betty (ed. and trans.) (1989), *The Singer as Interpreter: Claire Croiza's Master Classes*, London: Victor Gollancz

Greene, Harry Plunket (1912), *Interpretation in Song*, London: Macmillan

Lehmann, Lotte (1971), *Eighteen Song Cycles: Studies in their Interpretation*, Worthing: Littlehampton Book Services

Moore, Gerald (1975), *The Schubert Song Cycles*, London: Hamish Hamilton

—— (1981), *Poet's Love: The Songs and Song Cycles of Robert Schumann*, London: Hamish Hamilton

—— (1953), *Singer and Accompanist*, London: Hamish Hamilton

Schiøtz, Aksel (1970), *The Singer and his Art*, London: Hamish Hamilton

Memoirs, Biographies, Critical Discographies

Allen, Eleanor (2010), *Heddle Nash: Singing Against the Tide*, London: Jubilee House Press

Bessette, Roland L. (1999), *Mario Lanza: Tenor in Exile*, Portland, Oregon: Amadeus Press

Björling, Anna-Lisa & Farkas, Andrew (1996), *Jussi*, Portland, Oregon: Amadeus Press

Boagno, Marina (1996), *Franco Corelli – A Man, A Voice*, Dallas, Texas: Baskerville Publishers

Carreras, José (1991), *Singing from the Soul*, London: Souvenir Press

Caruso Jr, Enrico & Farkas, Andrew (1990), *Enrico Caruso: My Father and my Family*, Portland, Oregon: Amadeus Press

Castle, Charles & Tauber, Diana Napier (1971), *This Was Richard Tauber*, London: W. H. Allen

Cesari, Armando (2004), *Mario Lanza: An American Tragedy*, Dallas, Texas: Baskerville Publishers

Drake, James A. (1984), *Richard Tucker: A Biography*, New York: E P Dutton Inc

Elwes, Winefride & Elwes, Richard (1935), *Gervase Elwes*, London: Grayson & Grayson

Emmons, Shirlee (1990), *Tristanissimo: The Authorized Biography of Heroic Tenor Lauritz Melchior*, New York: Schirmer Books

Foxall, Raymond (1963), *John McCormack*, London: Robert Hale

Freestone, J. & Drummond, H. J. (1960), *Enrico Caruso: His Recorded Legacy*, London: Sidgwick & Jackson

Gedda, Nicolai (1999), *Nicolai Gedda – My Life & Art*, Portland, Oregon: Amadeus Press

Gigli, Beniamino (1957), *The Gigli Memoirs*, London: Cassell

Hastings, Stephen (2012), *The Björling Sound: A Recorded Legacy*, New York: University of Rochester Press

Headington, Christopher (1992), *Peter Pears: A Biography*, London: Faber & Faber

Henstock, Michael (1990), *Fernando De Lucia*, London: Duckworth

Jackson, Stanley (1972), *Caruso*, London: W. H. Allen

Kesting, Jürgen (1996), *Luciano Pavarotti: The Myth of the Tenor*, London: Robson Books

Levy, Alan (1976), *The Bluebird of Happiness: The Memoirs of Jan Peerce*, New York: Harper & Row

Matheopoulos, Helena (2000), *Plácido Domingo – My Operatic Roles*, London: Little, Brown & Company

Mannering, Derek (1992), *Mario Lanza: A Biography*, London: Robert Hale

McCormack, Lily (1949), *I Hear You Calling Me: The Story of John McCormack*, London: W. H. Allen

McCracken, James & Warfield, Sandra (1971), *A Star in the Family*, New York Coward McCann & Geoghegan

Melchior, Ib (2003), *Lauritz Melchior: The Golden Years of Bayreuth*, Dallas, Texas: Baskerville Publishers

O'Connor, Garry (2017), *The Vagabond Lover: A Father-Son*

Memoir, Totnes: CentreHouse Press

Pears, Peter (1995), *Travel Diaries 1936–1978*, Woodbridge: Boydell Press in conjunction with the Britten-Pears Library, Aldeburgh

Pettitt, John (2002), *Callas and Di Stefano: The Years of Glory*, Ilkley: The Odda Press

Ross-Russell, Noel (1996) *There Will I Sing: A Biography of Richard Lewis*, London: Open Gate Press

Schipa Jr, Tito (1996), *Tito Schipa: A Biography*, Dallas, Texas: Baskerville Publishers

Schnauber, Cornelius (1994), *Plácido Domingo*, Boston, Massachusetts: Northeastern University Press

Scott, Michael (1988), *The Great Caruso*, London: Hamish Hamilton

Seghers, René (2008), *Franco Corelli, Prince of Tenors*, Portland, Oregon: Amadeus Press

Slezak, Leo (1938), *Song of Motley: The Reminiscences of a Hungry Tenor*, London: William Hodge

Tauber, Diana Napier (1959), *My Heart and I*, London: Evans Brothers

Turnbull, Michael T. R. B. (1992), *Joseph Hislop: Gran Tenore*, Aldershot: Scolar Press

Williams, Jeannie (1999), *Jon Vickers: A Hero's Life*, Boston, Massachusetts: Northeastern University Press

Zucker, Stefan (2015), *Franco Corelli and a Revolution in Singing: Fifty-Four Tenors Spanning 200 Years, Volume 1*, New York: Bel Canto Society

Index

Index

More About CentreHouse Press

CentreHouse Press is an independent publisher, specialising in memoirs, travel books, plays, literary fiction, children's books and non-fiction. The press also publishes ebooks. We have published, in either paper or electronic form, the following writers: Jon Elsby, Andrew Elsby, Garry O'Connor, G. K. Chesterton, Peter Cowlam, Tony Phillips, Eliza Granville, Harry Greenberg, and Sam Richards. The press has also featured the work of artists Anne Boulting and Julie Oxenforth, and has worked with artists Thierry Naiglin, Dawn Hunter and M. Elena M. Rosillo.

For the latest news, visit our website, centrehousepress.com, or catch up with opinion and reviews at our blog, or find us on social media—

chpblog.centrehousepress.com
facebook.com/centrehousepress
@centrehouse

Coming Home
Jon Elsby

*C*oming Home looks, in the broadest sense, at the Catholic Church and the phenomenon of conversion. It considers, among other things, the varied components of Catholic identity; the complex, multifaceted relations between Catholicism and postmodernism, and between Church doctrine and pastoral praxis; and the controversies between so-called conservatives and liberals over the direction the Church should take in the future.

The Catholic Church, with its 2,000 years of accumulated doctrine and definition, claims to be the one and only divinely appointed repository of religious truth and wisdom, authoritatively taught and preserved for transmission to posterity. No other institution makes such a claim. It would be unwise to dismiss that claim in accordance with some dogmatic presupposition rather than weighing it impartially according to the evidence.

Coming Home invites the reader to consider all the evidence before making up his or her own mind.

Light in the Darkness
Jon Elsby

Christian apologetics is an important area of intellectual endeavour and achievement, standing at the boundaries between theology, philosophy and literature. Yet it has been largely neglected by historians of literature and ideas.

In these essays, the author attempts to establish apologetics as a subject deserving of respect in its own right. He analyses the apologetic arguments and strategies of four of the greatest Christian apologists of the twentieth century – Hilaire Belloc, G. K. Chesterton, Dorothy L. Sayers, and C. S. Lewis. He shows how different lines of argument support each other and converge on the same conclusion: that what Chesterton called 'orthodoxy' and Lewis 'mere Christianity' represents the fundamental truth about the relations between human beings, the universe, and God.

Wrestling With the Angel
Jon Elsby

Who am I? Am I an autonomous being, able to define myself by my own free choices, or a created being with a given human nature, living in a world which, in significant respects, does not depend on me? Are these two views necessarily opposed?

Wrestling With the Angel is one man's attempt to answer those questions. Raised as a Protestant, the author lost his faith in his teenage years, and then gradually regained it – but in an unexpected form. This is the story of a spiritual and intellectual journey from Protestantism to atheism, and beyond: a journey which finally, and much to the author's surprise, reached its terminus in the Catholic Church.

'*Wresting with the Angel* has the form of an intellectual autobiography, along the lines of Newman's *Apologia pro Vita Sua* but, like that older work, has much wider implications than that of a merely personal story. Elsby's style is engaging and the meaning of his prose – unlike much modern theology – clear.'
Stephen Lovatt

Orthodoxy
G. K. Chesterton

Chesterton wrote of *Orthodoxy* that it represented an attempt 'to state the philosophy in which I have come to believe' and to do so 'in a vague and personal way, in a set of mental pictures rather than in a series of deductions'. For most of its readers, it is the wittiest and most rollicking defence of the Christian faith ever written. Anticipating much modern theology, Catholic and Protestant, Chesterton's apologia is more personalistic than propositional. He understands that, in order to be credible, a belief system must appeal to the heart as well as to the mind. No one has set out more engagingly the reasons for believing in Christianity as the timeless truth about who we are, and rejecting the alternatives as fads and fashions. Jon Elsby, author of *Light in the Darkness* and *Wrestling With the Angel*, has written extensively on Christian apologists and apologetics, and has penned an illuminating introduction for this edition of *Orthodoxy*, which also contains brief notes and an index.